The Ring
with the
Emerald Stone

Maura Rooney Hitzenbuhler

First published by Dog Ear Publishing
4011 Vincennes Road
Indianapolis, IN 46268
www.dogearpublishing.net

ISBN: 978-1-4575-4687-7

This book is a work of fiction. Places, events, and situations in this book are purely fictional and any resemblance to actual persons, living or dead, is coincidental.

This book is printed on acid free paper.
Printed in the United States of America

Acknowledgments

With grateful thanks to my extraordinary proofreader, and long-time friend, Aine O'Brien Paulus, whom I was fortunate to meet in N.Y.C, after we were both living in the United States approximately a year.

To my daughter Tara Hitzenbuhler, a multitude of thanks for her excellent work in designing the cover of my book, The Ring with the Emerald Stone, getting me to meetings on time, handling my finances while I sign books, and the many tasks she does on my behalf.

For

James A. Rooney (recently deceased)

Thomas K. Rooney

Robert F. Rooney (U.S. Marine killed in action)

Frederick Rooney

Joseph Rooney

and

Patrick Rooney

CHAPTER 1

Exhilarated and a bit apprehensive was seventeen-year-old Maria, as she prepared for the trip, her first ever outside of England. Daphne and Penny, her co-workers, had invited her to join them on a tour of Spain, and she was delighted that they had included her. She was not as close to either of them as they were to each other. They did not reveal themselves to her, and she knew they shared secrets to which she would never be a party. Nevertheless, they had invited her to tag along, and this had made her very happy. If only she were more knowledgeable of life, knew as they did what to say to boys, if she were not so naïve, she believed, she would have a more solid relationship with them. The best she could hope for was to try to be less bashful and learn from them.

"Now Maria," her mother's voice broke into her internal conversation, "Stay with Daphne and Penny at all times, be alert to your surroundings, and don't stray from them for a moment."

"Yes Momma. Don't worry, we'll all stay together."

"You're all I've got, honey."

"But Momma, you weren't much older than I when you left Poland to go to America."

"Yes, darling, to America and then England, but I spoke English. You don't speak Spanish."

"Penny said just about everyone in Spain can speak English, because they see English and American films and television."

"Don't count too heavily on that, as some will, but many won't. The important thing is to stay in well-lit areas if you're out in the evening. Don't go out alone, and don't become too friendly with strangers."

"Yes, Momma."

Penny and Daphne want to meet strangers and dance with Span-ish lads. They say Momma is old fashioned. She's not really. It just seems so because she cares and worries about me.

"I'll be the soul of discretion, Momma."

"Are you imitating me, Maria?"

"Who better to imitate?" she laughingly replied.

"I don't want to be an over-protective mother, but you're only seventeen."

"Eighteen in two months."

"I wish you had let me get you a new suitcase rather than using that old beat-up case of mine."

"Daphne said to bring no new suitcases for it's important we don't look like tourists."

"With her cockney accent, Daphne hasn't a hope of passing for anything but English. Do as Penny does rather than follow Daphne's example."

"They're here," Maria said, hastily rising from her chair on hear-ing the doorbell ring.

"Yes, she's ready," Anna calls out as she brings her daughter's suitcase to the door, just as Maria opens it. Anna and Maria cling to each other in an embrace, her mother reluctant to let go.

"It's to Spain she's going, Mrs. Jablonski, not the hangman," Daphne told her. "This is the 1980s, we're all hip. Nobody will put anything over on us."

"Have a lovely time, and stay away from trouble," Anna heard herself say as they entered the car.

"We will Momma," Maria called back and waved as the taxi took off.

During the taxi ride Maria feels the burden of leaving her mother behind. Her job in the accounting department is her first job, and she has been working there only seven months. Her plan had always been to save money and take mother on holiday—perhaps back to Poland. Now sitting in the taxi on the way to the airport, her joy is overshadowed by guilt. This is her first separation from her mother, made worse by the fact that her mother has no other children to keep her company while she is away. Her mother doesn't speak to the neighbors other than to wish them 'good morning' or 'evening,' and so they view her as an oddity. There were just the two of them as far back as Maria could remember—no aunts, uncles or grandparents. Only her mother's mother survived the camps. Her mother left all that behind when she and her father left Poland for New York. After her father's death, according to her mother's recounting of these events for her daughter, her pregnant mother bought a ticket and began yet another life in England.

After the girls arrived in Madrid, however, guilt had not a fighting chance against the newness, the balmy climate, and the excitement of this city.

* * *

Anna sat alone in her apartment and thought about her daughter, wishing she was with her to protect her against any unsavory men the girls might encounter. She was feeling regret that she had not warned her daughter of the evil that abounded in the world. Maria was so child-like, so unprepared to wander into a world beyond their own small world. Anna worried also about her daughter's companions on this journey. Daphne had had an abortion when she was sixteen, and was now dating a jobless young man named George. The other young woman, Penny, at age twenty-one was a more mature young woman, but she too had taken up with an unemployed young man.

Anna reflected back on their religious heritage, which she never revealed to her daughter, and of her well-to-do grandparents and other family members, who had died in the camps, and of Maria's grandmother Ruth, saved because she was out for a walk with her nanny when the soldiers came to the home. The nanny's family took the child into their home, an outsider in the improvised family, but loved, until the young man of the family accosted her as she was changing the bed linen, and impregnated this fifteen-year-old girl. On discovering what happened, the parents of the young man told the girl she must leave both their home, and the town where they lived.

Ruth died giving birth and the child grew up in an orphanage where she was given the name Anna. At age thirteen Anna was sent to work on a farm, where in time she met a young farmhand, who had one goal in mind: to save enough money and go to America. Anna and Stan fell in love, married, and his goal became their shared goal. Through hard work and diligent saving, they believed they would reach their dream.

Penniless in America was not much better than being servants in Poland, and it was made worse by the unfamiliarity of this new country. They worked in different factories in New York. Stan, used to working outdoors, found factory work intolerable. Saturday afternoons, when he had finished his work for the week, Stan stopped at a construction site, where he questioned the crew on the possibility of employment. You need experience, he was told. When he saw a wall being built, he would ask the builder the proper way of doing it, and even assist in the building of it. He sat and talked with the workers on their lunch break.

"So you want to join our construction crew," a man he had never before seen on the site asked. When Stan said he would, the man looked upwards and said, "Could you climb up there and work in the sky?"

"I could. I have no fear of heights."

"Be here next Saturday and I'll try you out."

Stan left the dusty, airless factory to work in construction.

Anna continued to work all summer in the steamy factory, then in autumn enrolled in night school, where she attended classes after a full day's work. She, like Stan, wanted to earn more money than they could in the factories.

Their plan was to work, save, and put off having children for at least five years so that they might have a better future for themselves, and the children they hoped to have.

Anna agreed with the plan, but in less than three years she found herself pregnant. She could not bring herself to tell the hard-working Stan that she had let him down, and destroyed their dreams and hopes for the future.

To abort the child because it came before the scheduled time and spoiled their five-year plan was unthinkable to Anna. She owed it to her mother Ruth, whose whole family, except for her, died in the camps, and who would die giving birth to her, to preserve the line that had come close to extinction. Stan, although he had endured much hardship during that dreadful war, did not lose any members of his family in the camps. Yet she knew he would not go against his religious beliefs and consent to an abortion.

She was forced to make a most difficult decision, and to make it in haste. She would abandon her beloved husband in order to keep the child.

Taking enough money from their bank account for a ticket to England, and using her maiden name, she sailed to England.

On arriving there, Anna knew it was imperative that she find work immediately before her pregnancy was noticeable and her money ran out. To save money, she chose to rent a room, rather than a flat. Her plan was to wait until the baby was old enough to enter the school system before renting a flat.

In labor she arrived at the hospital's emergency area, she remembered, and answered the questions put forth to her—"no, she had never been seen by a doctor during the pregnancy, she had no insurance of any kind, no next of kin, and no telephone." Then the birth process began, which put on hold any further questions that might have been asked. Holding her newborn daughter in her arms erased all that came before this blessed event.

CHAPTER 2

Abdul's first glimpse of Maria was on the television screen as she stepped out of a tour bus in Spain. A reporter questioned this beautiful English teenager as the camera man came in for a close-up. I must meet her, Abdul decided, as her image faded from the screen.

While enjoying the flamenco and the sights of Madrid, the girls met a group of young women and men who nibbled on hors d'oeuvres with their drinks, and then a short time later moved to another pub and continued bar hopping throughout the night.

By morning Daphne was boisterously drunk, Penny vomited, and Maria, who did not drink alcohol and had never before been up all night, was having trouble staying awake. Daphne in need of black coffee, Penny now with nothing in her stomach, and Maria who would rather have gone back to their room to sleep, entered the first restaurant they found open at six o'clock in the morning. It was an expensive restaurant but in their combined misery they didn't notice.

After being seated, Maria, on checking the menu, brought this to the attention of her companions. Daphne answered, "Hell, I only want coffee."

"A cup of tea and some toast for me," Penny added. Maria put her head back against the chair and closed her eyes.

When the waiter took their order, Penny also ordered tea and a roll for Maria.

"She doesn't want anything, she's asleep," Daphne pointed out.

"A cup of strong tea will wake her up and get her going," Penny replied.

"That man sitting alone at the table behind you keeps staring at us," Daphne whispered to Penny.

"Maybe he wants to join us."

"By his clothes and his jewelry I'd say he's rich." Daphne smiled at him, whereupon he arose and walked over to their table.

"May I join you?" He introduced himself, but his name was unpronounceable to either of them and so soon forgotten. They in turn gave him their first names as he sat down next to Daphne.

"English ladies," he said in an accent that delighted Daphne and Penny. "Your friend, she is tired, is she not?"

"Yes, we've been sort of partying all night. She isn't used to staying up late," Penny explained.

"She is very young. I'd guess her to be about seventeen years."

"You hit it on the head. She is seventeen," Daphne smilingly told him.

He didn't ask or guess at their ages. He excused himself for a few moments while he went to speak to two men dressed in business suits. He returned to their table, and as they chatted, Maria's head fell onto Penny's shoulder.

Their gentleman friend beckoned to the waiter who immediately attended to their table. Daphne and Penny were soon enjoying a delectable breakfast of crepe suzettes with an abundance of fresh berries and bakery delights placed before them. He ordered tea for himself.

Penny, who was not unattractive but neither could she be called beautiful, was flattered to be here with this well-dressed man with a caring manner and foreign sounding accent that was like soft music to her ears.

Daphne ate and studied the man. He was tall with a complexion that was not produced by a tanning lotion. He had a winning smile and perfect teeth. Penny spoke to him so that she could hear his voice—a lullaby; a romantic sonnet was this voice of his. Reluctant to leave Maria asleep in the breakfast booth, and even more reluctant to depart from this newfound friend, Penny would have liked to remain at the table, but Daphne, refreshed by breakfast, voiced her desire to get postcards of Madrid to send back home. It was her wish to get cards from each place they visited.

"We must wake her," Penny said of the girl whose head rested on her shoulder.

"No, do not awaken her, I will stay here until she is awake and let her know you both have gone shopping and will return for her."

"We'll be back shortly, for there is a card shop just down the street from here," Penny said as she gently moved Maria's head and laid it on the back of the seat.

The two girls walked out into the sunlight discussing their gentleman friend and what a story they would have to tell the office workers. "After we get some postcards, we'll return and see what else he might offer us," Daphne smiled.

"If nothing else happens to us, this would be terrific enough to last forever," Penny said, dreamily, as she looked at her reflection in a store window.

Moments after the girls left, Maria woke up. To her surprise she saw not Daphne and Penny but a handsome young man sitting in the booth with her. *This dream is amazing in that it is difficult to believe it is a dream,* the girl thought, as she rubbed her eyes.

"Good morning Maria," he smiled in greeting, I'm Abdul," he added giving her a much shorter version of his name than he had given to Penny and Daphne.

He knows my name, yet we have not previously met. Why wasn't sleeping beauty scared when she woke from her long sleep and saw a handsome stranger standing over her? I'm scared, yet it is not an unpleasant sensation. Can one be pleasantly frightened? Daphne and Penny must have gone to the ladies room and before doing so, told him my name. They should be back any moment now and all will be explained. In the meantime, there is no reason to be alarmed for this is a public restaurant with several diners present.

"Your friends went shopping. You were asleep and so I offered to stay with you so that no harm would come to you. You must be hungry."

"Yes," she answered although until he mentioned it, she was unaware of it.

"I know of a very nice place not far from here that serves excellent food."

"I can't leave with you. My friends will be expecting me to be here when they return."

"Women can take so long to shop. We could be back before they return. I could leave a note for them at the concierge's desk. Are you willing?" he asks encouragingly.

"Yes," she answered with just a bit of apprehension.

"I will leave a note at the desk," he told her as he rose from the table.

At the desk, he took out a business card and pen from his pocket and wrote a brief note and handed it to the clerk, saying, "Make sure they receive this."

"Certainly sir." The clerk wished them 'good morning' with a pleasant smile.

Outside they walked side by side down the street, and then down a side street where they entered a restaurant which smelled of exotic spices. It seemed dark after the bright sunlit morning, and Maria stopped to let her eyes adjust, and to get her bearings, but almost immediately they were being guided into the depths of the restaurant's semi-darkness. Holding her hand, her new-found friend led her forward, through a beaded curtain to a small candle-lit table set for two. He pulled out a chair for her and after she was comfortably seated, he sat opposite her. A waiter entered this curtained-off area. Abdul ordered for both of them. She was about to tell him she did not understand what it was he has ordered, when he spoke.

* * *

"You were surprised that I knew your name. I must reveal to you, Maria, that I've seen you before our meeting. Not in person but on the television news. You were alighting from a tour bus. The moment I saw you, I was determined to meet you. A reporter was asking you your name, and also asked if this was your first visit to Spain. The camera favored you and proceeded to close in on you until the television screen was filled with your beautiful face. You had said you came from England to Spain on holiday with two friends, whom you introduced. I knew I had to meet you. You are even more beautiful in person. When I saw you in the hotel with your friends, I was determined to get to know you." He omitted the inquiries that had been made on his behalf and also that the three girls had been discreetly followed through the night and, as dawn advanced, to the restaurant.

Maria didn't know how to respond. Nobody except her mother had ever told her she was beautiful, and she believed that it was her mother's love for her rather than her appearance that caused her mother to make such a statement, and so she remained silent.

While Maria wondered why the table held no cutlery, Abdul picked up a triangle of pita bread. He scooped up some hummus, encouraging her to do likewise. Throughout the meal, she followed his lead, tasting and enjoying all the many foods that were brought to the table, During the course of their conversation, Maria learned that he was not Spanish as she had thought but had been to Spain many times and was very knowledgeable about this country that is new and exciting to her.

CHAPTER 3

On not finding Maria or the man who had bought them breakfast, Penny and Daphne went to the courtesy desk.

"Do you wish to check out?" the clerk asks.

"Well, no. You see a gentleman we met while having breakfast here, offered to stay with our friend Maria, while we went out to get some postcards. She had fallen asleep in the booth, as she was very tired after partying all night."

"I see," he answers not very sympathetic to the young women's plight. "You have not checked into our hotel!" *Prostitutes in our establishment*!

They could not recall the gentleman's name, but gave what they believed to be a very good description of their male friend.

"In what way can I be of assistance?"

"Maria would not have left without leaving a note to inform us where she was going. Please check to see if she has left a message."

"No message of any kind has been left by this woman you speak of."

Daphne, raising her voice an octave higher injected, "I want to speak to the manager."

"Please, Madame, lower your voice."

Daphne forcibly pulls the waiter who had brought them breakfast over to the desk. "Ask him about the man who sat with us and ordered breakfast. He spoke with him."

The waiter stated that he did not know who the man was who sat with them, and under further questioning stated he did not see a third woman.

The clerk, unseen by the two women, pressed a button and moments later security guards appeared. The clerk took one of the two guards aside, and told him what he knew of the situation, while the other guard tried to have the women follow him to the manager's office.

"Look, all we want is to find our friend, Maria," Penny diplomatically told the guard. "She would not have left the premises without leaving a note for us."

"I understand, but first I must ask you to come to the office where this can be discussed in private." They did so. The manager appeared kindly, but merely repeated what was already known. Daphne became quite irritated by this which led to her being chided for her bad manners and, adding insult to injury, he suggested that such behavior might be acceptable in England but was not tolerated in Spain. Penny believed the guards brought them to the office in order to remove them from the check-in desk where people might overhear their conversation.

The police, who had talked with the hotel personnel, dwelled largely on the fact that nobody at the hotel had seen a third woman, the woman who allegedly had disappeared. Neither Penny nor Daphne could produce Maria's passport or plane ticket, for Maria had these documents with her. The police took their statements, inquired further of them of this 'unfortunate' event as they called it, and assured them it would be looked into. The women, however, left the office feeling defeated.

* * *

Abdul offered to show Maria around Madrid.

"What time did you say on the card that we would meet with Daphne and Penny?"

"I left it open, urging them to enjoy themselves, and we would meet up with them somewhere along the tour."

"The tour will be heading to Seville this afternoon."

"After I've shown you Madrid, I will drive you to Seville, and anywhere else you might like to visit."

"That's very kind of you, but my trip is prepaid as are all my accommodations. "I cannot afford to stay in hotels other than those provided by the tour." *Penny and Daphne would handle this much better than I, she thinks, before continuing.* "You're a very kind and generous person, and I don't wish to offend you. Perhaps in my ignorance I have led you to believe I might accept joint accommodations with you, but I cannot. I am sorry if in any way I have given you to believe otherwise."

"My dear Maria, you do not offend me, rather, you intrigue me. I will provide you with your very own private accommodations on our travels."

Rather than alleviate her fears, he is confusing her. *Should she apologize for her assumptions? What would Momma's advice be?*

"Well, Maria, does my answer put you at ease?"

Embarrassed she smiled at the misunderstanding.

"Are you ready to tour Spain? My car is outside."

It was indeed outside, just a couple of car lengths from the entrance to the restaurant. A man who was behind the wheel of a BMW with tinted windows, stepped out of the car as Abdul approached. After opening the door on the passenger's side for Maria, Abdul entered the car. Donning sun glasses, he smiled. "Ready?"

"Yes" she answered as her body settled into the luxurious seat, "but first I must pick up my suitcase if I'm to stay over in Seville."

"What is in your suitcase that you might need?" he asked.

"Everything: my hair brush, toothbrush, nightwear, and change of clothing." Her mother did not approve of young girls wearing make-up, and so Maria, although she would have liked to experiment with make-up, had not as yet done so.

"While we ate breakfast, I had your suitcase picked up. It is now in my car."

Maria was speechless. *This man is unlike any I've ever known. Of course, I've never had a boyfriend and he isn't at all like the boyfriends that Penny and Daphne speak of. He is the genie released from the bottle. The genie usually gives three wishes and then takes back all due to some error or greed on the recipient's part. I must be cautious, and limit purchases for myself, so that I will have sufficient money to buy something special for Momma,* Maria decides. Looking towards the back seat of the car, she saw her familiar worn suitcase.

"Thank you."

"That suitcase is much too small to hold any but the barest necessities. We will pick up a few extra things for you to wear."

Abdul drove to a part of the city where shop windows displayed elegant clothing. *What is she to do, she asks herself,* as Abdul chose a store, and once inside spoke to one of the saleswomen. They were shown into a large room that looked, to Maria's eyes, like a room one might encounter in Buckingham Palace.

I'm out of my depth, she thinks, *and I don't know what to do.*

Abdul spoke to the sales woman in Spanish. They sat on the red and gold upholstered chairs while clothes were being brought in under the direction of this refined lady, and each piece was held out as though the clothes were bowing before them.

"Which of these would you like to try on?" Abdul inquired of her. "They have guessed at what size you might wear, but will know your exact size after you have tried on some of their clothing, and then they will continue to bring you clothing until you find what you would like."

The woman directed Maria to a fitting room behind a mirrored door. The first thing Maria did, now that she was alone, was check the price tags. On finding none, she was worried. *How can she choose without knowing the cost!* The blue silk skirt she deemed too expensive. Perhaps the lace blouse would be more affordable. She donned both and self-consciously walked into the room. Both Abdul and the woman smiled, and the sales woman nodded her head in approval.

You look fantastic, Maria. Absolutely fantastic," Abdul tells her.

"Perhaps I will take the blouse," she suggested.

"Only the blouse?" he asked, frowning. "Surely you would want the skirt to go with it?" Maria had planned to wash out her summer blouses each night and alternate the new blouse with the three other blouses she had packed. But, before she could convey this to Abdul, the woman softly clapped her hands, and two women entered the room each carrying more beautiful clothing. She dutifully tried on the clothes. Lingerie that would be most unsuited to the English climate was brought forth for her inspection, followed by formal wear. *What use would she have for these lovely gowns for she has never been to any formal event, and has no expectations of ever having the opportunity to do so.* However, the head sales woman and Abdul seemed to be enjoying this one-woman fashion show, and so she tried on many pieces of clothing she had no intention of buying. Once she had stated her decision to buy just the lace blouse, and a rather plain piece of lingerie, she relaxed, and enjoyed trying on these high-priced garments. Yet she was happy when it came to an end, and they could continue their journey. The bowl of fruit that had been placed on the low table before them had now been replaced by hot tea and finger sandwiches. When the salespeople left them alone, relaxing with a cup of tea, Abdul asked if she was satisfied with her purchases.

As they were about to walk out of the store, Maria stopped and said, "I haven't received the blouse and sleep-wear, nor as yet paid for them."

"It's all been taken care of, and has been placed in the boot of the car."

Maria was surprised by this efficiency. *Should I offer to pay for the two items now? No, he might be embarrassed if I hand him money in public. I'll wait until we're in the car,* she decided. There is yet one other request she had.

"Just one more purchase, please. Before we leave Madrid, I must get a postcard to send to my mother." Abdul suggested she wait until they arrived at the hotel to make these purchases, and he would have them mailed from the hotel. Maria smiled in agreement.

* * *

Abdul was very knowledgeable about Madrid and Seville, and all areas of this warm and sunny land. He was her guide and a most able one. She was amazed that he was so versed in the history of this country. He avoided crowds. The only time they were among people was on a boat ride in Seville.

Sometimes they arrived before a particular historic building was open to tourists, or at the close of the day, and to her surprise they were admitted. It was as though they were expected. Their accommodations were ready when they arrived at the hotel. True to his word, she had a private room, and not only a bedroom, but also a sitting room. She had gotten that much right, and felt good about it, as she remembered her mother's words, 'never put the cart before the horse.'

It would take her a long time, she surmised, to repay him for the expenses of this holiday. So that she could cut down on expenses, she would tell him the following morning that she must return to Madrid, and the accommodations provided for her there. Also she was somewhat uneasy about the trip since he was doing so much for her enjoyment, and she had nothing to give him in return.

A knock on the door interrupted her thoughts, and opening it she found a bell hop with an armful of boxes. She assumed he had made a mistake. The boxes all had the name of the store where she had shopped. He entered, and asked where to put the boxes which, although they were not heavy, were awkward to carry, and threatened to slip out of his arms. "On the couch," she told him.

"I'm afraid you've make a mistake. I selected only two small items. You must have brought someone else's clothes."

The man looked baffled. "I was told to deliver all these boxes to your room," he said.

Just then Abdul appeared in the doorway, and tipping the man, he dismissed him.

"No mistake. I took the liberty of choosing some of the items you tried on. I hope I have not offended you by doing so."

"I cannot pay for all these clothes."

"There is no need to do so. I have taken care of it, and I am most happy to do so."

She did not wish to appear ungrateful. Nobody had ever lavished such riches on her before. She knew from Penny's and Daphne's experience that their boyfriends did not do so. Daphne and Penny usually paid their share of the evening out, and often paid their boyfriends' shares. Of course, their boyfriends were often on the dole, whereas Abdul had told her he is a successful businessman. Yet, she was uncomfortable in having Abdul buy her clothes. She didn't know how to convey this to Abdul without offending him.

"Thank you. I must, however, pay you after I return home."

"What I would like is for you to wear one of the gowns at dinner tonight."

She remembered the pink gown, which she thought would be useless to her since it was too fancy for her lifestyle, and which she'd never have an occasion to wear, and believed that might be the gown he wished her to wear.

"The black gown," he requested.

"Yes, of course. I will be delighted to wear it."

"Will you be ready at seven?"

"Yes.

His handsome face broke into a smile as he left the room.

I should have told him, I don't wear clothes such as that dress. I should have spoken out before expenses got so out of hand. The other boxes! What are in those boxes? In haste she opened the other boxes. In clouds of tissue was the black gown, the blouse she had chosen and two other blouses similar to it but in other colors. She also found some flowered skirts as light as gossamer, a tailored green silk suit consisting of a jacket and matching long skirt. "Oh God," she whispered, "I'm up to my eyes in debt."

At seven o'clock sharp Abdul arrived at the door. He was dressed impeccably for dinner.

"You look magnificent," he greeted her as though she were royalty. "Where is the lace scarf that goes with it?" She reached into the pile of tissue paper, pulled out the scarf and put it around her shoulders. Abdul removed the scarf from her shoulders, and placed it ever so gently on her head draping one end so it fell gently down her back and the other fell loosely on the opposite side of the dress. They took the lift to the top floor. As they walked out of the lift, she placed her hand on his arm, which brought a smile to his face, as they walked towards the music coming from the dining room.

On hearing the music, she wondered if they would dance. Her mother, who danced well, had taught her how to dance. She would love to dance with Abdul. To feel his arm around her waist, and his body close to hers, as they dance to the rhythm of the music would be blissful.

They were shown to their table where to her surprise, they were not alone. At the large table other men and women were seated. They were either Spanish or from Abdul's homeland, Maria believed, for their skin color and black hair were similar to his. Some of the men, although in tuxedos or business suits, wore white head coverings with a cord that circled around the head. All the women were dressed in black, with tightly wound scarves covering their heads only, or their heads and foreheads. Abdul graciously made the introductions. The men slightly bent their heads towards her as they were introduced, and the women smiled in acknowledging her. None spoke. Although wearing a beautiful black gown and a lace scarf, she was an outsider in appearance and culture to these strangers—people who dipped into the many communal dishes as they ate. She was thankful that her glass and tea cup were solely hers. For all that, they were a congenial group who chatted, joked and laughed. As dinner came to an end, and the dining room music turned into full-bodied dance music, Maria hoped Abdul would dance with her, but he did not. None of the people at their table danced. This gown was made for strolling onto the dance floor and dancing the whole night through, not merely to sit in, she felt, as she tried not to let her disappointment show. It was difficult, for she would have loved to dance.

As she studied the dancers, she noticed that the women were wearing off-the-shoulder gowns, some held in place by fragile-looking straps and others miraculously held in place by unseen means. In contrast to the ladies dancing, all the women at the table wore gowns that circled the neck and had long sleeves. Hers had a mandarin collar, long lace sleeves like her fellow diners, and reached to her ankles. Even the lace blouse she bought had a high ruffled neck and long sleeves, although the negligee was quite revealing.

CHAPTER 4

In bed that night Maria had time to think about this unusual situation, and wondered why she had been chosen from among the many nice girls on the tour. This was the first time she had slept in a room alone. Although she had securely locked the door, she was scared. Her mother had told her to stay with Daphne and Penny, and she had not done so. What would her mother say if she knew she was traveling with a man she had just met? Her biggest concern, however, was that she was beginning to like him in a new and different way than she has ever felt before about anyone, and in her innermost being she knew she would be extremely sad when this trip was over. She believed she might be falling in love with Abdul, but never having had such an experience, she could not be sure. She tried to rein in her emotions and view the situation logically. She knew almost nothing of Abdul other than that he was gallant and obviously wealthy. Perhaps he had girlfriends in many countries! This was just a brief interlude, she reasoned, similar to two strangers taking shelter from the rain in a Museum, or under an archway. Yet she wanted this adventure to last forever and it pained her to think that soon they would have to say goodbye.

The following evening she wrote a brief message to her mother on a postcard, telling her of the beauty of Madrid and Seville. She did not tell her of her newfound friend. All that wonderful news she would reveal to her mother on her return for she could not do justice to this prince charming on a postcard.

After Seville, Abdul suggested a boat ride to Morocco.

Looking out into the water, Maria thinks, *this is the best holiday one could ever have. Yes, she will accompany Abdul to the magical place, for is not her holiday a marvelous dream. Dreams must come to an end, as this surely will, but until her return to England, she will travel with her bewitching traveling companion.*

They are approached by an elderly couple from Sweden who asked to have their picture taken together. Abdul graciously obliged them, thus making them very happy and increasing Maria's admiration of him. The couple walked away, thanking them.

"We could see Tangiers first."

"Other than associating Tangiers with the French Foreign Legion, I know nothing of it."

"Those woe-begotten soldiers of fortune were withdrawn in the 1950s."

"I was unaware of that."

"After Tangiers, Casablanca."

"Casablanca!" Maria smiled.

"You are familiar with it?"

"No. I remember seeing an old film on television that took place in Casablanca. My mother told me, when I asked, that Casablanca was in Morocco. Have you seen the film?"

"I am familiar with it."

"It was a beautiful love story that took place in a strange setting. That film put Casablanca on the map."

"Casablanca, I believe, was there long before that Swedish woman and her American co-star made the film."

"I mean for you yes, but not for many of my countrymen," Maria answered and then added, "I hope I have not offended you."

"I'm just teasing you," he smiled.

"Could we visit Rick's Café?"

"There is no Rick's Café, there never was one."

"Oh, my mother will be disappointed to hear that. She told me Europeans escaping Nazi Germany did so via Morocco and Rick's was an American café, a sort of safe haven."

"In 2002, a member of the U.S. Diplomatic Corps in Morocco decided to keep foreigners like your mother from being disappointed, and turned a run-down building into Rick's Café where everything is in black and white, like the film, and with lots of arches."

"Foreigners! I too am a foreigner here."

"Yes, but such a charming one," he answered with a devilish grin. After a moment he continued, "Every night the resident pianist plays "As Time Goes By" and other vintage favorites."

"How marvelous! I hope someday soon, I will be able to bring Momma to the newly established Rick's Café. It would make her so happy. Casablanca is her favorite film."

"That film depicted an event that was supposed to have happened during WWII after the American and British invaded North Africa. Casablanca is now a modern industrial city. Over one percent of the population is Christian, and less than half of one percent is Jewish."

"And the majority are?"

"Muslims. In 1860 Spain invaded and occupied Northern Morocco. In 1912, the French imposed a protectorate over the country. The ensuing struggle with France ended successfully in 1956, and the foreign legions were disbanded."

"Who were the first people to live here?"

"The Arab-Berbers were the original habitants. They were divided into a number of distinct tribes just like the original natives of America—the Indians."

"You said the majority of the people are Muslims. Are you also?"

"Yes. Does that, for you, change our friendship?"

"No. There are many Muslims in England, and other peoples, but I don't personally know any of them." He was about to comment on that but instead said, "I'd like you to see Fes, also."

"Fez! Aren't they the little hard cloth hats with the tassels the people in the film wore?"

"Fes, the capital city, not fez the head covering."

"Oops!"

"What language do the people speak?"

"Arabic is the official language. French is the language of business, government and diplomacy."

"I assume you know Arabic?"

"Yes," he laughed.

"French?" He nodded in agreement.

"English, Arabic, French, and Spanish," Maria uttered quite impressed.

"I know only English and some Polish as my mother was Polish before she became an English subject."

"So you are part Polish and part English?"

"Yes."

"The Moorish dynasties once ruled Morocco. Your Shakespeare made one of them known in the world."

"Othello! My mother would read a Shakespearean play to me, and we would discuss it before attending the performance. Othello had such a sad ending. That two people who very much loved each other could come to such an awful end is dreadful. My mother, ever practical, said mistrust and lack of communication, which are also a present-day problem, destroyed this couple."

Abdul laughed heartily.

Unlike the black car with the darkened windows that they drove in around Spain, a red convertible with the top down was waiting for them in Tangiers. Before disembarking, Abdul changed from his customary slacks and white shirts, to a long loose-fitting white garment, which he explained was more comfortable to wear in hot weather. Maria watched as Abdul walked among the people. Although he was dressed like them, he stood out among them.

How indescribably handsome he is, Maria thinks, falling in love with this Lawrence of Arabia image as portrayed by Peter O'Toole. *He is beauty and grace in motion.*

She watched as people on the street greeted him with respect as he spoke kindly to them. Some wanted to give them small gifts. He thanked them. One small boy hunkered down was pressing a design with a hammer onto a round metal disk the size of a dinner plate. When he got her attention, he expressed his wish that she buy it. He had put a lot of work into the plate. She had no use for it, but bought it. Suddenly she was surrounded by small boys trying to sell her their wares. Abdul spoke to them in Arabic, and they dispersed.

CHAPTER 5

When Anna Jablonski heard that her daughter had mysteriously disappeared, she was overwrought. In her grief, she blamed Daphne and Penny for her daughter's disappearance, herself for allowing Maria to make this trip without her, and God for permitting such a disaster to have happened. Disappeared. What was she to make of such an announcement? The very word slipped silently through her mouth. She could not do battle with its nothingness. Objects get misplaced and sometimes lost, not people. People do not disappear, which means she must be somewhere, but where? I must find this place. Anna prayed that God would protect her daughter in the alien surroundings of this unknown place, and bring her safely home. The police take statements, but will they be able to make Maria reappear from this illusive place, this never-never land of mist and nothingness.

Should she go to Spain? The police advise against it. "They will contact the police in Spain," they assure her, "and get to the bottom of this." What did the police in either country know of her daughter, or of her carrying this child in her womb during the long journey from America to England; or of her own mother, Ruth, saved by a miracle, who would give life to her, and she in turn would bring a child into the world who would grow into a beautiful young woman. Now it is all snatched from her in the indefinable, untouchable disappearance. The girls had said the hotel personnel had all agreed that they did not see Maria with them. How can that be? Why would they lie?

Penny and Daphne were being bombarded on all sides. They could not leave their homes except to go to work, where they were followed and questioned, and momentarily blinded by flashbulbs. At work the opposite occurred. Nobody spoke to them as they worked in silence. In this atmosphere, they even found it difficult to speak to each other, and that added to the haunting silence that surrounded them. In fear of being harassed should they leave the building, they ate lunch at their desks.

"My dad is the only one in my corner," Daphne lamented to Penny as they sat eating lunch. "He said if these foreigners stayed in their own country this wouldn't have happened. He said we've got too many of them here and they're ruining England. Every shop and mall is filled with them. My dad said they don't know our ways and do as they please, and talk to each other in their own language so we won't know what they are saying. My dad said, first the Irish came and as soon as they lost their peculiar accents, they could have passed for English, but those bastards didn't want to be English. Now we have Indians, Pakistani, and black people from every colony we once took possession of. Most of them don't work and become hooligans, while some of them go to our Universities, and get higher paying jobs than we English can get. And the whole blooming lot of them call themselves English. English, imagine that! 'This is the face of an English man,' my dad said putting his hands under his chin like this." Daphne demonstrates and laughs, remembering her father's words and actions.

"But Daffy, Maria was in Spain when all this happened, not England, and she and her mother look like English people."

"Her mother speaks with a foreign accent. Maria was born in England so that means Mrs. Jablonski has been in this country at least seventeen years, so why does she still talk like she does? My dad is Union Jack all the way, but he's on the dole and that makes him angry, which is understandable."

"What about your Mum?"

"She blames me for bringing all this trouble upon all of us. I wish we had never invited Maria to come with us."

"Your dad's understandably angry because he's been on the dole for over two years. That's makes men bitter."

"Bitter! He was a great father when we were growing up. He went all out at Christmas buying us whatever we asked for. In the summer he took us all on holiday. He loved doing things for us kids.

Now he hasn't got the money to do anything. He has to give Mum most of the dole money, so I give him a few bob every payday, so he can join his friends in the pub for a few pints."

They ate their lunch in silence for a while, and then Penny asked, "How could she have just disappeared like that? Do you think that nice man who bought us breakfast had anything to do with it?"

"The papers think so, but then those reporters are a bunch of jerks."

"He was so nice to us! I wish I could remember his name."

"Sometimes fellas don't give their right names, and that strange-sounding name he gave, now that I think about it, didn't sound like a proper name."

"What if she's never found, Daffy?"

"Stop calling me Daffy. My name is Daphne. I bet Maria is having a grand old time wherever she is and not wanting to come home."

"No, that's not like Maria. Besides, her mother's going bonkers over this whole thing."

"It's us that are taking the blame, and having to put with all this. The media is making her out to be an innocent child, and us like wicked stepmothers. How I hate this job. I wish I could find a better one."

"My Mum said we're lucky to still have our jobs after all that has happened."

"Your Mum's a howl. Have her come down and work here and do this bloody filing hour after hour, and see how we're being treated."

"She works very hard cleaning offices."

"If you hadn't blabbed to that reporter about leaving Maria asleep at the restaurant, so I could go out and buy postcards, I wouldn't be taking such a clobbering from the newspapers. Because of what you said, they pick on me more than on you."

"Sorry, Daffy—Daphne, I didn't tell that to the newspaper people, I only told it to the police, as they needed all the information we could give them to find Maria."

"So, have they found her? No. All that's being done with that piece of information is to make my life miserable."

"Mine also."

"What they've done is painted us both with the same brush, and it serves you right."

"I'm sorry."

"You should be."

The next day as they sat and ate lunch at work, the topic of Maria's disappearance was again mostly on their minds due to an article in the previous evening's newspaper.

"Imagine, Daffy, that rag of a paper saying that Maria was probably led into prostitution! She didn't even have a boyfriend. Her mother probably never told her anything about getting knocked up."

"Mine didn't either," Daphne replied, but I learned soon enough, and there's nothing wrong with me now, is there?"

"What I'm saying is it would be a terrible shock for her. You know what I mean, and she knowing nothing at all."

"We can't be blamed for that. That's her mother's doing."

*　*　*

Anna was a strong woman who believed she could handle any situation, but the mystery of her daughter's disappearance defeated her. In spite of her stress and anguish, she knew she had to pull herself together, and return to work.

Life was not easy for Daphne and Penny, who felt they had done nothing wrong, yet were being blamed for Maria's disappearance. The newspapers treated them harshly saying Maria was only seventeen while they were nineteen and twenty-one and should have taken better care of Maria. The Sunday Times described how the three girls had met. Daphne and Penny met on the underground while going to work. Penny got on the tube one station after Daphne, and after seeing each other getting off at the same station each day, going in the same direction and into the same building, they introduced themselves. Both girls work on the same floor in different departments. They had known each other approximately two years when Maria got off at their stop and entered the building in which they worked. They discovered that Maria worked on the floor above theirs in the accounting department. Daphne's and Penny's work consisted of some typing but mostly filing. Soon all three were meeting for lunch.

The newspaper interviewer, the girls believed, wrote his article portraying them as responsible for Maria's disappearance, for the rest of the article emphasized that they were out pub-crawling all night, were looking to hook up with men, and took up with a rather unsavory gentleman, then left the helpless Maria with him while she was asleep in the hotel restaurant.

"That Mr. Robinson from the newspaper is blaming us for what happened to Maria," Daphne shouted, clutching and shaking the newspaper. "The headline read: "Did the girls abandon their seventeen-year-old friend to a sex ring?"

"The <u>Mirror</u> practically calls us prostitutes," Penny cried. "All we wanted to do was dance and have a nice time," she continued to wail.

"What do these damn papers mean 'we should have taken care of her?' Maria was almost eighteen and I'm nineteen, that's only a year's difference," Daphne asked, then screeched, "Look at the horrible picture of us they put in the paper."

*   *   *

After Anna Jablonsky read the newspaper, anger flowed out of her like a dragon's fire. The Friday evening's newspaper ran a story about white slave trading. Anna locked herself in her apartment the whole weekend.

Anna had wanted to name the child Ruth after her mother. Stan, however, had said when the time was right for them to have a child, if the child was a girl he wanted her to be named Maria after his mother who died when he was eleven years old. Since she had deprived him of his daughter, she felt obligated to give the child the name he had chosen.

When the child was old enough to ask about her father, Anna told her he had died before she was a year old. Anna worked hard to give Maria everything she herself could never have dreamt of having. She regretted that she couldn't afford to move to a better neighborhood, but they had a good life. They were as close as a mother and daughter could be, Anna believed, sharing their innermost thoughts as sisters, best friends and companions, but now Maria's world had expanded to include her fellow workers. She had hoped to share with Maria, when the time was right, and the money saved, her great desire to take Maria to Poland on Maria's first trip abroad. When Maria excitedly told of her plan to go with her fellow employees to Spain, Anna felt forced to abandon, for a time, this great desire.

CHAPTER 6

Maria was happy to leave Fes, for this inland city was oppressively hot. Momma must by now have received the postcards from Madrid and Seville that Abdul had graciously offered to mail. What will Momma think when she receives the postcards from Morocco? Maria tried to visualize her mother's reaction. Momma wasn't much older than I when she left Poland for America. After my father died she had to care for a child while working to support us, thus ending any hope for a holiday. I know she wanted me to stay with Daphne and Penny throughout the trip, but how excited she'll be when I tell her of my wonderful adventure, and of Abdul who made it all possible.

He has been noticeably more relaxed and happy since we arrived in Morocco. Is it because we have gotten to know each other better, or is it because he seems more at ease with the people here? she wondered.

Before leaving Casablanca, to Maria's utter surprise, Abdul proposed marriage. The unexpectedness of his question left her without words, which embarrassed her. He gently kissed her on the cheek.

"Why not ask the question here?" he asked. "Paris is called the city of love, but it was here in Casablanca that Bogart and Bergman's great love scene took place."

It was for her a magical moment suspended in time. Although they were on a busy thoroughfare, they were removed from the crowds. The thought occurred to her that in the love scene between Bogart and Bergman, they were reluctantly saying goodbye. This was not the blossoming of their love but its dismal sad ending. She would not put a damper on this memorable moment by revealing her thoughts.

She felt honored to be asked to be his wife. Yet it was happening all too soon. They had met each other less than two weeks ago, and were just beginning to get to know one another. If she said "no" he would leave, and she would never see him again. It would be akin to the very sad farewell of Ingrid Bergman and Bogart. She did not want that kind of ending between Abdul and her. For Abdul and her there would be no Paris to remember—just a heart-breaking goodbye.

With his arm around her, she found her voice and softly answered, "Yes."

As he guided her towards the car she realized that her answer changed everything. She would need to let her mother know immediately. To-night she would write her a letter telling her all that had happened. Stepping into the car, she knew her whole world would be different, but in what manner she could not envision.

"I must introduce you to my father, and the family," he happily told her. "Tomorrow we'll fly to the United Arab Emirates."

"Where is that?"

"In the Persian Gulf."

Yet, she had no idea where that might be. Yes, everything had drastically changed. Her holidays which were coming to an end, suddenly became something completely unexpected. She had heard the expression "Love sweeping one off one's feet," but this might sweep her out to sea to a land as strange as the fabled Arabian Nights. The United Arab Emirates, she had not previously heard of, but believed the Persian Gulf must be near Iran, for she knew Iran had once been called Persia. It was all a muddle. After she was introduced to his family, she hoped to introduce him to her mother. She wanted so much to see her mother, and have a long chat about all that had happened and continued to happen.

Abdul did not sit with her in the plane. She sat with two women dressed in black in a curtained-off area of the plane. The men were dressed in lightweight summer suits or long light white airy garments and colorful woven cords around their white head coverings. Why, she wondered, did women have to wear black from head to toe in this heat while men wore light-as-a-handkerchief white flowing garments? The women that she sat among did not speak English, so she was cut off from their conversations. Nor were the magazines in English. There was no overhead film being shown, so she wrote a letter to her mother. The women smiled at her in a friendly manner and were helpful. *Would Abdul make an appearance?* she wondered. He did not.

Passport check-out was almost non-existent for their group. They held up their passports, and walked through and out into the street. Outside the airport jeeps awaited them. The three women were ushered into the back of one of the jeeps with a male driver in front. The other jeep carried Abdul and other men. The jeep with the men left first. As soon as she entered the jeep it took off immediately following the first one. The women traveled onwards without any communication among them. The sand on each side overflowed onto the road partly covering it. It whirled up into their faces stinging the faces like tiny pebbles. On the strand in England she remembered how fine and soft the sand was. Here it was gritty and coarse, with the consistency of dirt. Her clothes became peppered with it. She could feel the sand in her mouth, nose and, more painfully, in her eyes which began to feel sore and irritated. She would welcome some of the rain that fell in abundance in her homeland. The sand looked endless, and was mesmerizing and disorienting.

After what seemed like a long time, to her great relief they had left the desert behind, and were now driving through crowded streets. Her weariness from traveling eased as she became engrossed with the people all attending to their business, accustomed to the various food smells, and the din of the crowds. The drivers in the jeeps were impatient with the people who ignored them, even when they came dangerously close to running over them. Maria was in no hurry to continue, for she enjoyed this confrontation which permitted her a small amount of time to study the people, who were selling, buying, and haggling over price. The food stands had strange colorful items that smelled different from any food item she had ever seen. She would have liked to leave the jeep, and walk among these merchants and buyers but alas, she knew she could not do so. The jeeps were making their way slowly through the crowds that mostly ignored them, and the people packed in this small area did not move until the jeeps were literally pushing them forward.

On coming to a more elite area of the city, the car she rode in stopped at the entrance to a large building richly adorned in sun-drenched colors of pale apricot, yellow and cinnamon. As they entered, Maria was held spell-bound by a magnificent mosaic of blue and yellow tiles on a white background, until one of the women who had accompanied her tapped her arm, and then looking at her companion, shook out her clothing. Maria did likewise. The jeep ahead of them did not stop at the building, but continued on. After shaking the sand out of their clothing, they walked briskly for some length before they entered a large room with many pillows, frothy curtains, and couches. A tea tray had been placed there, and Maria and the women drank some tea. There was no cutlery on the tray and so in following the women, she too ate from a dish with the help of pieces of pita bread. After eating, the women reclined on pillows, and beckoned Maria to do so. Now that she had had a meal, she succumbed to sleep almost immediately.

Maria was awakened by a knock on the door. A young woman came into the room without waiting for them to answer. She led Maria to a bathroom where she could wash her face and hands and comb her hair. After her sleep, she was glad to find her eyelids were no longer red and irritated from the sand. Taking her hand, the woman led her out into the open area through a courtyard that had many beautiful flowers and trees, and then out to a waiting jeep. The women who had traveled in the jeep with her were now seated in the back of the jeep, and moved closer to each other, so that she might enter.

They drove to a modern-looking building that looked like an office building. She did not know why they had brought her here, or what to expect. Abdul had said that most of the women spoke English. If so, why was she traveling with two women who could not. They accompanied her into the building, which turned out to be a doctor's office.

Within ten minutes she entered the doctor's office alone. The doctor was dressed in an attractive deep blue dress that reached her ankles and had long sleeves. A pale blue scarf was loosely set upon her head and casually pulled back over her shoulder and so fine in texture that it did not hide her hair.

To Maria's relief this woman spoke English. She was a gynecologist and told Maria that she had been brought to her office to determine her purity. She asked her if previous to meeting Abdul she had

had a boyfriend? "No, she did not." "Did she ever have an intimate relationship?" Although she had answered no, she was nevertheless required to submit to an internal examination to verify her statement. Maria lay on the doctor's table and the doctor proceeded with the examination.

After several moments, the doctor smiled and said, "You pass." This puzzled Maria and prompted her to ask, "Passed what?"

The doctor paused before answering. "You have never been with a man."

Maria did not know what the woman spoke of, as she had already said that she didn't have a boyfriend.

"You are to be married into a renowned family. The young man in question has yet had no wife."

Encouraged by the doctor's friendliness and her fluency in English, Maria wanted to stay longer with this woman but, in a friendly yet businesslike manner, she ushered Maria to the door where she wished her happiness and many sons.

Apparently no courtship period was to take place in which they might get to know each other, nor would she be part of the wedding planning. Many of the women could speak English and would help her select clothing she would need for the occasion. Cost did not seem to be a consideration. When she told the women of her desire to have her mother present at her wedding they listened but had nothing to say on the matter. She wanted to speak with her husband-to-be about this, but saw little of him in the days and weeks that followed. When she saw him he was always with other men, whom she was told were his brothers and cousins, and it was not permissible for her to approach him at such a time. Nobody could have so many brothers and male cousins, she felt, and so believed she misunderstood what the women had told her. The house was big enough to accommodate a great many family relatives without any of them coming upon each other.

She was brought to a large room in the women's quarters where they gathered to chat, laugh, and sometimes rise from their cushions and dance, while others clapped, all enjoying the gaiety of the evening. The women there spent much time dressing for these women-only occasions, for no men ever entered these quarters.

The evening before the wedding, Abdul sent for her. He smiled at her and she knew she loved him with every fiber of her being. Yet, she was uneasy about these feelings. How could she fall in love with him? How could she not? Some of the young women had older husbands, and none had a husband as handsome as Abdul. She should feel blessed. *I should be the happiest person on earth, or in heaven,* she thought. Yet, she had a feeling of being isolated, different, an outsider, and lost without her mother. If Abdul, had met her in England, dressed in western-style clothing, looking as he did like a film star with his handsome good looks, her mother and friends would have thought him fascinating, and a most desirable choice. Her mother had said one always had a choice. Yes, she had, and she had made the choice to marry Abdul. Here all was confusing, which she believed caused her to doubt her decision.

If only my mother were here, Maria thought, *everything would be well.*

Abdul presented her with beautiful jewels, and, waited for her reaction.

"These are exquisite," she told him in awe of these precious stones. Yet, she could not envision herself wearing these expensive jewels. They looked like what the Queen of England would wear, or a potential queen. She would feel foolish adorned in such as these.

"Tomorrow we marry," he smiled at her. "Are you happy?"

"Yes," she replied, although filled with doubt and feeling like a prisoner. If her mother were with her all would be perfect, she thought, and added, "I'd love to have my mother at my wedding."

His face went blank. She had no idea what he was thinking. Did she ask at the wrong time? The women had said if their first night together went well, he would be very generous to her, and should she give him a son, he would grant her anything within his power to give. In her excitement to see her mother, she forgot what the women had said, and desperately wanting her mother to be with her on her wedding day, had spoken rashly. *I must be more patient,* she chided herself.

"Perhaps after we're married she can come here. I would like very much to see her," she amended her statement.

He nodded his head and left the room.

Was his reason for choosing her due to the differences in her appearance from the other women here? If so, she found that strange and very shallow. Now, reflecting on how she had instantly fallen in love with him due to his physical appearance and charm, how frivolous were her reasons as well? *What would her mother think of such shallowness*

CHAPTER 7

The marriage ritual was strange and foreign to Maria. As part of the marriage rites, Abdul went into one of the very large rooms with the other men where they celebrated the occasion of his marriage, while she was swept into another room filled with women who ate from the wedding banquet, after which they listened to music and danced singly or in groups. They insisted she enter the merrymaking although she was feeling sad that she was not dancing with her spouse on this their very special day. As evening progressed they belly-danced, and when they found she had never belly-danced, one of the women stood behind her and, with her hands on Maria's hips, gently guided them in a circular movement to the rhythm of the music, while another woman, Jasmine by name, stood in front of her gracefully moving her hands while demonstrating how the dance should be performed. Maria was fascinated by the dance, and the joy and freedom of these movements erased her sadness as she truly entered into the celebration.

As the evening wore down, they watched the film, <u>West Side Story</u>. They wanted Maria to show them how to dance, as the characters in the film danced, but she had never danced like that. What would she teach them? She would forego the waltz since one needed a male partner to waltz, and proceeded to teach them how to polka as her mother had taught her. They enjoyed this very much and all wanted to try it. The room resounded with so much noise from the stamping of feet that it took a while before any of them heard the knocking on the door, and opened it. One of the male servants was standing at the door inquiring as to what was causing the loud noises coming from the room. They informed him it was a new dance they were learning. He was confused, but accepted their answer, and conveyed this information to the men at their wedding celebration.

When chimes were sounded, the women kissed and hugged her before leaving. Maria was told to stay until called for. She sat alone for some moments, until an older woman entered the room and requested Maria to follow her. The woman led her to a bedroom with a bed so large it would take up every inch of space in the bedroom her mother and she had shared. This woman helped her bathe and dress in the nightwear the other girls had helped her choose. After brushing Maria's hair, she was told to wait and her husband would come to her.

She was not sure what to do when he would come. Her mother had told her what not to do or permit when with a boy, but she had not told her what to do in a situation like the one she now found herself in. She had received information on what to do when dating, but nothing on what to do, or expect, on being married. Abdul entered the room.

It was a strange feeling being in bed with a man, a man she hardly knew. In the time she had known Abdul she had never been this close to him or been touched by his long sensitive fingers. This then was marriage, she figured, as he touched parts of her nobody had ever touched before. She was being lured into a soothing dreamlike state. Then without warning he hurt her. Instinctively, she tried to pull away from the source of the pain but could not for her actions made him hold her closer. She felt deceived. He had lured her by sensations she had never before known, and then he had abruptly hurt her.

Moments later he let go of her. She jumped out of bed. From a relatively safe distance she looked at him. His eyes were closed, and an expression of peace and contentment lay on his face. Slowly, she returned to the bed. After a while he rose, pulled his robe around his body, bent over and kissed her, and headed towards the bathroom. She lay there feeling sore.

If the night went well, the women had said, he would be most generous. Generous enough, she wondered, to permit her mother to come here? Did the night go well? Would her trying to pull away from him mean she had failed? This whole night confused her.

On emerging from the bathroom, he got into bed beside her. She hoped he did not wish to continue. "It only hurts the first time," he whispered. "Your mother should have told you what to expect."

"My mother didn't know I was to be married," she answered in defense of her mother.

"Sleep well, Maria," he softly replied and turning on his side, was soon asleep. She arose and went to the bathroom.

* * *

Abdul was not unknown to Scotland Yard. He had been a student at Oxford, where he excelled on the debating team. He was a well-spoken, quiet, engaging person who was well liked. He wore only western clothing, and completely fitted in with his fellow students, who were unaware of his family wealth and connections, and knew him only by the name he used at Oxford. His independent ways brought him to the attention of the police for he had a tendency to side with, and once walked in protest with, those whom he saw as being wronged or mistreated.

Scotland Yard's more recent report on Abdul confirmed that Abdul and Maria had been legally married according to Islamic law. Maria had freely entered into this marriage. Shortly after they were married, they went to the Swiss Alps, where Abdul skied. Due to his athletic expertise his bodyguards had a difficult time keeping track of him on the slopes. Abdul and Maria took long walks together, and could be seen a few times walking around the town, where they made some purchases. The people in the town remembered them as a very happy couple.

The Yard's report was wholly different from the recent reports in the newspapers. There was no kidnapping! Maria was lawfully married to Abdul. If their relationship had changed since their stay in Switzerland, well, that was the nature of marriage, some worked out well, while others did not.

* * *

As Maria packed a small valise to go to the coral-filled waters of the Gulf, she thought how nice it would be to be there, or anywhere, alone with Abdul. The only time they had been alone had been for a brief time in Spain and Morocco, but even in Morocco they had been joined by his kin and friends for dinner, and who remained with them for the rest of their stay in Morocco, and for the two blissful weeks in

Switzerland. Otherwise, Abdul was seldom without his extended family.

Well, if they must make this trip with his family members, Maria felt happy that Jasmine, whom she greatly admired, her very likeable husband Ramiz, and their three delightful children, would be sharing this holiday. They were going to the yet unspoiled beaches near Ras Al-Khaimah. They rode in two land rovers. Abdul sat at the wheel of one and Ramiz drove the other. The children wanted to ride with Abdul and so the two boys sat in their vehicle while their younger sister rode with her parents.

When they came to an area where they had the road to themselves, all those riding in the cars got out save the drivers who behaved like schoolboys as they raced each other, blocked one another, and gleefully passed the other on the road with the children cheering them on. After much daredevil driving they all continued their trip to the beach near Ras Al-Khaimah. Their game had come to an end with each man gleefully proclaiming himself as the winner.

On the beach, the children wanted to play ball, and their expectation that Abdul and Ramiz would join them was fulfilled. The young boys, dressed in cotton knit shirts and shorts, kicked off their sandals, impatient to start the game, while, Ramiz, in slacks and a green knit shirt, threw his sandals onto the sand. Abdul, who remained in traditional dress minus his footwear, was playfully tossing the ball in the air. It was agreed that the eldest boy would play with his father against Abdul and the younger boy.

Ramiz, although heavy of build, was remarkably fast on his feet and swift in cornering the ball. Abdul moved as a ballet dancer as he jumped for the ball, and when he kicked it, his long white clothing swished around his tall lean body which moved with extraordinary grace.

Jasmine, wearing a pale yellow shirtdress, with the buttons close to her neck open and her long sleeves folded back to the elbows, looked at Maria, breaking into her concentration. "He is handsome, is he not?" There was no doubt of whom Jasmine spoke.

"Yes, he is. Have you known Abdul for a long time?"

"Yes, you might say we grew up together. As children we were very competitive. Rivals, you might say. I love him like a brother."

Why does Abdul wear Arabic clothing while Ramiz and the children wear western-style clothing."

"Would he look different to you in western clothes?"

"Perhaps, but he'd still be very handsome."

"He is a traditionalist, always was, as is his father. His father, however, never wears western-style clothing while Abdul, when in a non-Muslim country, does."

"Abdul was wearing western-style clothing when I met him in Spain, but in Morocco he changed into traditional dress."

"It makes sense to wear the traditional menswear here in the Emirates or in any hot climate. White is cooler and those garments are very light-weight and catch the slightest breeze, even from the movement of one's legs while walking. Unlike slacks, there is no tightness around the waist, and there is more freedom of movement which makes them better suited to our climate."

"It is strange to see some wear the traditional dress while others wear western clothing."

"Not strange in Dubai. There is a great mixture of dress here and all clothing is acceptable. Dubai is the most modern Middle East metropolis."

Maria, who felt very comfortable in a flowered skirt and a long-sleeved cotton blouse, asked, "Why is this area called the United Arab Emirates?"

"That all came about through tough negotiations by Sheik Zayed. He got seven small sheikdoms to join together: Abu Dhabi, Dubai, Ajman, Fujairah, Ras al Khaimah, Sharjah, and Umm al Quwain under one banner. Small countries, especially those squabbling with one another, could be easy prey for larger countries, especially if the smaller countries have a resource such as oil. The UAE has the third largest reserve of oil."

"Then this Sheik Zayed must be a hero here."

"After the death of Sheik Zayed, outside critics said the UAE wouldn't last, but it has and is the only United Arab states in the region."

"I gather that is why there are fantastic hotels, fabulous shopping malls, and so much prosperity here!"

"Yes, our traditional Bedouin lifestyle and customs continue alongside very western versions of rampant consumerism, and we all manage to harmonize such disparate and opposing forces. Before oil was discovered, the region was a backwater where the sheikdoms were nothing more than tiny enclaves of fishermen, pearl divers, all with rivalries and conflict."

"The Texas of the East!" Maria concluded at which Jasmine laughed, then added, "I think the bigger boys have had enough soccer."

Walking towards the land rovers, Jasmine took out the coolers filled with water, juices and chopped fruit, and placed them on a cloth on the sand, as she called to the sweaty ballplayers. They stopped for cold drinks and to briefly relax before going to the hotel for showers and supper.

"Did Abdul remember to tell you we'll be staying overnight?"

"Yes," Maria answered.

The happy crew of ballplayers sat in the sand contentedly drinking and splashing themselves with cold drinks. Maria was pleasantly surprised at the way Jasmine and Ramiz's children clung with such familiarity to Abdul and how playful he was with them. The boys seemed to be always holding onto him and when the little girl, tired from the day's activities, sat herself in his lap, he circled his arms around her. He will make a very good father, Maria happily believed. *Yes, she was fortunate to be loved by such a good man as Abdul,* she mused, *and looked forward to someday having his child.*

At the supper table Maria was delighted when Jasmine stated that their spouses must dance with them before going to the gaming tables.

"What about the children," Maria asked.

"We never take the children to any hotel that does not provide supervised activities that the children would enjoy," Ramiz answered.

"I don't dance," Abdul softly stated.

"Do not tell me that, after all the dance lessons I've given you," Jasmine admonished him.

"Apparently, I was not a good student," Abdul smiled in reply.

"You will dance," Jasmine pronounced with a measure of determination mixed with pleading.

Although awkward on the dance floor, Abdul never stepped on her toes. It was difficult for Maria to understand how Abdul could be so fluid and graceful playing soccer, and yet dance so stiffly. Yet, with his arm around her and his body pressed next to hers, she was happier than she could have dreamed of being.

Jasmine and Maria left the gaming tables early so that they might change before walking out in the early morning darkness. Camel drivers in the distance made a picturesque image on the desert sand as they traveled in slow motion under the star-filled sky. After viewing this vision from the past, Jasmine said, "These camel drivers live as our ancestors did."

"Has prosperity left them behind?"

"They are more prosperous now, but they cling to the old ways."

Abdul and Ramiz joined them and the four of them traveled onwards, until they came to an area with an enclosure of horses. Abdul, Ramiz, and Jasmine all mounted horses. Maria declined. Then the three of them raced along the sand to a designated point and back. Jasmine kept pace with the other two as she, in her wide-legged pants, straddled the horse. Although Abdul won, it was only by inches over Jasmine's horse. Both Jasmine's and Abdul's horses raced neck and neck most of the way with Ramiz's horse coming in at a respectable distance behind them.

Maria lay awake from the excitement of the day, while Abdul, exhausted from the soccer game and horse riding, fell asleep immediately. As she lay awake, it saddened Maria to think how her mother must have felt when she did not return to England with her friends.

When she had asked Abdul if she could get stamps to mail her mother a letter he was silent for a moment before answering. "Yes," he had said and then requested that she give him any letters she wanted mailed and he would take care of them. She did so. She wrote many letters to her mother. She would have liked to have written to Penny and Daphne but she did not know their addresses. They had traveled on the underground, each of them getting on at different stations, all heading to the same building to work, but she had never been to either of their homes, nor had they to hers until the morning they left London for their holidays in Spain.

Time moved on and Maria waited in happy anticipation for a reply but no word came from her mother. *Had something happened to her mother?* she wondered. *Was her mother sick?* She wrote her mother again. Months passed without a piece of mail from her. Worried that her mother had not replied to her letters, she approached her husband and asked that her mother be brought there. He told her it was difficult to get a passport to leave England, or any European country, to travel to the Middle East. He left the room without further comment. She wondered how she could present her case to her husband, so that she would not merely be dismissed. When she asked the women they changed the subject. "We cannot speak of those things," one of the older women, on seeing her forlorn appearance, gently told her. "We leave such things to Allah." She cried, realizing the hopelessness of the situation. The older woman reached out and held her, and for a moment, Maria felt as though she was once again in her mother's arms.

The women, to a great extent, dressed for each other and danced for each other and this seemed strange to Maria. Sometimes the wives and their husbands went in groups on trips. Paris was one of the favorite places for the women to go to buy clothes, and they also spoke about attending the Fashion Houses of Madrid. They did not seem to know that it was in Madrid that she had met Abdul. To the hilarity of all, as they spoke they imitated the way the glamorous models walked down the runways.

They had many children among them, but Maria could never determine which children were born to which of the women. Maria very much wanted to have a child. Her choice would be a daughter, but she was given to know that a girl child brought no status, or great jubilation among the men. Alone at night, she thought of her mother and how desperately she wanted to see her. She wondered what Daphne and Penny would think of her husband. If communication between Abdul and her were better, he would understand how much she needed her mother, and life would be perfect. She felt she could bear almost anything if her mother were with her.

She loved Abdul and believed he loved her, yet when she tried to verbally reach him, she failed. They never truly had a conversation of any length, which was a cause of concern to her, but apparently did not bother him. He certainly didn't confide in her. Communication between them was flawed, and she did not know how to fix it. She remembered what her mother had said of Othello:

mistrust and the lack of communication, was what destroyed his marriage to Desdemona. Often she had seen Abdul in prolonged conversation with male members of the family. *Was she not as close to him as they were? Would this situation change in time? How much time,* she wondered, *would it take for them to freely speak to each other.*

As time went on Maria became a part of the women's lives. They gleefully did the polka, listened to music and danced. What she enjoyed most was the time she spent with the children who loved to touch her hair and tell her they too wanted blue eyes.

Suddenly one morning she woke up sick to her stomach and vomiting, and was astonished and hurt that the women laughed at her misery. We must celebrate, they told her as they danced around her. Amid the celebration they told her that a child might be growing inside of her. What they said proved to be true.

Finding herself pregnant she was joyfully happy, but also sad, for at a time like this she felt the absence of her mother almost unbearable. She watched in amazement as her body expanded. As it became large, Abdul removed himself from their bed. In the anxious days that followed she had the comfort of neither her spouse nor her mother and her happiness diminished. She wished she could exchange all the beautiful jewels Abdul had given her for a plane ticket to England, or to send the money she might obtain from them to her mother, so that she might come and be with her during this time. Out of her misery she recalled what the women had said: Abdul would give her anything within his power to give, should she have a son. So in time she felt her request would be granted.

CHAPTER 8

Maria gave birth to a son. The baby was passed from arm to arm among the male relatives. She had worried that his fair complexion and blue eyes would cause him to be rejected by these tanned, dark-haired people, but his fairness merely made him more special. He soon became his grandfather's favorite among his grandsons. Abdul referred to the child as his son, and all the other males referred to baby Waheed as Abdul's son, without mentioning that the child was also hers.

It was over nine months since she had made her earnestly sought request to Abdul. Now that she had given him a son, she would again approach Abdul with another idea that would make it possible for her to visit her mother, and her mother to see her first grandchild. First, however, she had to go through the waiting period. When the waiting period was over, Abdul would return to their bed, and she would make her request. There was much rejoicing. Abdul bestowed more precious jewels on her, but did not grant her request. She found herself sinking into depression. The jewels, alas, could not bring happiness, and she found no pleasure in them.

When their son was ten months old, she made the request that the three of them, Abdul, Waheed and she, visit her mother in England. When he said he would not go to England, she asked that she and the child be permitted to visit her mother. Her request was not granted.

Maria had been persistent in her request; for to stop would mean she had abandoned her mother. Like the old woman in the worn book belonging to her mother, who unceasingly pleaded with the judge, and in order to stop her from pestering him any further, he granted her request, she too had persisted, but to no avail.

She had nobody to intercede on her behalf—nobody to appeal to. Even her mother could not help her in this situation. Hopeless, all seemed hopeless, but all she had left was hope, and she knew she must hold onto it.

Abdul sent word that he was coming to her, and so she waited. She had never waited so long prior to this and wondered what had caused the delay. Hour after hour she waited throughout the night until she fell asleep. When she awoke the next morning and realized he had not come, she cried. He was the one who had brought her here, married her, and now rejected her. Even if he wished to dissolve the marriage, she doubted she would be permitted to return home. In losing his favor, she would have no standing whatsoever among his people.

As the day wore on, she became aware that all the women knew what had happened the previous night. She suspected the men also had been informed that her husband had summoned her without going to her. She had insisted on making a request that he did not wish to grant, and as a punishment he had called for her, then did not make an appearance. Her shame was paraded in front of her wherever she went as though she wore a scarlet letter on her chest.

Abdul's harsh discipline had become a public embarrassment for her. She could feel the women's sympathy. She found herself walking with her eyes downcast. Her feelings towards Abdul were in turmoil. She had been bewitched by his handsome face and captivating smile, but she had had no idea that the person beneath would remain a stranger to her, a stranger who kept her walking on sand rather than solid ground. *How,* she wondered, *did he perceive her?* All she had in the world now was their son Waheed, who was a most delightful child.

Shortly before Waheed's first birthday, while walking to the nursery as she usually did in the morning after breakfast, she forced herself to look happy for his sake, and indeed when in his presence she was happiest. As she walked to his crib, she noticed he appeared to be asleep. Why does he sleep when the babies around him are active and vocal?

"Wake up sleepyhead," she called to him as she approached the crib, calling him by name. Standing over him her heart froze. Waheed lay lifeless on the small mattress. Two other women were in the nursery, and heard Maria gasp in horror, then scream.

Soon people were rushing into and out of the nursery. In the midst of the commotion, Abdul arrived, followed by a doctor. Maria sat in a daze on the floor. The full realization that her son was dead stunned her into silence, as she stared blankly ahead. Abdul sat down on the floor beside her, and with his arm cradling her they sat in silence. Due to her dazed frame of mind, Abdul's gesture was lost to her. After several minutes the doctor beckoned him, and Abdul gently removed his arm from his wife, rose and walked towards the doctor. They spoke in hushed tones for a few moments, and then left the room together.

Some of the women brought Maria to her apartment and laid her down on the bed. After the initial shock wore off, she walked to the nursery, half hoping Waheed was alive. The possibility that he had died was too unbelievable to penetrate her mind. Yesterday Waheed was a healthy, happy baby. There had to be some mistake, perhaps it was all a bad dream, she felt as she remembered his face and laughter of the previous day. When she arrived at the nursery his crib was empty.

Maria demanded to know where her son was. The other women had never before seen the quiet reserved young mother act this way.

"Tell me where he is," she insisted in a raised voice.

One of the women who had slipped out of the nursery returned with the doctor who Maria thought might explain to her what had happened to her son, but he, against her protest, forced a needle into her arm.

Abdul came to her the following morning. He explained that one of the other women went to the nursery before dawn and put a pillow over Waheed's head, smothering him. The woman was disturbed by the attention the boys' grandfather showered on Waheed, thus replacing her three-year-old son, his previous favorite, in his grandfather's eyes.

"Who among them would do this?"

"Laila."

Laila who stood behind her, placing her hands on her hips to help her sway while belly-dancing, Maria remembered. A friend! A sister! Whom can I trust?

"She will die for this horrible deed."

Maria wondered, since nobody saw Laila perform this dreadful act, what proof was there.

"Are you sure Laila did this?"

"Yes, she confessed. The execution will take place tomorrow at dawn."

"Execution! By what means?"

"She will be stoned. We both must be there."

"Stoned? I don't want to witness that."

"You must. I will throw the first stone, and then you will throw a stone. Just one stone each is all that is required of us. Others will finish the task."

"I cannot participate in her stoning," Maria protested in horror.

"Do you not care that our son was murdered?"

That was the first time she heard Abdul refer to Waheed as *their son.*

"You must participate. Our part will be brief. If you wish, I can arrange for a woman to take you inside after you have thrown a stone."

Maria shook her head in silence.

"Not to do so would bring dishonor to Waheed, and disgrace upon me and my family. You will do it," he insisted, as he hurriedly left the room.

Maria was distraught. What she had wanted from Abdul was consolation in their shared loss, the feel of his arms around her, being able to talk about the one thing they had in common, their child. She had expected that they would reach out to each other in this calamity, but that didn't happen. Instead, Abdul had demanded that she participate in the death of a young woman by stoning, thus making Laila's young son motherless. Might forgiveness, she asked herself, better honor Waheed rather than this inhumane form of death for a woman who, in seeing her son being ignored in favor of another child, had momentarily lost all reasoning? If only she had known how Laila felt, and had spoken to her, perhaps she could have saved Waheed's life and Laila from this terrible death.

Maria slept fitfully, her dreams filled with nightmares of running barefooted over hot sand with Waheed in her arms, as crowds of people followed throwing stones at her. As they were about to catch up with her, her cloak slid off and looking down she saw that she carried not Waheed but Daoud, the son of Laila. She awakened trembling uncontrollably, her nightclothes soaked in sweat. It was hours before she was able to fall asleep again. More frightening dreams followed.

It seemed she had just fallen asleep when she was awakened by one of the older women, Sarah by name. It was early morning. Since she had had nothing but bad dreams during the night, her body was not rested. She lacked the energy to rise, but the woman insisted she must make haste, for Abdul and the rest of the household were long awake and preparations had taken place. Maria looked at the clock. It was fifteen minutes past five o'clock. She thought she heard water flowing. Rain! For a moment she was back in England listening to the falling rain. As she felt the woman pushing her out of bed, that relaxing moment was pushed from her mind. No rain was predicted for this region's dry earth. At the insistence of the woman, she entered the bathroom, where she showered. This was as close to water as she could get. While she was in the bathroom, the woman laid out a long black silk fitted coat, and a black scarf.

When Maria returned to the room, she found a tray of hot tea, bread and honey on a small table in the room. She drank the tea but could not bring herself to eat. The woman spoke to her about needing to eat, but Maria shook her head.

After she had dressed and put on the coat, the woman proceeded to button the slim coat from neck to ankles, and fixed the scarf on the poorly combed hair of the unresponsive girl.

The woman walked with her out into the early morning calm.

"It will be brief, just minutes, and soon over," the woman soothingly consoled her.

After walking a short distance, they came to a courtyard that Maria had never before seen. The silence was deafening as a crowd of people stood motionless in horror. Then Sarah walked with Maria over to the lone figure of Abdul. He did not acknowledge her presence. The woman then left to join one of the groups of spectators in their silent vigil.

Maria tried not to focus on the reason for their presence here in the courtyard, or on their dead son. After several minutes, a small figure covered from head to toe in a black garment was led by two men to a post less than twenty feet from where Abdul and Maria stood. The crowds became quite noisy. The men left the woman there, and walked towards where Abdul and Maria stood, handing Abdul a stone about the size of a woman's fist. Abdul received the stone, and reaching out, he took Maria's hand and placed the stone in it, closing her reluctant fingers around it. Then he took the larger stone that he'd been given. Abdul waited quietly for a few minutes and then threw the stone. It hit its mark and Maria heard a low moan. "Now," he said, but his wife stood frozen on the spot. She could not raise her hand. "Now," Maria, he demanded, but still she could not participate in the ritual death of this woman. Laila had sunk down, and now looked like a black rock on the ground before them. It had been a horrible night, Maria thought, and it is now proving to be a dreadful day.

For the first time since they stood there, Abdul looked at his wife. She could see the anger in his eyes, and it frightened her, yet she could not do as he commanded of her. The stone she held fell to the ground, as though the stone itself had decided on this solution.

Abdul raised his hand for a moment, then lowering it, walked from the courtyard. His young wife followed him. Nothing happened for several moments, but just as they entered an open-air passageway off the courtyard, a selected group continued what Abdul had begun. As the pounding stones hit their target and bounced on the ground, a great noise came from the people. Maria fell to her knees and wept. This involuntary action further displeased Abdul.

"You have dishonored our son, and brought shame upon me and my family." "I'm sorry. What you asked was beyond my ability to do," Maria weakly answered, greatly distressed by what had just taken place.

"Do you not care that she murdered my son and yours?"

"His death grieves me terribly. Her death will not restore him to us, and it makes her young son motherless. Showing forgiveness to Laila would have been a better source of peace for me than taking her life." Maria knew that that thing that looked like a black rock was Laila kneeling under a black covering. With dread she now saw that she knelt as the stoned woman had. Would Abdul, due to some offense of hers, cast the first stone at her? This woman's husband had not been among the spectators. Why did he not plead with Abdul on his wife's behalf? He did not throw a stone, but neither did he do anything to prevent it. Unfortunately, Laila's marriage had been less than desirable. Her sole reason for being, her whole joy in life, had been her son. To see her beloved son being replaced in his grandfather's affection weighed heavily on her, and led her to a reckless, deadly decision. If Laila had planned this murder, Maria was convinced she would have had time to consider the consequences of her actions on herself and on her son. Therefore, it must have been a rash act committed by her after seeing Daoud's pain at being displaced in his grandfather's affection.

"Stoning is a gruesome form of death."

"Why does death by stoning affect you so greatly?"

"It is barbaric!"

"Is hanging a more merciful way to die? To be hanged by the neck? In the days of King Henry VIII and his daughter Elizabeth I, to be drawn and quartered was a popular form of execution by your countrymen. Even your royalty did not escape going to the executioner's block to have their heads chopped off. Stoning has been in practice since biblical times. Even Jesus was present when a crowd gathered for a stoning."

"Yes. Then he asked the person who was without sin to throw the first stone. None came forward, and the woman was saved. Would any of the people who threw stones today have been able to come forward as Jesus had asked?"

Not answering her question he continued, "Do you realize the gruesomeness of being drawn and quartered? A man was partially hanged, and then taken down and quartered alive by having his body cut from the collarbone to his sexual organs, and then cut across. Sometimes his entrails were removed, and often he was tied to a wagon and dragged through the town. Barbaric?" Abdul said, as he turned and walked away.

Maria's feelings for Abdul had drastically changed after witnessing the stoning. Looking at his departing figure, she wondered if he would throw the first stone if she found a way to leave him and was brought back. Suddenly she felt terribly alone.

Sarah, who had left the courtyard, and had been waiting for Abdul to leave, approached Maria and helped her to stand, then led her back to the women's quarters.

"What punishment would he place on her for disobeying his command to throw a stone," she wondered later in the day. Should he summon her and not show himself, that would no longer hurt her, nor would it bother her if everyone from the eldest to the youngest members of this extended household knew she was being shunned by her husband. Her son was gone. Her husband, at the time of their greatest pain, thought only of revenge on Laila, and punishment for her. She had nothing more to lose.

As the days and weeks passed, he did not summon her. She wondered if he would in time lose his anger towards her. She had, however, no desire to share his bed. She remembered the pain of their first night together. It had been unexpected but was soon over. Back then she had no idea of the pain that lay ahead for her, a lingering pain that would remain as part of her existence.

Three months after Waheed's death, some of the women became very excited. They and their husbands were going to Monte Carlo on holiday. The women looked forward to doing some clothes shopping. Seeing Maria standing silently in a corner of the room slightly curbed their excitement.

"Give me your measurements and I'll get you a stunning gown," Jasmine, who had showed Maria how to belly-dance, spoke.

Some of the women had told her that Jasmine was not her given name; it was a name she had chosen for herself. Regardless of what name Jasmine was known by, Maria knew that Jasmine would always be a bright and fascinating woman. She thanked her, but turned down the offer.

Maria's jewels were merely hard stones and no comfort to her as she had lost interest in her appearance. Shortly before they left, she heard that Abdul would be among the group leaving for Monte Carlo. This then, she felt, was her punishment for disobeying him by not throwing the stone. She felt a tinge of pain on this discovery but had no great desire to join them, and felt her sorrow would only cast a pall over their holiday.

Shortly after their return, everyone noticed that Maria had lost weight and no longer took care of her appearance. Sarah took her aside, and touching Maria's hair, muttered, "Oh, darling, you haven't been brushing your beautiful hair." Then she took a brush from her bag and commenced to brush Maria's hair. After a few moments while still brushing the young woman's hair, she asked, "What food did you like to eat in England?" Maria, taken aback by this question managed a smile, something she had not done in what seemed a very long time. "Tell me, child, and Abdul will see to it that whatever you'd like to eat will be prepared for you. See," she said, holding Maria at arm's length, "you have lost much weight." On a sadder note, she added, "Your beautiful face has lost its healthy glow and your eyes have lost their brightness." Putting the hairbrush aside, the woman placed her arm around the young woman, and sitting down drew Maria to herself.

"Why are you so sad, Abdul loves you."

"His actions belie what you say."

"Abdul is his father's favorite child. After four girls were born to this wife, Abdul arrived. There was great celebration. Oh my, what a celebration! We all received beautiful gifts as part of the celebration. Yes, the boy was given everything. You might say he was spoiled, but we all only saw his tenderness and the beguiling smile on his handsome face. Is he not handsome?"

"Yes, he is very handsome, but a stranger to me even after a son was born to us. The loss of our son was the most agonizing event of my life and his, yet he did not speak to me of our mutual grief. In this worst of times when we might have consoled each other in our shared pain, he abandoned me."

"You come from a different culture, whose ways are not our ways. Women know best how women feel and how to console each other. Men, likewise, understand the ways of men. You do not allow your sisters to lament with you. Abdul receives help from his brothers."

Maria understood what Sarah was trying to convey, but still clung to her own cultural ways, although she realized they were not perfect either. Men in England often sought sympathy in the unspoken silence of their male friends, usually in a pub, while women gathered at the home of the woman to comfort her in her grief. She wanted what should be but often was not—the sharing of pain by the two most greatly affected. If her mother were here, she knew, her mother would help her through this most difficult time. Her mother! Maybe people from different cultures were not so far apart. Her mother would have helped her through her greatest crisis. The difference was that these 'sisters' were not as close to her, which was probably mostly her fault, for she still felt like an outsider in the group. She had wanted Abdul and her to console one another since this loss was for both of them, the greatest loss that had ever befallen them.

The woman who held her in her arms temporarily soothed her pain, and in helping her see it from Abdul's point of view, gave her the first small relief from grief since Waheed's death.

"Revenge is not the answer, love is stronger and more healing, and yet after this tragedy, Abdul left on this family trip without me," Maria softly uttered as though speaking to herself.

"The male members of the family most likely suggested this trip for him, for he suffers inwardly. It was probably decided that you were in no condition to enjoy any kind of travel at this time."

"Perhaps not, but why wasn't I given the choice? Surely I am the best judge of how I feel, or what I can undertake to do?" Maria, having at her disposal a caring person to confide in, asserted herself now in words as she had never done before.

"Yes, but the men in consoling Abdul, most likely recommended he join this trip. I do not believe it was to slight you, but rather that their sympathy was confined to him and what would be best for him at this time." Into the silence that followed, Sarah spoke, "Tell me darling what you'd like to eat, and it will be ordered and cooked for you. It is Abdul who requested that I ask you this." Maria smiled up at the woman. "Good, you smile. Your smile is a good sign. You will never forget Waheed, but life goes on and so must we. Yes, it will take time for you to recover from this, but you will."

Maria was grateful to the older woman, yet her heart ached for her son. As Sarah had said, only time would heal this wound inside of her. Her mother's presence would be a tremendous help at this time but that was denied her, and so she now held not one but two great losses in her young life.

Still finding it difficult to live with Abdul's rejection, she felt that inasmuch as she loved Abdul, living with him was too painful, and if the possibility of escaping ever presented itself, she would risk leaving him.

CHAPTER 9

When the holiday makers returned, it was decided that, should Maria wish it, every fortnight two of the women would accompany her to a nearby shopping center, a very elite place. She did not know for sure who made this decision on her behalf, but believed it had to be Abdul. This announcement, however, did not brighten her spirits.

Remembering Laila's son was now without a mother, Maria walked into the nursery. It was the first time she had been there since Waheed had died. The women were playing with their children or rocking them to sleep. Then she noticed Daoud sitting in a corner by himself looking very much alone and sad. "Daoud," she addressed him. He looked up at her from the bench he was sitting on, and stared at her as though he had committed some offense. She picked him up and, sitting on the bench, held him on her lap. He seemed fearful and sat very still. He had been watching and waiting for his mother each morning. He did not know why his mother didn't come to play with or read to him. The other mothers did not exactly ostracize him, but rather didn't know how to relate to the child of a woman who had committed such a vile act. It was, in their eyes, as though the child was tainted by his mother's deed.

As Maria gently rocked Daoud, she sang him a nursery song in Polish that her mother had sung to her when she was a child. As she sang, his stiff body loosened, and he laid his head on her breast. Here was someone who needed her, she thought, and then shortly after realized that she too needed someone to love. She would try to help this motherless child, and so decided to come to the nursery every morning after breakfast to spend some time with him, as she had once done with Waheed. Soon she was singing children's songs to him with hand gestures which he greatly enjoyed, and they laughed as their hands touched. In the cool of the evening, she would return to the nursery and take Daoud for a walk in the inner courtyard. She saw his face light up in a wide smile when she entered the nursery, and it gave her much joy. After a while some of the other children, who had ignored Daoud, would come over and sit with them, and Daoud knew that he alone could sit on her lap, and that he was special to her.

Jasmine, walking into the common room to retrieve a scarf she had left behind, saw the woman who had been talking to Maria, leave.

"So you have been talking to Sarah?"

"Yes."

"She is Abdul's father's wife."

"Is she Abdul's mother?"

"No, his mother is dead."

"What caused her death?"

"Her indiscretions."

"What do you mean?"

"She fell in love with another man, and was planning to leave with him. His father discovered her plot, and had her brought back."

"He took her back and forgave her?"

"How innocent you are Maria. He had her stoned in the same courtyard where Laila met her death."

"How dreadful," Maria uttered in horror.

"She knew the consequences of her folly."

"What happened to the man?"

"He had a rich and powerful father and his punishment was banishment."

"That is not the same as losing one's life. Why should she have died in such a manner and he be allowed to live the life of the wealthy abroad?"

Jasmine laughed, before continuing. "Two years later he was murdered by another woman's husband, who accused him of having had an affair with his wife. The man who murdered him was a Christian. It is said his father never recovered from his son's death. His father died shortly after." Maria sat in silence, appalled by this news.

While tying her scarf around her neck, Jasmine spoke, "None of us can have everything we desire."

Wishing to know more, Maria continued the conversation

"What would have been the consequences if a wife ran away, not with another man but because her husband beat her or treated her cruelly?"

"The same as if she left with a man. You don't have to worry about that," Jasmine laughed, "for Abdul is a kind and gentle person."

"If your husband died, would you have to remarry?"

"If Ramiz should die," Jasmine stated, "I will not remarry. My father is in agreement with this; he provided me with a good education and I should be able to support myself. My father is rich but very much a part of the old ways. He believes a woman must forfeit her life if she has committed adultery."

"Even if the woman in question is his daughter?"

"Yes."

"Are you happy in your marriage?"

Jasmine laughed. "When I was given in marriage to Ramiz, I was very disappointed. He was almost twenty years older than I and could not be called handsome. His first wife had died and he had been without a wife for quite some time."

"After I got to know him, she continued, I fell in love with him. I remember our wedding night. I did not want to get into bed with him. I thought he'd be angry, but instead he asked me if I knew how to play cards! When I said I didn't, he sat down on the bed, and beckoned me to join him as he shuffled the cards. 'I'll teach you,' he said, with a twinkle in his eye and a half-smile on his face. Soon we were enjoying ourselves. He was an excellent teacher. We played cards until the early hours of the morning. Then he kissed me, and as he was about to leave, turned and said, "When you're ready, Jasmine, I'll be most happy."

"Ramiz has a fantastic sense of humor, and we enjoy being together. When we are in Monte Carlo, he brings me to the gambling tables and provides me with chips. He seems happier when I win than when he does. We go together to whatever entertainment the casino has to offer. He particularly likes it when a good comedian is performing. I go shopping with the women where I buy clothes to wear at our gatherings, and I also buy clothes that will delight my generous, lovable and witty husband."

"You must be the happiest woman in the group."

"And to think I was once angry with my father, and disappointed by his choice," Jasmine laughed. "My father is very pleased that I am happy in my marriage. Years later when I asked him why he chose Ramiz for me, he said to spare my life! He wanted, he said, a son-in-law that I wouldn't tire of, and someone who was mature enough to be able to handle a strong-minded woman," Jasmine added with an amused smile. I told him now that I had given Ramiz two sons and a daughter, I did not wish to have any more children. He asked if Ramiz agreed with that. I told him my husband, on hearing it said, 'so be it.' If I had chosen my marriage partner, my marriage would probably have been a disaster. My father is a very wise man." Maria admired this woman.

"Don't be sad, Maria, the dark spell will in time give way to much happiness. You will one day have another son." After a brief silence, Jasmine said, "Abdul was much desired by many and that desire was squashed when he honored you by marrying you. Your position is enviable."

Maria, who had not been aware of this, was astonished. After a brief silence she asked, "You are so seldom seen, how do you spend your day?"

"Ramiz, the children and I have breakfast in our apartment. One of us, depending on our schedules, takes the children, our five-year-old daughter Raina and our two sons, aged eight and ten, to school. Since I have a law degree, I'm on the board that attends to the family's legal matters. Ramiz is on the financial board. We're both part of the Diplomatic Corps, as is Abdul. It was Ramiz who put my name forth for this position, and convinced its members of my suitability for the task. As yet, I am the only woman in the Diplomatic Corps. This is our most interesting job. Anytime we're home, we have our evening meal with the children."

"When you and your husband go to the gambling tables in Monte Carlo, do you wear the traditional black?"

"No. We like to blend in with the crowd. Ramiz wears western formal wear, while I am covered in the traditional manner, but in formal wear, the long sleeves that are beautifully embroidered, and the gowns of a light-as-breeze chiffon, or silk in vivid colors with matching head scarf."

"I would like to have an occupation, too."

"Learn the language more fluently and you will."

"I'd very much like to be more fluent in Arabic but I would need to go to the University. I'm not free to come and go as you are."

"Speak to Abdul. I believe he would be happy to provide you with a tutor."

"I will."

After Jasmine left, Maria thought, *it would be wise to learn the language for I may, though I'd rather not think about it, be here for many years. Might Abdul, in time, treat me as an equal as Ramiz treats Jasmine?*

Abdul was hurrying across the outer courtyard when he heard his name being called. Turning he smiled as he said, "Father," and reversing his direction, walked towards the older man. The men brushed the sides of each other's cheeks in the motion of a kiss, then hugged each other.

"It is good to have you home again. Did your trip go well?"

"Yes, very much so but I'm glad to be home." Immediately changing the subject, he stated, "I fear life is not good between you and your wife."

"You have just arrived and word has gotten to you! Maria still grieves over the death of Waheed. She doesn't seek the women's assistance in her sorrow."

"Our ways are not her ways. There is a cultural barrier. Our women are foreign to her. Therefore, it is you who must speak to her."

"Speak to her! I cannot get through to her. Each time I am with her she asks that I bring her mother here, or that I permit her to go to visit her mother in England. As you know, that is not possible. The newspapers and television in Europe at the time I brought her here stated she was missing—abducted, and other such wild stories. We did nothing to correct their misinformation, and now would be a bad time to do it, especially in Maria's present frame of mind. She has written many letters to her mother, and given them to me to mail but, of course, I could not do that. She even suggested before Waheed's death that we all go together to visit her mother. Seeing her mother is all she speaks of. That world is closed to her. See, Father, how impossible it has been for me. She wants the one thing I cannot grant her."

"Her mother is very important to her; no father, an only child, and no other family members, as I remember, just the two of them, mother and daughter, what a close relationship they must have had. This is the first separation for each of them. You have lost your son, she has lost her son, and her mother."

After a moment, his father resumed speaking.

"Since Maria's unhappiness is caused by her separation from her mother, why not invite her mother for a visit?"

"Father, you do not know the extent of what you ask? European mothers-in-law control their married children's lives. Not only their daughters', but to some extent their sons' lives too."

"Do you not think Jasmine will have a strong voice in whom her and Ramiz's children will marry?"

"Jasmine is a diplomat. She will be guided by reason."

"Yes, she is an excellent diplomat when listening to and aiding others towards the best possible solution for all concerned parties. However, when emotions come into play, as they do with those closest to us, the playing field takes on a different dimension. Emotions muddy the water."

"Let me put a question to you, Father. If Maria's mother comes here on a visit, she may decide to stay here indefinitely, since she has no other children or family needing her attention. I cannot force her to take a plane back to England. My options would be very limited, and whatever steps I take, would have a very negative effect on Maria and our marriage. Under these circumstances, what would you suggest?"

His father answered with a question, "What do diplomats do when they become entangled in a no-win situation?"

"The one holding the better hand usually wins by default."

"In your situation, who holds the stronger hand?"

"It's a draw. No winners." Abdul answered.

Both men walked in silence.

Moments later his father addressed him again.

"How do you both stand with each other? Does she reject you?"

"No, nor does she welcome me. She just lets what will be, be. Before my son's death, I knew she loved me. I could feel it in the depths of my being when we were together, when she freely reached out to me."

"Has she not confronted you about the letters she sends, yet receives no reply?"

"No."

"She trusts you and she is compassionate and patient; these are highly prized virtues. However, she is not happy. It is not good to have an unhappy wife. It could eventually mean trouble for you."

"I will try harder to please her."

"Why did you go to Monte Carlo with the family, and not take her with you?"

"I discussed it with the family, who believed she was in too much grief to enjoy such a trip."

"Do you not think she might have seen this as a rejection of her on your part?"

"No. She was in no condition to travel, and would have found no enjoyment in being there. Also, if she covered her head, her non-Muslim eyes would stand out. Besides she no longer cares how she looks. It is only with encouragement from Sarah that she has begun to brush her hair. She no longer wears the jewelry I have given her: the sapphire to complement her eyes, nor the rubies that gleamed against her pale skin. I brought back beautiful clothing for her, but she has not worn any of it."

"The late King of Jordan had blue eyes as has his son, the present King. Monte Carlo is not England and no questions would arise."

"You do not think it risky? Interpol will not take notice?"

"Risks abound, but we cannot let them hold us hostage. All that really needs to be hidden is her hair. On our airlines or when you are both alone or with the family, she would be quite safe and would not need a burqa. The only traveling she'd do would be among our people. So she'd be perfectly safe."

A silence settled gently between them as they walked.

"In the evening, Maria walks in the inner courtyard with Daoud," the older man stated.

"With Daoud?"

"Yes, and it is the only time she is not in sorrow."

"Why? It was his mother who murdered Waheed."

"Yes. Your wife does not apparently believe in 'an eye for an eye.' The child is innocent and missing his mother, and she, with compassion, is helping him through his loss."

"I did not expect her to be nasty to the boy, but neither did I expect her to mother him. Laila murdered our son."

"The blame is not solely with Laila."

Abdul looked at his father in surprise.

"Waheed was my favorite grandson. I loved him, but I should not have neglected Daoud in my affection for him. It was through my actions as much as hers that my beloved grandson died. My sorrow is great, and through it I admire Maria, whose son was taken from her, and while still grieving, has the capacity to show such kindness to this child."

"Father, you cannot take blame for loving one child more than another. You are blameless in my eyes and in the eyes of Allah."

"Thank you, Abdul. Alas, it is difficult for me to forgive myself." Then he added, "Maria is an exceptional woman."

As the two men took leave of each other, their embrace was not the customary embrace but a lingering one, as each held onto the other for support and comfort.

CHAPTER 10

Clad in a burqa, Maria joined two of the women preparing to go shopping. They would be driven there by a servant of the household, who'd drop them off to browse and shop until his return three hours later. They had been coming to this elite Plaza every two weeks for the past four weeks. Maria did not particularly want to be there, but she came for a glimpse of the world, even if it meant seeing it through a mesh screen. The only time she was obliged to wear the burqa was when traveling with women alone.

It bothered Maria that she alone must wear this restrictive burqa. When she asked Abdul why this was so, he answered, "Because there are a lot of foreigners working here in the UAE. As a European, you would attract attention from men much more than our women, unwelcome attention, should you not be covered when alone with the women. You know that when we're together, you can wear whatever you wish for I am there to protect you from harassment. It is on those trips with the women that I wish you to be completely removed from those who would freely address you."

Protect her! She appreciated his concern and somewhat understood it, yet underneath the burqa, she felt like a prisoner. *Even criminals in a chain gang tied together*, she thinks in exasperation, *can view the world from a better vantage point than I. This hot, tiresome garment robs me of the freedom to interact with others, but then,* she reasons, *that is its purpose. It also makes it difficult to see clearly any item I might wish to purchase.*

"Their own women," as Abdul referred to her companions, were not much freer than she was. Their long-sleeved black garments covered them from their neck to their ankles. The black scarf not only covered their heads, hiding their hair completely, but also covered their foreheads. Was it the "foreigners" Abdul spoke of, or was it she that he lacked trust in! This freedom seemed like a very lopsided arrangement to Maria.

Maria marveled at Jasmine's freedom. Even the traditional long black coat Jasmine wore when traveling was outstanding for she had a seamstress pipe it down the front in emerald green, and had the buttons changed to match. When she donned an emerald scarf on her head, this woman who walked to the beat of a different drummer, yet abided by the rules, looked stunningly beautiful. Jasmine is wise enough to adhere to the law, never crossing the line, but often balancing upon it.

Getting out of the car, the women walked together. These two women were not fluent in English but with words, and hand gestures made themselves understood. Looking at the window displays the two women with Maria try to decide what shop to enter. Maria feels she cannot buy clothes, as she had not worn any of the beautiful clothes Abdul brought back from Paris. While the gowns are beautiful, they are not what she would have chosen; the strong colors, which would look lovely on a dark-haired woman, are unsuited to her fair complexion.

While wearing the burqa she feels like a walking hay stack, one of these round ones that were common before machinery made the hay into blocks. Hay stacks reminds her of the English countryside, where her mother used to bring her on picnics in summer. They never owned a car but took a bus to a beautiful location usually a spot by a river or pond and spent the afternoon there, returning home by bus in the evening. Her mind dallied there awhile until the heat under the burqa brought her back to the present. She had said she didn't like to wear black garments out in the hot sun, and Abdul had given her a blue burqa with a white head piece, saying he knew blue was her favorite color.

Maria, hot and tired from walking, under this detestable garment, asked that they stop for a cold drink. They brought her to a table within twenty feet of where they would purchase their drinks, for they were instructed to protect her by not losing sight of her for even a moment.

While she struggled to ease the bundle of material into a chair, she became aware of a lone man who sat at the next table. Normally she would have ignored such a person, but he had hair the color of hers, was dressed in western-style clothes, and was staring at her. Mostly, he was looking at her hands which mystified her. After several moments, he took out a pen and a piece of paper from his pocket and began to write.

Well, I suppose he has lost interest in my hands, she surmised. Just then he rose and placed the small piece of paper discreetly on her table and walked away. After a moment, she reached out, and picking up the paper read it.

"I realize I must not speak to you, but I am curious, most curious as to where you got the ring with the emerald stone you wear on your right hand? I gave such a ring to a woman whom I lost contact with many years ago. I believe the ring is one of a kind. If you can enlighten me on this matter, I will be much obliged to you. Just write a reply and put it on the seat as you leave and I will pick it up."

Quickly she fumbled in her handbag and found a pen. Under cover of the burqa she wrote on the back of the paper she had received from him: "I am Maria Jablonski from England, who came to this country over two years ago. The ring in question was given to me by my mother, who is just a working woman, who could not afford a specially made, one-of-a-kind ring. Can you help me escape and return to my mother in England? If you can do so, I will gladly give this ring with the emerald stone to you, for I have nothing else to give. Will you help me?" She could not see what she had written, but wrote as clearly as possible in the hope he would read her message, and help her.

He returned to his table with a cold drink, and sat down. Standing up, she bumped into his table, dropping the note beside his hand, then patting down her burqa, she settled back into the seat. He put his hand on the note, picked it up and left.

He was, apparently, working on one of the many construction sites, for much construction work was taking place. Would he betray her? Why would the ring her mother gave her be of interest to him? She was risking her life, she knew, by connecting in any way with this foreigner, but she desperately wanted to go home to her mother.

She could not continue to live as a stranger in this strange land, or separated from the world in this hot cloth container. How long would it take to die by stoning, she wondered, and how painful would it be? Sarah had told her Laila would have been sedated before the execution. Would she be given a sedative to null the pain, or would Abdul be so angry with her, he would deny her that small relief? Maria evaluated the positive and negative aspects of her actions in her mind, for she could not put such thoughts on paper. The positive: Be able to see her mother again; go home and have a normal lifestyle. The negatives she did not want to think about, but knew she must. If her attempt to escape was discovered, she would risk death by stoning, never to see her mother again, having to leave Daoud behind. Then another thought that she had not previously considered entered her mind. She was asking a man, a complete stranger, to risk his life in order to free her! Suddenly her cause seemed doomed. Why would a total stranger risk his job and his very life for her?

The approaching women put an end to these life-and-death thoughts. They brought three large cool drinks. As they refreshed themselves, they sat leisurely at the table beside her. For the moment she was grateful for having the cover of the burqa, for she did not want her troubled countenance exposed.

After a brief spell, they wished to take Maria to the jewelry store. When she protested, saying that Abdul had showered her with more jewelry than she had need of, they suggested she buy a piece of jewelry for Abdul. What might Abdul want that he did not already have? Yet she went, thinking how she would have enjoyed buying clothes or toys for Waheed. Before he died, plans were already being made for his first birthday. When he was born, his grandfather had bestowed rich lands on him, and others had lavished him with money and gold.

She did not know what Abdul's accumulated wealth was, nor did it matter to her. If she wanted to make a purchase she just used the name, Wahida, meaning the moon, as her signature. The other women used their own names. Maria had accomplished what she had wanted, and was glad when it was time to return.

After returning Daoud to the nursery, Maria saw Jasmine hurrying towards her.

""I've been looking for you," Jasmine said. "I want to give you this," as she handed the younger woman a box. Taking the gift, Maria pulled the ribbon off, opened the box, and lifted out the scarf exclaiming, "It's beautiful, Jasmine, and what lovely colors. The light and deep pinks, pale apple green and touches of black. It is absolutely beautiful."

"When I saw it in the store, I thought "they are Maria's colors," Jasmine laughed.

"They are," and reaching out she hugged Jasmine.

"I saw you walking with Daoud!"

"Yes. He misses his mother very much, so I spend some time with him after breakfast, and we also walk in the courtyard before dinner. As you know, a young woman comes to the nursery every afternoon to teach the toddlers English through games, nursery rhymes, and stories. I have been doing somewhat similar with Daoud, but in Polish, and I'm wondering if my doing so will confuse him?"

"No. When my daughter was about a year old, and learning both languages, I added a third by speaking to her in French. To this day, she speaks English with a French accent." Both women laughed.

"How long do the children stay in the nursery?"

"That depends on their parents. I left my eldest son there until he was about a year and a half. His younger brother stayed a little less than a year there because he had an older sibling to play with. They did not need tutoring because Ramiz and I spoke to them in both languages, and provided them with books in both languages. Raina spent the shortest time in the nursery. Daoud is the oldest child in the nursery. Laila probably kept him there to be with other children, since he is an only child. When he is five years old, he must leave there, and attend school with the older children. I have heard, however, that he must leave here soon, as his father plans to live with his relatives, and he will take his son with him."

"Permanently?"

"Yes."

"I will miss him." After a few moments Maria added, "How are you related to the family?"

"By marriage. Ramiz's and Abdul's fathers are cousins."

"And Laila, how did she fit in?"

"Abdul did not tell you?"

"Did not tell me what?"

"She was one of his sisters."

"His sister?" Maria was aghast.

How could one have one's own sister stoned? Suddenly she found herself afraid of Abdul. How could he possibly care about her mother, a woman he did not know, and bring her here? She had to leave this place, but how? Would the older man with the blond hair help her?

"Sorry, perhaps I should not have told you."

"No. I'm glad you did," the younger woman replied in a barely audible voice. "You said he had other sisters, what of them?"

"The other sisters are both beautiful and desirable women. They made good marriages. Laila was the plain one without much of a personality, which is understandable living with such lively, outstanding sisters. Although the oldest, she was the last to marry."

"Life wasn't kind to her," Maria added on a sad note.

"Should I stay with you for a while?"

"No. I'll be all right, thank you, and thank you for the lovely scarf."

Jasmine left to join her family at their dinner table.

Two weeks later, the three women were heading back to the shopping plaza. Maria eagerly looked forward to this trip. Would the blond-haired man be there? Would he contact her or having read her note, decide he did not want any part of this dangerous scheme? If he were there, and did not contact her, it would mean he did not wish to get involved.

She wished she knew how to pray. Her mother had never brought her to a house of worship, but read to her from a well-used book of a people of long ago; the story of a people who so often found themselves oppressed. Her mother especially enjoyed reading the lives of the women from this book, of Sarah, Rebecca, Rachel, Ruth, Judith and Esther. All her friends had some religious beliefs, and most of them belonged to the Church of England. Her mother was adamant that she not go there with her friends. Right now, however, she wished she knew how to petition God. If she could talk to God, he might free her from her bondage.

"You're very quiet, Maria," one of the women stated.

"She is stacking up in her mind what she wants to buy," the other one laughed.

"Ah, she will make up for time not used a fortnight ago," the first woman added.

"I'm returning the gold chain I bought. See, Maria, its closing is not tight. It will loosen and get lost."

They left the car and walked to the shops. "I hope he returns on time. We waited almost an hour for him the last time, yet he insists we be there at four o'clock on the dot." The other woman's response was, "perhaps we should report him."

"We may not be provided with another driver!"

"I will talk to my husband and see what he says," her friend added, and the subject was dropped. After they had exchanged the chain and made some purchases, they decided it was time for a cool drink.

The foreigner came, and to Maria's relief, sat at a nearby table drinking from a bottle. She did not want to leave without having some indication of his willingness to help, or his refusal to do so. His refusal would be understandable as he was a guest worker in this country fulfilling his obligation. Working here in the UAE, he would be aware of the consequences of helping her.

The women, now refreshed, wanted to continue, and were coaxing her to go with them, joking about her laziness.

"You two are used to wearing a hot, tiresome burqa," she answered deciding to give full blame to the burqa. "Go ahead. I will finish the last of my drink and follow. Moments later, believing he was not going to make contact, she rose to leave. As she did so, the worker dropped his wallet and bent down to retrieve it. She felt what seemed like a thick piece of paper being slipped into the heel of her shoe. Straightening up he did not look at her, but proceeded to put his wallet into his pocket.

Maria did not know what to get Abdul that he did not already have. She paid little attention to the elegantly decorated shop windows, for she was concentrating on the paper in her shoe, rather than any gift she might purchase. Turning around, her two companions saw her walking towards them. Afraid the paper might work itself out of her shoe as she walked, she told them that she needed to use the rest room. To her dismay she found that any rest room would not do, they must use the one in the hotel further down the street.

Safely inside the toilet booth she retrieved the paper. It was actually many small pieces of paper lightly glued at the end. On the topmost piece of paper she read from a list of questions:

"Are you married?

Do you have a child?

Are you pregnant?

How often do you come to the shopping plaza and how long do you stay?

What time does your driver pick you up? Does he ever arrive earlier than the time allowed?

Write your answers on these post-its and if you see your contact, me or another construction worker, stick the post-its underneath the table as close to the center as possible.

Do not sign your name."

He is going to help her! Perhaps not! But then why would he ask all these questions if he did not plan to help? Could it be a trap? Was he just gathering evidence to use against her? Would he betray her? After many internal discussions, she decided she had to trust him if she had any hope of seeing her mother again. She had everything to win, or everything to lose. She would have to risk death in order to live free. He, on the other hand, was risking his life for her without any reward except for the emerald stone ring on her finger. If this ring had value, her mother, she knew, would have sold it during one of the bad financial times they had been through, when everything of value got sold. His willingness to help her both amazed and troubled her. Why would he risk all?

CHAPTER 11

On her next trip to the shopping mall, Maria, who had answered all the questions, waited for an opportunity to give them to the foreigner. She was fearful now. She feared Abdul, and she feared the foreigner. She was putting her life in the hands of a stranger, a man who had never seen her face, who had no proof she was who she said she was, yet was willing to help her! Why? Were her actions bringing her close to the execution block? Yet, there was no turning back. Would Abdul throw the first stone? Suddenly, something hit her. It hurt.

People were pulling at her. "She just blindly walked into the street light!" One of her companions said, "Are you hurt?"

Maria shook her head and in doing so realized that the movement was painful.

"We have to get you back to the hotel and see how badly you're hurt."

Not yet. She couldn't go yet. She had to make contact with her foreigner.

"Come Maria, we must get you to the hotel and have you seen to by a doctor."

"No doctor. First let me rest a few moments until I get my balance," she replied as she sat down.

"Is it bleeding?"

She put her hand towards her forehead. It was sore to the touch, but she did not feel any moisture.

"No, just a bump." *Darn it, I should have been paying attention to where I was walking rather than thinking of the blond-haired man,* she thought. Suddenly through the mesh she saw a young man, a boy really, approximately her age or younger, sitting at a nearby table. He looked very much like the older man, the one from whom she received the post-its. Perhaps the boy was his son. She removed the list of answers from her pocket, and stuck them under the table.

"We must go to the hotel where you can lie down. We'll walk on each side of you to steady you."

Maria rose, and for their benefit, held onto the table to steady herself.

"Abdul will be furious with us when he sees the bump on your head," one of them fretted, as they took up their positions on either side of her.

"Perhaps if he hears of this accident, he will release me from wearing this detestable thing."

They walked slowly to the hotel. While her head was sore and throbbing, Maria felt like dancing, for although she couldn't stay, she had made contact. The boy who looked so much like the man would surely pick up her note. She would have to wait to receive any further message he might have, but he could proceed with the information she had given him, and in two weeks' time she would receive further instructions.

At the hotel, one of the women explained what had happened. They were shown to a room. With the burqa removed, the three women examined the damage. A bucket of ice was brought to the room. However, with the time taken to sit at the table and evaluate the situation, plus the slow walk to the hotel, the ice was applied too late, and a rather large bump now showed on her forehead.

"Can we get you a cold drink?" one of them asked. "or hot tea?" the other chimed in.

"Hot tea," she replied in true English style.

"Perhaps we should request a doctor."

"No. I will be fine after I have some tea and have rested."

"Abdul will be angry when he sees your forehead," one of the women repeated worriedly.

"He is away on business. If not completely gone, the bump will be greatly reduced on his return, and not noticeable."

This made the women, who always followed orders, relax. They ordered room service.

"Are you able to sign for this service?"

The women laughed. "Yes, of course. This hotel is owned by the family."

So that is why they were insisting we come to this particular hotel. She didn't want a doctor. She was safe here, she reassured herself. These women would not abandon her.

The tea was soothing. The women drank their cold drinks, and in a short while she closed her eyes and fell asleep.

When she woke up, she looked at her watch, and discovered she had dozed off for about thirty minutes, and was now feeling relaxed. The women were sitting by the window. She watched these women who made no demands on life, enjoying the simple pleasure of people-watching. In less than a half an hour, they would need to be at the designated location for their driver. As Maria fixed her hair to cover the bump, the women turned from the window.

"Did you have a nice rest?"

"Yes, I'm feeling fine now."

Maria and her non-Muslim friend carried on a secret correspondence. He questioned her about her background. He mentioned he was Polish, and wanted to know if she could speak Polish. "No, she did not, except for a few words, and some Polish expressions her mother sometimes used." To her relief he said he would help her, but that she must be patient, yet ready to move with very little notice, and she should not by word or action reveal to another soul, not even a close friend, what they were planning.

She would very much like to confide in Jasmine, and even get her opinion and hopefully her blessing, but she knew that would be unsafe, for Jasmine was very fond of Abdul her kin and friend since childhood. Jasmine might tell Abdul, not only to save their marriage which Jasmine mistakenly believed was salvageable, but to save her English friend from an action that might cause her to forfeit her life.

After many weeks she received a note saying the plan was in place and they would now take action. She would arrive at a table as usual carrying no baggage. As soon as possible she should find an excuse to send the two women to a store. Immediately after they were out of sight, she should walk towards a van in the alley between the restaurant and bakery. They would proceed from there.

On the appointed day, Maria was nervous but not fearful. The women had left to get ice cream. What she hoped and prayed for was finally happening. She could not, would not, think of the risk, but only of getting safely out of the country and seeing her mother again. She followed instructions, but saw nobody. Then the back of the van which faced the alleyway opened and the boy and his father and two other men stepped out of the van. Mr. Krakowski introduced himself, as he pushed a bundle of clothes into her arms.

"Quickly get into the van and put these clothes on, and hand me the burqa and whatever else you are wearing. You will find a wide elastic bandage which you will need to tie tightly around your breasts to hide them." She felt strange dressed in boys' clothing, and was astonished to see her burqa move out of the alley on feet that weren't hers. Mr. Krakowski, his son Karol, and Maria got into the back of the van. The other man drove.

As they drove down the highway Mr. Krakowski cut her hair into a boy-style haircut, and while he was chopping it off, said, "You must keep the cap on at all times, and try to walk and talk like a boy, but speak only when asked a question until we are through customs. We have just enough time to get to the airport for the flight out."

"I have no passport or ticket!"

"All that has been taken care of. You will be addressed as Karol, and must answer to that name as you'll be using my son's passport. He will be using another person's passport, one belonging to Darien. Darien was a 16-year-old boy who died a few weeks ago after falling off the scaffolding. He was a very nice young man, and a good worker. He would have gladly helped in your escape. We didn't tell the authorities of his death, but after praying for his immortal soul, we buried him on the construction site."

"Why aren't I using this unfortunate man's passport and Karol his own passport?"

"The height difference! Darien and Karol were once the same height. But, in the past two years, Karol has grown up like a weed. You are noticeably shorter, as was Karol, when he was issued his passport. As for the tickets, I have all three of them. The driver will burn the bag of your hair, and the clothes you wore under the burqa will also be burned."

"The man in the burqa will pass as me!"

"Yes, who is to know who is under one of those things? He will stay with the women until just about fifteen minutes before the driver arrives, and then make his escape, and dispose of the burqa. That will give us almost an hour. It was necessary to time this as closely as possible to make our escape. It takes thirty to thirty-five minutes to get to the airport, and if all goes well, and I pray it will, we'll be in the air before they've discovered you are missing."

"What if the plane is delayed," Maria thought but does not give voice to her thoughts. The driver said goodbye to them at the airport, and wished them a safe journey. Mr. Krakowski handed each of them a small carrying bag so that all three of them had hand luggage. They passed through customs, and were headed for the plane just twenty minutes before the flight.

"Your father must be nervous; he hasn't spoken a word since we sat down."

"He's praying."

Moments later they boarded the plane. It left on schedule.

After arriving in Poland, they went to the Krakowski home where Maria met Stan Krakowski's wife and their younger son. Ellie Krakowski, a most pleasant and endearing hostess, had a big meal prepared for them. Maria was astonished by the amount of food placed before them. It was more plentiful and of a greater variety than any meal her mother had ever prepared, even for the holidays or important occasions. If it were not for the eagerness of her to see her mother, Maria felt she would like to stay with this kind and loving family who made her feel like she was part of their family. It had been explained to her that they could not go directly to England without causing suspicion.

Stan Krakowski believed that Abdul's family would check the destination of everyone who left the country at the time Maria's absence was discovered. Going to England might raise suspicion whereas their decision to make Poland their destination was a wiser choice due to the fact that many on the construction site were Polish. It was nearing Christmas, and the Polish crew always went home for Christmas, Stan explained to his wife who asked many questions. She considered her husband a hero, a hero who would never receive recognition for his exceptional deeds outside of his own immediate family. He explained the preparation for the escape, and the escape itself in great detail to his family, but he omitted a very vital part of the story, Maria believed, by not mentioning the ring, and what part it played in all of this, which was a mystery to her. She was about to remedy this omission but hesitated, then decided not to speak of it for it had been her mother's ring. Since he had a wife, it puzzled her as to why her mother had had it.

From Poland, Stan booked tickets for Maria and him to fly to France. Maria remembered how easy it had been to enter the United Arab Emirates. The women walked through customs alongside the men, who without stopping, held up passports as they passed through. Yet, what an ordeal it was to leave! She shuddered to think of their fate if the plan had not succeeded. Stan's loving wife would be without a husband and their two sons would be without a father. Her own fate, if she were found leaving the country, she knew, but banished from her thoughts.

Maria stayed overnight with them and Mrs. Krakowski made a huge delicious breakfast. Immediately after, the family bade Stan and Maria goodbye. Several hours later, Stan and Maria, passing as father and son, arrived in France. They would take the Chunnel rather than a plane to England as a safer measure.

Arriving on the English side of the Chunnel, they were met with a heavy downpour of rain.

"England," Stan spoke while turning the palms of his hands upwards.

"How often I wished for rain while in the UAE," Maria laughed, "but not this deluge."

"Be careful what you wish for," Stan laughed.

"Do you not wish for things?"

"Yes, I do, although I have been blessed with so much. My most heartfelt wish was that Karol and I could get you safely out of the UAE, and we have succeeded in that. Here we are on English soil."

Drenched from the rain, Maria told him, "When I wished for rain, it was a light refreshing shower I had in mind, not this soaker. I feel like I've been swimming while fully clothed."

"I should have taken an umbrella from home with me," Stan said as though thinking aloud, and then with a strong voice added, "Wet, damp and chilly, but safe."

Maria, who did not want to seem ungrateful to Stan, could not divulge that she missed the sun and brightness of the Emirates. She had forgotten how dank, drab and colorless England was in winter. As they looked at the darkened streets through the falling rain, in the grayish brown of the city Dickens wrote of, Maria remembered the brightness of the desert sand, citrus-colored buildings, and the hot sun. Suddenly through the rain they smiled at each other, for their hearts sang. Miracle of miracles, they were free. "Home" Maria uttered in gratitude.

"Nothing quite compares to it," Stan added.

"I can hardly wait to see the expression on Momma's face when she sees me."

"Nor I."

They took public transportation as far as they could before hailing a taxi. Looking out the window of the taxi through the early morning mist, to Maria's eyes, everything looked dreary. She remembered how brightly the morning sun trumpeted the day, shining against the pale cantaloupe, honeydew, and lemon-colored walls of the buildings. Momma would have liked being there, Maria knew, for rainy, damp days made her arthritis more painful. People in England and other cold climates liked to holiday in warm sunny climates, but as much as they enjoyed these holidays, they were always happy to come back home to England, family and friends.

In the early hours of the morning, Stan and Maria arrived at Anna Jablonski's apartment.

"Soon you'll be out of those wet clothes, and comfortably seated by the fire," Stan smiled.

He doesn't know my frugal mother, Maria thought. *Momma never lights a fire in the daytime, only in the evening, except on Saturday and Sunday, when it is very cold,* Maria remembers.

It was beginning to look like Anna Jablonski was not going to admit them, as no amount of knocking on the door brought a response. They needed to wake Anna Jablonski without waking any of the neighbors. Stan wondered if Anna was awake, but living alone in a rather rundown neighborhood, and not expecting a visitor, she might refuse to open her door.

Maria urgently called out in a loud whisper, "Momma," but to no avail.

Stan, taking out a piece of paper from his case, gave it and a pencil to Maria and asked her to write a note, and slip it under the door in the event that Anna heard the knocking on the door, but was afraid to open it. Maria did as Stan suggested.

They were both very tired, and not being able to gain admittance to her home after all they had been through to arrive here, brought tears to Maria's eyes.

Drawing her to him, Stan consoled the young weary woman before asking, "What time does your mother rise to go to work."

Before she could answer, the door opened and Anna stared at these early morning callers, until Maria whispered, "It's me, Momma."

Anna, with tears in her eyes, grabbed her daughter in an embrace, repeating Maria's name over and over in disbelief. Gathering herself together, she invited them into the living room.

"I'll put the kettle on," Maria said as her mother stumbled into a chair.

"Where were you? Why are you wearing men's clothes? How did you arrive? I thought you were...." But she could not finish the sentence.

This is Mr. Krakowski, my rescuer, Momma. We'll have some tea and I'll explain everything to you," Maria said as she bent over the back of the seat her mother sat on and put her arms around her.

"First take off those wet clothes, Maria." Her daughter went into the bedroom to change as her mother requested. Turning to Stan she said, "I am sorry I don't have any men's clothing for you to change into, but I do have a large robe you can wear while your clothes dry."

Anna and Stan exchanged a long, expressive gaze, but spoke not a word of the momentous emotions they shared—this young woman, this Maria, their daughter.

"Thank you," Stan finally whispered.

Anna left him alone for several moments while she retrieved the bathrobe. Stan looked around the sparsely furnished apartment with its badly worn couch and armchairs. No pictures, ornaments of any kind, vases, or clocks were present. The only clutter in the room were the books carelessly put back in place. Returning with the bathrobe, Anna directed him to the bathroom to change. She had turned on the hot-water unit so that they could bathe comfortably.

The apartment never seemed so small to Maria while living there. It was as though the spaces had shrunk. She then realized that she had become used to wide open-spaced rooms, bright elegant décor, that looked even larger in their pure white and citrus colors.

"Why did you not send a card from the places you visited as promised? Nobody knew where you were," Anna asked as Maria and Stan returned to the parlor.

"I did Momma. I sent cards from Madrid, Seville, and from Tangier, Fes and Casablanca."

"You traveled to all those places? I received cards from none of them."

"Didn't you receive my letters from The United Arab Emirates?"

"You were there? What were you doing there?"

Maria was shocked to realize that Abdul had not sent any of her cards or letters to her mother as he had said he would. He had deceived her! After waiting in vain for a response from her mother, and wondering why her mother had not replied to the letters, she had come to the conclusion that her mother was vexed with her for not returning to England as planned. In not acknowledging the correspondence, she assumed her mother had hoped to force Maria to return home, not knowing how almost impossible that was.

"I wrote you Momma, a great many letters, which Abdul said he would post for me. Apparently he did not."

"Who is this Abdul?"

As they sat down with tea, some bread and jam and biscuits, Maria gave an account of what happened in Spain, and Morocco, of meeting Abdul, falling in love, and marrying Abdul, and then feeling like a prisoner and desperately wanting to see and be with her mother.

Anna poured out a second cup of tea for all and Maria told of losing her baby and being forced to witness the stoning of the woman who smothered him.

"You had a child?"

"Yes, Momma, a beautiful baby boy."

"That dreadful woman killed your son. If only I could have been there to protect you and the baby, to have helped you through this terrible loss," Anna spoke as she folded her daughter into her arms.

"She did it during the early hours of the morning when the whole household was sleeping. Nobody could have foreseen this horror. Absolutely nobody."

"My first grandchild, the child I never saw, did not even know existed, was murdered. Oh, you poor child, how greatly you have suffered."

"Yes, it was terrible. That was the worst period of my life."

"Did the child look like your husband?"

"No, he was fair-skinned with blue eyes and blond hair."

"How old was he when he died?"

"Ten months old. The family was already preparing for his first birthday."

"That woman deserved to die. How could she have killed an innocent baby? She deserved to die," Anna repeated.

"No, Momma, nobody deserves to be put to death."

"Your son didn't, she did."

"A stoning is a terrible sight to see."

"If I had been there, I would have thrown the first stone."

"No, Momma, you wouldn't have."

"Yes, I would. That woman was a lunatic. She knew she would die for this terrible deed, yet she did it! That's insane, and yet you defend her."

"In civilized societies the insane do not receive the death penalty."

"It's that liberal-minded way of thinking that lets criminals loose to strike again," Anna said in a flat voice, for she was annoyed that Maria could defend Laila. In the brief silence that followed, Anna continued, "That husband of yours, did he defend her?"

"No, he cast the first stone."

"Good for him, I'd say," Anna said with determination.

"Laila, the woman who was stoned was his sister."

Anna is nonplussed. After a moment she said, "They kill babies and relatives indiscriminately!"

"Murderers are punished there as they are here."

"Well, no jury in England would have let her go free. Did you attend the trial?"

"No, there was no trial, Momma. The elders voted on it, and pronounced her death sentence."

"Did you throw a stone at her?"

"No."

"Were you asked to do so?"

"Yes."

"How did they take your refusal?"

"Abdul was very angry."

"And the others, those elders of whom you speak?"

"I don't know. They did not communicate with me on the matter."

"Thank God you're out of that dreadful country, and away from those people."

"No group of people is all bad or all good."

"Stoning is gruesome."

"Not any more gruesome than being hanged or beheaded."

"You have begun to think like them! You have changed, Maria."

For the first time since this conversation began, Stan weighed in, "Maria has been exposed to life beyond this little island. She has a wider view of the world in which we all live. She was a child when she left and is now a mature young woman. There is no turning back to what was, Anna. You must accept her for the woman she has become."

Anna was not ready to accept what Stan suggested. For a while longer, she wanted to hold onto the Maria who asked her opinion, and took her advice. This change was all two sudden, too abrupt, and she felt at a loss.

CHAPTER 12

"Did you not ask Maria what her religious affiliations were, my son?"

"She told me she and her mother had never been to any place of worship, nor had attended any religious function."

"She may be Jewish."

"She lied to me?"

"No, Abdul. We do not know for sure. A great many Jewish people were sent to the concentration camps. What we do know is that her mother's family was interned in concentration camps in Poland during WWII where they all died except for Maria's grandmother. Maria's mother, if Jewish, either turned away from her religious beliefs due to this, or she may have believed it wasn't safe to be Jewish, and abandoned her beliefs to keep her daughter safe."

"Our best source of finding Maria is through her mother. Wherever one is, there will be the other," Abdul weighed in. Maria must have had help in leaving the Emirates, yet she knew no other Europeans living here. After a moment, Abdul, deep in thought stated, "If that is so, it may take a while but we'll track them down. They have not landed in England. We will try the other European countries beginning with Spain and France to further the search there. We won't leave a stone unturned until we find them, and find them we will."

"Might the mother return with Maria to Poland where the mother grew up, a place that was familiar to her?" Abdul questioned.

"Yes, or she might still hold the horrors of what happened to her family in Poland, and be determined never to set foot there again," his father answered. "We will, however, also search for her there. Do not worry, Abdul, we will find them."

"I'm sorry Father, to put you to so much trouble on my behalf. I have been reckless in what I have done. Now after what she has done, I feel nothing but hate for Maria," Abdul said with vengeance.

"I doubt that, son, you are presently angry with her, and have feelings of being betrayed. Maria is an unusual name for a Jewish woman! It tells me her mother may have been trying to hide the fact that Maria was Jewish."

"Her father may have been Christian."

"Yes. It is strange that we cannot find a Jablonski that could qualify as a father to Maria!"

"Perhaps her mother never married Maria's father," Abdul suggested.

"That is a possibility."

* * *

"How could a simple holiday have turned into such a nightmare? Thank God you have returned, but how did you manage to do so," her mother asked in amazement.

Stan, who had been sitting in silent awe of what Maria had gone through, now spoke of receiving a note from a burqa-clad woman, who claimed to be Maria Jablonski from England, and who was seeking help in getting home. He spoke of how much he owed to the young man who died in a fall from the scaffolding, and whose passport made it possible for all three, his son, Maria, and himself to leave. Leaving for Poland close to Christmas would not draw attention to Polish workers, as it might at any other time of year, or if they had been heading to England. As another safety factor, after leaving his son in Poland, Maria and he flew to France, and took the Chunnel as the less suspicious route to England.

"We are indebted to you, Mr. Krakowski. Thank you so very much for risking your life, and bringing my daughter home. Do you have other children?" Anna inquired.

"Yes, besides my fourteen-year old Karol whom we spoke of, my wife and I have a ten-year-old son, Piotr," he answered, and then turning to Maria said, "Maria is a very pretty name. It was my mother's name."

Anna wondered if he would expose her lie to Maria, and damage or destroy her relationship with their daughter. She had made a very rash decision a long time ago, and had over the years regretted it. Not that she would have given Maria up, but that she had given Stan no voice in the matter. Too late Anna realized she should have told Stan that she was carrying their child. Now on seeing Stan, the pain of that decision, and the shame of it achingly returned. No, he would not reveal her past mistake to Maria because he was a decent man, and one who had mellowed with age, but mostly he would hold his silence to spare his daughter any additional pain.

"You said you loved this man, Maria. Sometimes opposites attract," Stan told Maria. "You saw him as a 'matinee idol,' someone wholly different from your average young Englishman. Many years ago, it was in the 1920s, I believe, there was an actor who played the part of a sheik. This particular actor, his name was Valentino, was endowed with an irresistible fascination in the eyes of young women. Young women and not-so-young women swooned over him. He was everything the average American or Englishman was not—handsome in a brooding way, with dark smoldering eyes, and black hair. He wasn't the Arab sheik he portrayed in the films, but a young man from Italy. No doubt Abdul fell in love with you. You are a most attractive young woman, and altogether different from the women of his country. You came from countries that are vastly dissimilar. When the attraction you each saw in one another waned in day-to-day difficulties of life, the cultural differences surfaced."

Nobody spoke for several moments after Stan finished speaking. It was then that Maria remembered her mother's words, *Mistrust and lack of communication destroyed the lovers in Othello* Suddenly tears filled Maria's eyes. Seeing Maria's sadness, Anna stood up and held Maria closely. "You are now safely home, darling; it was an experience, an adventure that you had, that will always be a moment in time to remember."

"I loved him, and may still do. I don't know any more how I feel," Maria quietly affirmed. "When he was loving and kind, it was so wonderful. When things got bad, they were painfully bad. When my baby died, my whole world collapsed around me. Then all I wanted to do was escape, leave that place behind me forever."

"Now that you are home, we both can start living again."

Taking a ring off her finger, Maria handed it to Stan. "I promised you this ring. It will never repay you for all you have done for me, but as I told you back there, I had nothing else to give you," and she handed the ring to Stan.

He took the ring, studied it for a moment, and then lifting her hand, placed it back on her finger. "It is yours, Maria. I want you to wear it always. When times get bad, as they occasionally will, look at this ring and remember your deliverance, and march bravely onwards."

After finishing tea, Stan leaned back in the armchair.

"It is imperative that you both leave England as soon as possible. It would be safer Maria, if you do not let anyone know you have returned, nor leave the house until you leave for your new destination. In that case you carried on the plane is another set of Karol's clothes." After a pause, Stan continued, "You will need new names. This is essential to prevent you from being found by Abdul, his family or others hired to find you."

Anna is stunned. She had thought now that Maria was home they would be safe, as did Maria. Frightened, they looked at each other and then at Stan.

"First have your names changed. What names do you think you would like?"

Anna was the first to respond, "Ruth, I'll become Ruth." Maria was at a loss to come up with a name. After several moments, her mother began to suggest names, Rachel, Sarah. Maria remembered the kind Sarah, the wife of Abdul's father. But no, she would remove herself completely from that household. Suddenly, Maria said, "Portia."

"Portia!" her mother questioned her daughter's choice, and then added, "Yes, that is a good choice."

"Well, it's shorter than Desdemona," Maria quipped.

"Now we need a surname," Anna spoke looking towards Stan.

"Cahill."

"I knew an Irish man some years ago with that name. He was a very nice man and I'm sure if he was aware of it, he'd be happy to extend his name to you."

"Ruth Cahill," it sounds strange but I'm sure I'll get used to it in time."

"I'd like the name Desdemona," Maria solemnly announced.

"Desdemona! Her mother asked. "Surely you will not choose the name of that Shakespearean woman who was murdered by her husband?"

"I feel a kinship with her. If Mr. Krakowski hadn't succeeded in getting me back to England, her fate would have been mine. In fact, he risked his own life, and put his son's life in danger to bring me home."

To avoid any additional thanks, Stan Krakowski, spoke, "When you change your name from Maria to Desdemona, you may need to shorten it for everyday use."

"To what?"

"I'm not sure, Des, perhaps," her mother weighed in.

Maria made a face.

"How about Mona," Stan asked.

"Mona Cahill, yes, that sounds good to me," Maria smiled.

"Yes, and you'll get to keep your first initial," Anna added.

"When you are ready to leave here permanently, do so under darkness of night."

"Where should we go?" Anna asked. "France, perhaps?"

"I would recommend Ireland or Scotland," Stan advised.

"Neither Maria nor I have been to any of these places."

"Ireland has a similar climate to here and its people speak English. Scotland has a colder climate as you probably know since it is north of England. What do you think, Maria?"

"I think we should go to Ireland."

"You will like it there I believe, although I've never actually been to Ireland. From what I hear, it is a beautiful country. I have worked with some Irish people on the job site, and as a people, I'd highly recommend them."

"How do we proceed?" Anna wished to know.

"First we'll get in touch with Scotland Yard and tell them the whole story. After you have your names changed, you can get new passports; you will need to decide whether you wish to live in a city or the countryside, and then you will pack and leave for Ireland. I'd suggest you stay in a 'bed and breakfast' until you find a place you'd like to rent, and then seek a job. After you get to know the country better, should you decide you'd like to live in a different part of the country, you will be free to do so."

"Mr. Krakowski, will you and Karol return to the United Arab Emirates after your visit to Poland?"

"No, Maria, that might be risky since we're all of Polish origin, and we all left United Arab Emirates at the same time."

"You'll lose your job!"

"Yes. I have, however, been working there for the past six years, going home only for Christmas and for three weeks in summer. We have purchased things we otherwise wouldn't have been able to afford, and during these past six years we have been able to put money aside for our sons' education and have established a savings account. The wages were excellent. We have been very fortunate."

"If you had not helped me, you would have continued working there, would you not?"

"Yes, but only for a short time. My wife and sons would like us to be living together as a family. I have been too long absent from the family, and it is time for me to return home permanently. So as soon as you are all set for Ireland, I will leave England."

"We only have one bedroom but this couch pulls out into a bed. You're welcome to use it," Anna tells Stan, "and we really would appreciate it, if you would stay with us until we're ready to leave England."

In bed that night, Anna pondered the past, and the changes in Stan. *He is still a good, hard-working man, but greatly mellowed. No longer the stern rigid Stan of long ago, whose reaction to the news of my pregnancy I had feared. What would his reaction, and more importantly his actions have been? We definitely did not want a child at that point in our lives, yet his strong religious faith would not have permitted an abortion. What a dilemma this pregnancy would thrust upon him. He relied on me to prevent a pregnancy with nothing but primitive methods at my disposal. I failed him. I thought I was doing the right thing, removing myself and the unborn, unwanted child.*

We were so young, so poor, owning nothing but our dream. A child at that time would have dashed our hopes and dreams to pieces.

"With new names, and help from Scotland Yard, the family could now purchase their tickets to Ireland. They heeded Stan's suggestion that a trip by boat would be safer than a plane flight, and he secured passage for them.

The night before they were to leave, Maria made an unexpected discovery which she revealed to her mother and Stan the following morning at breakfast, a meal she herself was unable to eat.

"I'm pregnant."

The sausage on Stan's fork did not make it to his mouth. Anna stood with the teapot in her hand staring at her daughter. "Pregnant," she mouthed just above a whisper, as she lowered the teapot onto the table, and herself into a chair.

"Oh God," Anna uttered aghast. "You must have an abortion before we leave England."

"I'm not going to abort this baby."

"You could wait until it is born, and then give it up for adoption," Anna responded, "but by then you may have gotten attached to it, and it might be more difficult to do so. An abortion right away would be best. You have to have it taken care of before we leave England, an abortion cannot be had in Ireland."

"No mother. I'm keeping this child."

"Her mother was astonished at how Maria had changed. Maria, who never spoke in her own defense, was now adamant about keeping what Anna saw as an unwanted child.

"Surely Maria, you want to put that dreadful period of your life behind you. You cannot do that, and give birth to his child, a child that may look like this man you have escaped from."

"I will build a new life for this child in a new country."

"Another man coming into your life may not feel as you do about this child."

"I would never marry such a man."

An awkward silence prevailed over the breakfast table. Coming to Maria's defense, Stan spoke, "Like mother, like daughter."

"Momma and I don't look alike," Maria, not understanding, answered.

"Your mother once fiercely protected the child she carried, as you now are doing."

Anna looked deeply into Stan's face. Would he say more?"

"A new baby will enter with you into your new start in life," Stan smiled at Maria. Congratulations, Maria. It is wonderful news, but do not make this known to anyone, not even Scotland Yard, for if a child is involved, Abdul's child, their attitude would surely change.

CHAPTER 13

Father and son walked the inner courtyard undisturbed by outside distractions, and greatly disturbed by Maria's disappearance.

"You have gained for us many friends, Abdul. Your diplomatic skills are the best the family has."

"But I have failed in my marriage. You had said father, that an unhappy wife was not good. I should have taken care to change that situation. I was busy doing other things, and I did nothing to alleviate her unhappiness."

"She has left the country, or we would have found her."

"But how father? She did not pass through our neighboring borders, nor did she leave by ship, therefore, she had to have gone by plane, but how?"

"You say she did not use her Arabian passport."

"No, she left that behind."

"She could have sold some of the jewels you gave her to obtain a false passport, and sold some for cash."

"No. She took nothing with her. All her jewels and clothes, except whatever clothing she wore that day, are still in our apartment, and she didn't have currency of any kind."

The two men walked in silence for several moments.

"I loved her, I gave her everything I could, and she left without a word or a note of any kind."

"You say you had no hint of what she planned to do?"

"None, whatsoever," the younger man answered and then angrily added, "I want her brought back."

"To punish her?"

"To punish all those who might have helped her, for she could not have accomplished this without help from someone."

"Where would this help come from?" The women who went shopping with her said they always stayed together, and Maria never removed the burqa, tried to speak with anyone, nor did anyone speak with her."

"How could she possibly have left with no passport or money?" Abdul wondered aloud. "I have lost that which was most precious in my life, my son, Waheed, and now my beautiful wife has left me." He spoke like a man weighed down with sorrow. I am constantly negotiating on behalf of others, and here in my own family, my own wife's problems, I ignored. I could not envision her leaving me; not only because it would be almost impossible for her to leave this country without me, but because we loved each other. How blind I have been."

"Do not blame yourself, for that would be most unproductive. I have some of the best people working on it, but they have been unable to find any trace of her. If we find her and bring her here she will be executed. So either way Maria will never again be a wife to you. Therefore, it might be better to put her out of your thoughts completely and remarry."

Although I may be partially to blame, what she has done is unforgivable. Her actions have created a quandary. I cannot take her back as my wife, yet I cannot let her go." His father does not respond. Abdul speaks again. "You had your first wife, my mother, executed. She, however, had violated the marriage contract by favoring another man. Maria would never have done that. Yet Maria's action destroyed our marriage, and brought the death penalty upon her."

"Having my first wife stoned was perhaps a kindness to her. The man she ran away with was a despicable person. He tired of her, and consorted with other women. He became involved with a married woman whose husband fatally shot him. He had no money of his own. His father held onto the family fortune, and rightly so, as the son would have gambled it away. That would have left your mother in a foreign country without protection or financial means. She would have been destitute. So perhaps I saved her from a fate worse than what our laws prescribe.

The two men fell into silence before the older man spoke, "I did not want to add to your burden by telling you this, but perhaps I should."

"Tell me what, father?"

"I now have confirmation that Maria's mother is Jewish, therefore, Maria is Jewish."

"Jewish! No, that cannot be. Her mother is Polish and Maria was born in England. Maria looks Polish."

"Intermarriage sometimes produces children who look different from a parent. Your son did not look like any of our people. He looked like his mother."

"But father, no Jewish parent would name a child such a prominent Christian name as Maria."

"Perhaps, she felt she would be safeguarding her daughter, and helping her fit into English society if she did not have a Jewish name."

"She deceived us."

"No, son, her mother's passport on arrival in England showed her religious affiliation listed as non-believer. She was, perhaps, leaving a painful past behind her. I believe Maria, protected by her mother, knew nothing of her Jewish heritage."

Abdul was too stunned to speak.

* * *

They said their goodbyes before going up the gangplank of the boat that would take them to Ireland. Anna walked ahead followed by Maria and Stan.

"Since it's almost Christmas, I wish you both a Merry Christmas."

"Merry Christmas, Stan," Anna, turning around, smiled at Stan, "and may you have a safe trip home. Thank you so very much for all you've done. I will be eternally grateful to you for bringing Maria home."

"Thank you Anna. I too am eternally grateful that I had the opportunity to help her, and that all went well." Then turning to Maria, he addressed her, "I do hope you like your new home, and you will have a safe delivery and a healthy child. Perhaps, Maria, you will send me an occasional postcard or yearly Christmas card, to let me know how you're doing. Here is my address, he said handing Maria a piece of paper with his name, Stanislaw Krakowski, and his address written on it. In walking up into the boat, Anna heard Stan say, "I've always wanted a daughter. For me, Maria, you'll always be that daughter." Maria smiled, looked at the paper and kissed him.

"I will gladly write to you and be most happy to hear from you. I have no memory of my father, but since you've come into my life, I like to think of him as being exactly like you."

It was time for her to board. They hugged each other and parted. "If the baby is a boy, I'll name him Stanislaw," she called to him from the top of the gangplank.

The last thing she saw, as she entered the boat, was a most marvelous smile on Stan Krakowski's face.

Anna, now known as Ruth, before leaving England, had spent time at the library where she went to seek information about Ireland, and returned home with three interesting possibilities. Of the three, she favored Kinsale which was nestled on the southern coast of west Cork, in the south of Ireland. She noted that it was one of the oldest and most picturesque coastal towns in the country, and near Cork City. She wanted a small town, but one with easy access to a city, where she might find work. This seemed like a good choice.

The boat would land in Dun Laoghaire Harbor on the South side of Dublin City. From the city, a train or bus service could be obtained to take them to any place in Ireland. Bed and breakfast accommodations could be expensive if used over a long period, so they would need to look for a flat immediately, Ruth surmised. Her plan worked well in her head, but would it do so when put into action, she wondered.

Ruth looked over at her daughter who was seated on a bench reading a magazine. *What would life be like for her pregnant daughter? Did the people here like foreigners? Should she reveal that she and Mona were Jewish? In this Christian country, would it make a difference? Would there be a Jewish population—even a small one?* She chided herself for neglecting to check the population of Jewish people, and where the majority might live in Ireland.

Why was she now worrying about these things, she asked herself, when she had never previously declared her religious beliefs or attended a synagogue? Then she answered her own question. *I want to be free to be me, and accepted on that basis. I want a new start with nothing hidden, nothing to fear. Will I find that in this new place?* Then the harsh realities from her past, as they so often do, seeped into her mind. *Why should this place be different?*

If Mona had known she was Jewish, maybe none of these awful things would have occurred. Then again, Mona could not have told her Muslim husband that she was Jewish for she had not known it, and that lack of information may have inadvertently protected her daughter. If in their search for Maria, should they find she was Jewish, would they abandon their search or would they continue and perhaps seek revenge, believing she had deceived them by keeping it a secret? Money could not buy the most important things in life Ruth knew, but, to those who have it, it could buy allegiance and dedication. She did not wish to alarm her so young, vulnerable, and pregnant daughter with the possibilities running through her mind, and so she had to be vigilant in protecting Mona. This secret burden she would carry alone, or at least until she knew how their new fellow-country people would react if it should become known.

Deep in thought, she heard Mona speak to her.

"How beautiful, Momma. Look at the sail boats in the harbor and beyond."

"Yes," it is indeed beautiful. I've never before lived close to a body of water."

"Yes, plenty of water, for it is but a small island surrounded by water. The closest piece of land west of where we'll be living," Ruth said, looking out into the sea, "is America."

"America"

"Yes," a woman who overheard them speak answered, "In the west coast of Ireland, the people usually refer to America as the closest parish west of them." Mona and Ruth smiled at this way of referring to America.

"Are you new to Ireland? From England is it you've come?"

"Yes to both questions," Ruth answered.

"You don't sound English," the woman said to Ruth.

"Well, I'm originally from Poland."

"Quite a few Polish people have come to Ireland in recent years. Their English is usually not as good as yours."

"I've been in England a long time. My name is Ruth Cahill, and this is Mona, my daughter, who was born in England," Ruth informed the woman, introducing her to Mona who smiled in response.

"Hello Mona, nice to meet you both," she answered affectionately, pressing her hand to Mona's arm. "I'm Mairead Coogan."

Mona, who had never heard a Cork accent, had been enjoying listening to this woman they had just met, while standing at the rail waiting to get off the ferry. "When I was a child we walked everywhere or cycled and occasionally took public transportation, now everyone seems to have a car, and this generation can't imagine having to walk to where one wants to go." Mairead smiled in remembering.

Mona is surprised that her mother and this stranger spoke to each other as though they were old friends. Momma did not make any close friends in England in all the years she'd been there. She bade people in the flats a 'good day', etc., but that was all. Mona thought, *I miss Daphne and Penny. Momma did not like Daphne and thought Penny was too old a friend for me. Penny was like an older sister. Daphne had said when she married George, she wanted Penny and me to be her bridesmaids. Her sister, June, whom she did not like, would have to be her maid of honor, because her Mum would insist on it. I was not able to say 'goodbye' to them. Here, I have no friends. I will never again hear from Penny or Daphne, nor will they ever know what happened to me or where I am.*

How can Momma, who spent all her life answering to the name Anna, seem so comfortable with her new name, whereas I have such difficulty abandoning Maria for Mona, and must constantly remind myself to answer to this new name, because inside of me I am still Maria.

Neither did Momma need to change the color of her hair. Stan believed and Momma agreed with him that since my face was in newspapers, and on television as in missing persons, if I dyed my hair brown it would make a huge difference in my appearance. People would not associate the new me with the other me. It does make a great difference, a difference I don't like. When I look in the mirror I am this stranger with the chestnut brown hair posing as me, and I wish I could have the old me back.

Momma packed two extra boxes of hair dye in our cases to make sure we had enough brown hair dye until we had an opportunity to purchase more in Ireland.

Looking at Mairead, Ruth said, "You apparently are returning home?"

"Yes, I enjoy visiting my children and grandchildren, but I love being back home again."

"Where do your children live?"

"One lives in London with her husband and children, another of my children lives in Germany with his wife and children, and my youngest is in Switzerland."

"Are they married to citizens of these countries?"

"No, none of them. My daughter in England and son in Germany have Irish spouses. My youngest daughter isn't yet married. They want me to come live with them, or live with each of them for several months at a time. I'd be like a gypsy running from one country to another, with no permanent address. I cannot do that. I couldn't leave Ireland. With my husband dead, and with them overseas, they say there is nothing to keep me here. That's far from the truth. I have longtime friends and neighbors I've grown up with, and my little cottage where Mike and I raised our children. Here I am at home. Oh, forgive me, rattling on like this. Where will you be going when we disembark?"

"To Kinsale," Ruth answered.

"Kinsale is it? Sure I'm going down that way myself. I'm from Cork, we'll be traveling south together," Mairead laughed.

CHAPTER 14

Ruth, who was carrying two rather heavy cases, was glad to reach the solid granite wall of the train station. Mona had a case on wheels, and another case that held her mother's portable sewing machine. Mairead walked briskly along carrying a large bag in each hand. The train ride was pleasant and the scenery beautiful, but Mona was too tired to appreciate it. In the city they changed trains, and settling into a train going southwards, Mona closed her eyes, and fell asleep.

Sometime later, Mona woke up, but had not as yet opened her eyes when she heard her mother in conversation with Mrs. Coogan say, "The main reason we left England was because Mona, who was only seventeen at the time, and on holiday with friends, met and married what appeared to be a charming young man. He was not. I won't go into the horrible details; it is sufficient to say, the marriage was detrimental to her health and life, and she had no choice but to leave him."

"How dreadful," Mrs. Coogan said with sympathy.

"O God," thought Mona, shocked. *Was her mother going to reveal to this woman her marriage to Abdul and all that followed? She had never known her mother to get so chummy with anyone. Why now? Should she open her eyes in order to stop her mother from revealing all! No, it was too late.* Her mother had already begun the saga of her daughter's dreadful marriage without ever revealing who the father was, or his nationality. This omission led the woman to believe the father was English. Her mother went on to say how Mona discovered she was pregnant the day before they left England. She decided, Ruth said, that Mona should have a new start in life, and not inform her hus-

band of her pregnancy, for to do so would have forced her to stay with this despicable man. They hoped to start afresh in Ireland.

Mairead Coogan, extended her sympathy to Ruth and her daughter adding how sad it was, but that Mona was fortunate to have Ruth to take care of her, and that the child would not have one but two mothers.

These feelings of Mrs. Coogan did not sit well with Mona, nor did her mother's lies. She would have liked to have had a say in what half-truth they would invent to cover her condition. Yes, she would need her mother's help with the baby, but the child did not need two mothers. *Surely after all I've been through,* Mona thought, *Momma would treat me like an adult rather than a child. I can't let this pregnancy put me back into that old position of being Momma's little girl.* She had not previously given much thought to the fact that she still called her mother Momma, as she had as a child. Would the change upset her mother? Would she agree to be called Mum? Penny and Daphne called their mothers "Mum."

Just then, Mrs. Coogan left to use the restroom. Mona opened her eyes and said "I heard what you told her."

"Before your body expands and becomes noticeable, and to avoid rumors, or be met with unspoken questions, we need to make it known to at least one person right away that you're pregnant and have had a husband. This is a small town, Mona, a place where everyone knows each other and where word of mouth spreads fast. I chose a very nice, sympathetic woman to pass on the news."

"You think of everything," Mona softly answered with a mixture of gratitude and apprehension. *With a child on the way, I'll still be dependent on Momma. Even with a child of my own, I'll still be a child to Momma. In her home I'll never have a chance to be an independent person in my own right.*

"Momma, now that I'm a grown woman and about to become a mother for the second time, I thought, perhaps I should now call you Mum."

Ruth was taken aback by her daughter's suggestion.

"We've had to make so many name changes, darling," her mother softly answered, "but you'll always be my little girl and my best friend."

"No, Momma, we cannot be both. We can have a mother and child relationship or an adult relationship."

Ruth is surprised at her daughter's persistence. Not being "Momma" to her daughter, Ruth felt the old and precious tie between them being torn apart.

"If it's important to you, and obviously it is, then we will make the change. I don't like the word 'Mum' so perhaps you can call me 'Mother.'"

Mona put her arms around her mother. "Mother, it is time to let go of that little girl, and become better acquainted with the adult me," Mona smiled.

Mairead on returning sees them in an embrace and smiles.

In Cork they received directions from Mairead to Kinsale and said their goodbyes. With the help of people along the way, they found the realtor's office. Mona, refreshed from her nap, looked at her surroundings, and liked what she saw. People they didn't know bade them good evening in passing, in their strange musical accents.

The realtor came into her office with teacup in hand, and mentioned they don't really have many people come to the Real Estate Office at this time of year since it was so close to Christmas. "I'm Catherine Shaw," this very attractive woman introduced herself.

"I'm Ruth Cahill and this is my daughter Mona."

"Nice to meet you both," she replied extending her hand to them.

"We've just recently arrived and need a place to stay. We thought we'd try a bed and breakfast first before committing ourselves to a permanent place," Ruth explained.

"That is a good plan. You might, however, be able to rent a cottage for a few weeks before you decide to buy, which would be less expensive than a B&B. There are just the two of you, aren't there?"

"Yes, just my daughter and me."

"Where are you from?" Catherine asked although she had detected that Ruth had a foreign accent and her daughter an English one.

"From England," Ruth answered.

"What brings you to Ireland?"

"Mona, at seventeen, while on holiday with friends, met and married what seemed like a charming gentleman. He was not. The marriage was a dreadful mistake. It was imperative that she leave him. However, the day before we were to leave England Mona discovered she was pregnant. We left without telling him of the pregnancy, as a child would have forced her to stay with him. I thought it best to move away and begin anew. We had been planning for some years to move out of our neighborhood in London which had begun to deteriorate. Now that we needed to move out of England, we thought we might move to Scotland, Wales or Ireland, and decided on Ireland."

"Well, I hope you'll be happy with your choice. I have done a lot of traveling abroad, but I'm always happy to return to Ireland. Of course, I grew up here. Mine was the first generation to travel in my family."

"This is a beautiful country."

"It has changed a great deal since I was a schoolgirl. Back then we had few foreigners, but now the world has changed. People move from country to country. We have Asians, Eastern Europeans, Africans and others living here now. We are becoming a mosaic of people of all stripes, sounds, and cultures," Catherine laughed, then continued on a more serious note.

"Mr. Donovan has his cottage up for sale. Nothing fancy but you could rent it for a couple of weeks before making a commitment. He's a very nice gentleman. He had been living there alone for some time before moving in with his son and daughter-in-law on the other side of town. You could fix it up very nicely. It is walking distance from the stores, which is good if you haven't a car, and the bus stop into the city is only minutes away."

"Could we see it?"

"Sure thing, just leave your cases in the office and I'll take you over. You've been traveling all day, no doubt. I'll make you a cup of tea before we look at it."

"I wouldn't want to trouble you."

"No trouble at all. Come into the back and I'll put on the kettle." They had tea and scones with butter and jam which they enjoyed before heading out into the night.

"You'll have to pay the rent, of course, and can stay in the cottage until you decide what you want to do. It's not far, so we can walk to it," Catherine said as she set a brisk pace.

Opening the door to Ned Donovan's cottage, Catherine said, "A bit of fresh air is needed in here." Failing to open the window in the living room, she affirmed, "I'll have him fix that. The yard behind the cottage comes with the cottage but the grazing land beyond its walls is now owned by his son. But then, I doubt very much that you'd be interested in grazing land!"

Cozy, Ruth thought, *and with possibilities,* as she walked through the two small bedrooms, and into the living room and tiny kitchen. The kitchen had a gas range, small refrigerator, sink and a non-built-in cabinet. Very little storage space, Ruth realized, but then she reasoned they had at the moment very little to store. A small table with four chairs completed the kitchen. There was a sink, toilet, and a bathtub with a shower overhead in the bathroom which looked like it was an addition onto the back of the house. "He'll rent it furnished, and is willing to sell it furnished or non-furnished with very little difference in price," Catherine said.

Two fireside chairs, a rocking chair, a table that could seat four, a glass case with dishes on the top shelf and books on the two bottom shelves furnished the room Catherine called the parlor. Each bedroom had free-standing wardrobes from a century or more ago and large brass beds, plus a small night table and a chair. The only built-in closet was the clothes closet in the entrance hall of the cottage. The wooden floors in the bedroom had no covering except for wooly sheepskins on the floor where one would set down one's feet on getting out of the brass beds.

Catherine did not intrude on their inspection of the cottage, but waited in the kitchen to hear what they might decide upon. Ruth muttered and shook her head looking at the paper on the walls, especially that in the parlor. A continuous turf fire would have burnt in the fireplace throughout the winter months. The wallpaper, whatever color it had been, was now all faded into a dull brownish color.

"What do you think, Mona?"

"The bedroom paper must have been very attractive at one time."

"Yes," Ruth agreed, "but it would be much easier and less costly to remove it and paint the walls."

As they entered the kitchen Catherine greeted them with, "Well, what do you both think of it?"

"It could certainly use a fresh coat of paint and some new wall-paper," Ruth answered.

"He doesn't want to put any money into the place. He expects to rent or sell it as is, and he has set the price most reasonably. If he has a buyer he might be persuaded to have it painted, but not papered. I can't, of course, promise you he will do so."

"I'm in a precarious position at the moment. I need to find a job, and we will need to think it over, but would like to rent it until then."

"Fair enough, Ruth. What kind of work are you looking for?"

"I've always worked as a bookkeeper. Can we move in tonight?"

"Yes, of course, since you plan to rent it. It's getting awfully late and you have both been traveling all day. Why not get yourselves a good night's rest. I'll have a friend drop off your cases tonight, and we can discuss it in the morning."

"Thank you. A good night's rest will be welcome," Ruth replied.

They said their goodbyes and Catherine left.

"Mother, do we have to sleep in these beds that others have slept in before us?"

"Mona, darling, if we stayed at a B&B or even in the finest hotel, many people would have slept in those beds before us and others after we had left," her mother laughed as she opened the ancient wardrobe. Ruth found two sets of sheets in plastic bags and two wool blankets on the top shelves alongside several pillows. Pulling the coverlet off the bed, she pulled out a set of sheets. "Put the kettle on for some tea while I make up the beds. I saw some crockery and cutlery when I checked out the kitchen," Ruth called out to Mona who had gone into the kitchen.

Having made the beds, Ruth entered the kitchen. "I don't suppose, there is any food here, since nobody has been living here."

"There is a tin of tea and a tin of cocoa. I think I'll have some cocoa instead of tea, there is also a tin of biscuits."

"That's not much for you to eat and you carrying a child. "I'll go out and see if there is a shop open where I can get something more nourishing.

"It's dark out, and I can wait until morning to eat."

"But Mona," a knock on the door stops Ruth in mid-sentence. Going toward the door she opens it and finds a young man and Catherine standing there.

"This is Tim from the bar down the street, and he has kindly agreed to help me bring the cases to you," Catherine said. Tim grinned as he stood next to Ruth's two cases and the sewing machine. Catherine had the case on wheels in tow and a covered plate in her hand.

"I thought perhaps you hadn't had much to eat in the course of your busy day, so I brought some ham and cheese sandwiches," she said as she handed the plate to Ruth. Tim brought the cases into the hall.

"Thank you. How much do I owe you?"

"Nothing," she replied as she waved her hand in dismissal. "Good night."

"Good night to you both," Tim added and they left.

As they sat down and ate the sandwiches, Ruth spoke, "Not hungry you said and you've downed half the sandwiches in record time."

"I did not want you going out alone at night in a strange place," her daughter stated. "These are good sandwiches," she added feeling comfortably fed.

"It was very nice of Catherine to think of our needs as she did, now get ready for bed, while I get some nightwear out of the cases. We'll unpack tomorrow after I get the Sunday newspaper and check the ads for a bookkeeping position."

In bed that night Mona felt trapped, trapped in Abdul's home, and now in Momma's cottage. With a baby growing inside of her there would be no independence, no job, and no prospects of one for many years until the child entered school. She was ashamed of her ingratitude towards her hard-working mother, who continued to provide for her and the child. *Mother's practical solution to abort the child had merit,* she acknowledged. *Momma speaks of all her family members being murdered during that awful war, yet to put an end to Abdul's hold on me, she would have this child aborted. She also tells me it would be easier for me to find a 'suitable' man here to marry if I were without a child. Whatever plans Momma had for me, and Momma is a great planner, I have destroyed. I am a burden to her. Yes, even those we love can, at times, be a burden to us.* Mona surmised.

CHAPTER 15

Mairead Coogan carefully removed the tea set from its accustomed place in the glass cabinet. Every ten weeks she performed this labor of love. It was her night to have the knitting group at her home. She had spent the day cleaning her living room and bathroom and baking an apple pie. She was especially excited about this evening for she had a lovely piece of news to impart to the group of women. Yes, all was in order. The bell rang. The women arrived singly or in groups with their knitting bags in tow. Taking off their coats, they seated themselves around the fire, and took out their knitting. She would let them settle in before imparting what she had to say.

"Only five days before Christmas," Rita said as she laid her almost finished angora sweater on her lap. "It seems to come faster each year."

"You sound the opposite to my grandchildren, who are impatiently awaiting Christmas," the woman making the yellow baby sweater laughed.

"Aw, to be a child at Christmas," the youngest among the group. who was making an Aran sweater, sighed.

"You will be one of these days, second childhood it's called," the knitter of the angora sweater laughed, and others joined in.

"I should be at home getting things ready for Christmas, but if I stay at home, I'll never get this shawl made."

Mairead took her knitting basket off the shelf. "I met a Polish woman and her daughter on the boat home from England," she announced.

"Visiting away from home at Christmastime" People traveling at this time of year do so to get home, not away from it," the woman working on the crib blanket stated with a frown.

"She is Polish, but has lived in England for a long time, with her daughter, a beautiful girl named Mona who was born in England."

"Where were they traveling to?" the woman with the yellow ball of wool asked.

"They plan to settle in Kinsale," Mairead continued.

"Why here rather than Dublin? There are no Polish people around these parts," the woman rapidly knitting the Aran sweater asked.

"Because the woman said her daughter fell in love at age seventeen. She married a man whom she later found to be a horrible person," Mairead solemnly spoke. The ladies' needles slowed down or stopped altogether. She had their full attention.

"So she ran away?" the woman with the half-finished mittens asked.

"Well, Mona, Ruth's daughter, discovered she was pregnant. If he found out she was pregnant it would have made it impossible for her to leave her wretched marriage, so they left without telling the husband. The mother brought her daughter to Ireland to put it all behind them and start over." A silence followed.

The woman who had been knitting a shawl spoke, "They say marriages are made in heaven. That might be so, but we live them here on earth."

"You've got a point there, still it is rather a drastic solution to just up and leave. Perhaps he might have changed when he had a child," interjected the woman with the angora sweater, who was now pointing her needles at the group. Some agreed with her, others were dubious.

"Could it be that there was no father?" the yellow bootie maker asked in a loud whisper.

"You think perhaps she made up the story of the girl having made a disastrous marriage?" Mairead asked incredulously.

"It just doesn't add up as a viable reason to move to a whole different country when she could get a divorce in England," the mitten maker joined in.

"How far along is the girl?" the bootie maker turned to Mairead.

"The daughter is only a couple of months pregnant." Ruth said it was due in June.

"It seems to me they left England before anyone could notice her condition," the maker of the baby blanket pointed out.

No knitting was being done as they pondered the possible reasons these two women had for their arrival on Irish soil. They spoke in whispers although no one was in the cottage other than the women themselves.

"So you think it was the girl's pregnancy that brought them to Cork?" Mairead asked as she rose to put on the tea kettle."

"That's the only logical explanation we can come up with. Of course, there could be another reason which we don't know of, and the mother didn't reveal, but one thing is certain, Ruth gave you what sounds to me like a 'cock and bull' story," the owner of the angora sweater stated.

"The poor girl," Mairead added as the water came to a boil.

"Yes, it must be very difficult for the young girl," they all agreed.

"But why did the mother tell such an unbelievable story," the mitten maker insisted.

"We may never know for sure, but I'd say she was obviously trying to protect her daughter," Mairead answered.

"No imagination," the blanket maker concluded.

"Yes, no originality," the woman sitting next to her agreed.

"Tea is ready, come to the table," Mairead invited, as she placed her apple pie down before them. The women took their places around the table, but questions continued.

"What if the mother thought the man who impregnated her daughter was unsuitable, and there was no wedding, and then the mother found the girl was pregnant?" the Aran sweater maker suggested.

"Perhaps he had a criminal record, or was a rapist," the shawl maker weighed in.

"Oh God," Mairead groaned. "Do you think this lovely girl was raped?"

"Well, sadly, that would be a good reason to leave their former lives behind them." The mitten knitter spoke. "That poor girl," she sadly concluded and all sympathized.

They left Mairead's home that evening with none of the good feelings they had arrived with. By twilight of the following evening the news of Mona's pregnancy had traveled many miles.

Ruth not only got a part-time position as bookkeeper, but she interviewed for and got two such jobs. One she would begin at eight in the morning until noon, and the other from one o'clock in the afternoon to five in the evening. Fortunately, they were just a twenty-minute walk from each other. She planned to apply for a bank loan, put the bulk of her savings down as a deposit, and buy the house.

That evening, Mona sat down by the fire and wrote Stan Krakowski a long letter telling him all that had happened since they left England, and wishing him and his family a wonderful Christmas. As she wrote, she could visualize the four Krakowskis seated around the dinner table, which was laden with an abundance of delicious food, lovingly prepared by Stan's wife Ellie. *How lovely it would be to be there,* Mona thought, *during Christmas. Did they put up a Christmas tree,* she wondered, *or sing carols? Did uncles, aunts, cousins, and grandparents join them as they celebrated? Did they exchange gifts? Mother never put up a Christmas tree but they exchanged a gift on Christmas Eve, and mother always treated the two of them to a nice meal the day after Boxing Day, since every establishment closed down for Christmas Day and Boxing Day. What,* she wondered, *would it be like to be part of a family larger than two, to have brothers and sisters to gather together with grand-parents, uncles, aunts, and lots of cousins?*

Abdul's family was large, but I never felt completely a part of it. I never quite fit in. They were not my grandparents, my uncles and aunts or cousins. Abdul was often away on business trips. That fort-night in Spain and Morocco was more beautiful than any lavish advertisement for a romantic holiday could convey. Yet in his home, with so many family members present, I was alone and lonely. Karol's family made me feel at home. Karol and Piotr treated me as a sister.

Suddenly she felt ashamed of her thoughts, as though she were betraying her hard-working mother by indulging in these fantasies. Having finished the letter, she addressed the envelope. She would get a stamp at the post office and mail it.

Christmas came with many festivities in this village of quaint buildings and cordial people. Since it was a pleasant enough day for a walk, Ruth suggested they walk down to the harbor. No stores would be open, so she prepared a flask of tea and, putting it along with some biscuits in a canvas bag, they walked down to the water.

"I've never lived close to water," Mona observed.

"Nor I," Ruth replied. "I don't know what the rest of Ireland looks like but this is a most beautiful area to live in." Mona nodded her head in agreement.

A knock at the door at seven o'clock on a Saturday morning woke Ruth from a deep sleep. Grabbing her robe she hastily put it on as she walked to the door.

A refined gentleman in his early sixties was standing there. "Sorry if I arrived too early, I am Ned Donovan." It took a moment for this to register with Ruth.

"Mr. Donovan," Ruth smiled, "Come in."

"I'm an early riser being I've worked the farm all my life. Catherine has got you all settled in, I see. This here was made by my daughter-in-law this morning," he added as he handed Ruth the still warm soda bread. "She thought you'd like some soda bread with your tea," he said as he sat himself down at the table, and taking out his pipe he filled and lit it.

Ruth, who had been embarrassed by her 'just got out of bed' appearance and her old worn bathrobe, began to feel quite at ease with this easy-going farmer.

"Would you like some tea?"

"No thanks, I've just had breakfast. I assume that Catherine told you how to light the pilot light to the heater and the oven?"

"Yes, she did. She has been very helpful."

"She's a good woman, Catherine is. She never married. Her younger sister did, but a year later she died in childbirth. It was very sad indeed."

"Did the child survive?"

"She did, yes. She must be eleven or twelve years old by now. The father left for England about a year after the death of his wife, leaving little Una with her grandparents. Catherine helped them raise the child." After adjusting the tobacco in his pipe, he continued. "It was touch and go for a while when she was a toddler, whether the grandparents could have her, or whether the father would return and claim the child. Elizabeth, his second wife, however, saw to it that that would not happen. They have four children of their own now and Elizabeth never wanted the child from her husband's first marriage. So, Elizabeth's refusal was the Shaw's lifeline after the loss of their daughter, Mary."

"That should not have stopped a beautiful woman like Catherine from getting married."

"No, it really didn't I suppose, although she, more than the grandparents, has been raising Una. They're like mother and daughter. Catherine is a most attractive woman, but Mary was always considered the beauty of the family."

"Does the child resemble her mother?"

"Just a bit. She looks more like the father, but she has her mother's delightful personality. Well, I'd better not keep you from your plans for today," he said as he rose up and was about to leave, then hesitated a moment, "Where did you say you were from?"

"I didn't, but I'm from Poland originally."

"Catholic, I presume?"

"No, I'm Jewish," she offered, and waited for his reaction. She had not planned to impart to him or to anyone else this particular piece of information. He was so comfortable in his own skin, and thereby so easy to speak with, she had lowered her guard.

"We don't have a temple or synagogue in these parts. You'd need to go to Dublin to attend one. Whenever you'd like to go, I'll take you to the train station. My daughter, Ciara, lives in Dublin. She'd be happy to show you where it is located. I don't know if you attend a morning or evening service but, no matter, you could stay with Ciara overnight the night before, if it's in the morning you'll be attending, or the following night, should it be an evening service you wish to attend."

"I wouldn't want to inconvenience your daughter."

"No inconvenience, Ciara would be happy to help," and having said that he bade her 'good morning' and left.

Moments after Ned Donovan left, Mona entered the kitchen.

"I thought I heard you speak to someone," she said, looking around the kitchen.

"Mr. Donovan came by and brought the soda bread that his daughter-in-law made."

Realizing she had told Donovan that she was Jewish, before even mentioning this very significant fact to her daughter, forced her to make haste in getting this matter settled.

"Sit down, Mona," she said as she placed two cups of tea on the table, "I have something important I need to tell you, something I should have told you a long time ago."

Mona looked perplexed. *Had they not always shared their important information?*

"Something you should have told me a long time ago?"

"Yes. It goes way back to World War II long before you or I were born." And so, Ruth went back in time to earlier generations, so that Mona might know the family history. Ruth told of the family struggles, with all the truth that she knew of it, until she reached Mona's father. That would have to remain a piece of fiction in order not to destroy her and Mona's relationship.

"Oh, Mother, I'm so sorry for all you and our family had to endure, and all because you were Jewish. I can understand why you kept this a secret. You are an extremely brave and strong woman."

"Now that you know the family history, I have something else to share with you. I am going to go to a synagogue in Dublin someday soon. I thought I might do so before Passover and then you and I can observe Passover together for the first time here in Ireland. If my visit to the synagogue is a good experience, I hope you'll join me there on the High Holy Days." After sipping some tea, Ruth continued with a laugh, "What a weight that has been on my shoulders."

"This was a weight upon your shoulders?"

"Yes. I was trying to protect you, maybe unnecessarily, but with my background came a lot of mistrust. Now I feel liberated and I want to observe Passover. You remember the events I used to read to you. It was safe to have a bible because it gives the Jewish history and Christian beliefs. You remember the story of how the Jewish people left Egypt under the leadership of Moses?"

"Yes."

"Well, that is what is remembered at Passover. This is the perfect occasion to establish who we are—our true identity—the day of remembrance of our ancestors' flight out of slavery in Egypt. In those terrible final hours of the tenth plague when the first born child in every Egyptian family died, the Israelites, who in following God's instructions, had splattered the thresholds of their homes with the blood of a lamb so that the angel of death passed over them, and they were spared. That is what is celebrated on Passover." Freedom comes with a huge price, but Ruth chose to ignore that part of the story until a later time. "You too, Mona, have escaped from your captives. Abdul's and your first born could not be saved but now another child grows within you."

"We have come a long way since World War II, Mona. The holocaust decimated my family. The free world did not come to our aid. Our suffering and deaths were ignored. Even God seemed to abandon us. It was as James Joyce said of another people and their situation, 'God was paring his finger nails,' when these atrocities were occurring. Parents could not protect their children from the onslaught of those dark terrible times. Now, I believe we are in a safe place. We have new identities, and a new beginning."

Ruth laughed in her excitement at the prospect of being 'whole' as she described it. "So let us reclaim our heritage, and observe our past freedom from slavery, and your more recent deliverance."

Mona was happy to see her mother so alive with enthusiasm for the holiday.

After a long pause, Ruth asked, "How do you feel about all this?"

"I don't know. I have never previously belonged to any religious group. This is all very important to you Mother, but not to me. You have always known you were Jewish, even though you kept it hidden, but it has never been a part of my life, and I do not know if it ever will be."

Ruth was dismayed. Revealing who she was, and is, had not had the expected results from her daughter. She somehow thought they would be of one mind on this issue. She had finally handed down to her daughter her peoples' history and her daughter had rejected it. Well, not so much rejected it, Ruth surmised, but she did not see it as a vital part of who she was, and that saddened Ruth. *Perhaps I waited too long to tell her,* she chided herself.

Into the silence, Mona spoke, "That's your history, not mine."

"No, darling, it is our combined past, of who we are as a people, passed down through the ages."

The women sat in silence, each with her thoughts; Mona feeling sad that she had disappointed her mother, Ruth saddened by regrets and feelings of loss.

CHAPTER 16

Mona was excited to find a letter that had been pushed through the mail slot, and was lying on the floor in the hall. It was the first personal letter since their arrival in Kinsale and addressed to her. To her delight it was from Stan Krakowski. On opening it, she read of his apology for not sending her a Christmas card, as he had not received her card with her new address until after Christmas. He hoped she was well, and he was happy to know they were both adjusting nicely to the new surroundings. He asked if they would be getting a telephone installed, as he would on occasion like to telephone her.

She would have liked her mother to have a telephone installed, but her mother had said they had no need for one, because they really knew nobody they needed to phone, that telephones were expensive, and should they need to use a phone in an emergency they could use the pay phone in the pub down the road.

Stan wrote that her family in Poland spoke of her often, and all sent their love. She was delighted that they thought of her as family. He also wrote that he would like very much to think of her as his godchild, and hoped she might think of him as a godfather. This brought a smile to her face. She already thought of him as a father figure in her life, and was very pleased by his suggestion. He ended by wishing her and her mother a Happy New Year.

Ruth left for work each morning, and Mona shopped for and cooked their meals, washed their clothes, and cleaned the house so that her mother would be free of those chores and could enjoy her weekends.

Mona wished she too had a job. If she had had a job in Ireland before she became pregnant, she could have worked until shortly before the birth of her child, but now nobody would hire a pregnant woman.

In late March, Ruth caught the flu and was unable to work. She knew she would have been paid during the time she was sick, but having been recently hired, and due to her conscientious nature, Ruth asked Mona to go into Cork city, and take over her bookkeeping tasks until she recovered.

"No, no doctor."

"But mother, you're very sick with this flu, and need to be seen by a doctor."

"No dear, 'this too will pass.'"

"I could ask Catherine to check in on you while I'm at work."

"Don't you dare," her fiercely independent mother replied. "I've always managed alone, and will continue to do so. Don't even mention to Catherine or any of the neighbors that I've come down with this nuisance of a bug. I don't want people dropping in on me. I wish to be left alone. Sleep and liquids will take care of it."

"What if Catherine or another neighbor sees me, rather than you, at the bus stop?"

"Should they ask, tell them I'm taking a few days off, or that I am allowing you to keep in touch with the work that you were trained to do," and then, she waved her hand denoting how trivial the question was.

Mona did not pursue the matter further in fear of aggravating her mother, who was greatly annoyed that this illness had taken hold of her, especially at a time like this and she newly employed, nor did Ruth take kindly to the idea of being pampered in any way.

"No, Mona," her mother replied to Mona's offer to stay home, and take care of her until she recovered. "You can do nothing to rid me of the flu. I want you to stay away from me, so as not to become stricken with this awful bug. You have a baby to consider, and must keep well."

Mona obeyed her mother. For three weeks, she took the bus into the city where, with joy and anticipation, she did the accounting. For the first time since they had left England, she met other young people. Although she could not join them on Fridays after work at the local pub as she would have liked to, she enjoyed the brief mid-morning and mid-afternoon tea breaks in their company.

As the flu began to subside, Ruth worried about her daughter. She would have liked to be able to phone Mona at work and hear how she was doing, and to ask if she needed any help with some of the more involved accounts. *Was she eating the lunch she brought from home between jobs or was she delayed by Mr. McCain who, on his leisurely lunch break, had the habit of stopping by to inquire how she was doing?*

Ruth also worried about the young woman, Rose, whom Mona spoke of. Ruth had seen her at work, but didn't know her. *Pretty little thing she was*, she remembered. *Those girls go out to the pub Friday evenings for beer, talk, and singing. They were not a rough crowd like Daphne's friends were. It was Mona's association with Daphne and Penny that brought her to Spain and on the disastrous journey to the Emirates. Of course,* Ruth thought, becoming more relaxed, *Mona will not be going on holiday for a long time to come. As I came directly home to Mona each day from work, so too will she come immediately home to me. Was Rose another wild card like Daphne?* she pondered. She could never understand why her daughter and Daphne, who had nothing in common, had become friends. *Opposites attracting, no doubt.* thought Ruth.

As soon as I get my strength back Mona can stay safely at home, and wait for the child to be born. Our next purchase will be a house phone, and a cellphone, Ruth decided, and with that thought in mind, she fell asleep.

Mona was happy to see that her mother had recovered, but saddened to leave the job and the friends she had made there, especially Rose. Mr. McCain, for whom her mother worked, sent home Ruth's paycheck weekly with Mona, and on Mona's last day on the job, he gave her a substantial check of her own.

Mona grew restless at home. Sometimes she read in the library instead of at home in order to be among, and have brief encounters with, people. Mona's days were always brightened when Una dropped in for a visit, to ask how Mona felt and to talk about the baby Mona carried. Una was like a younger sister to Mona, each of them being the only child of the family, and subjected to a very protective adult. They shared their innermost feelings, fears, and hopes and developed a strong friendship. *If only we were closer in years*, Mona thought, *we could be best friends.*

To her surprise and delight, Stan phoned her asking how she was doing, and to tell her that he and his wife planned to make a visit to Ireland around the time the baby was due, to celebrate the birth of the child with her and her mother. This news was warmly received by Mona, who now not only looked forward to the birth of her child, but also to a visit from Stan and his wife.

Mona's statement, that she would have the child baptized in the church, stunned her mother. After the jarring effects of this announcement, Ruth, reflecting on it, realized everyone they associated with in the country was Christian, but it was mostly Stan Krakowski's religious affiliation, she believed, that had most influenced Mona's decision. He, who had earlier told her he felt like a godfather to her, had now spoken to her about choosing godparents for the baby.

Mona wanted Rose to be the godmother but Ruth discouraged that idea. Mona had known Rose for a mere three weeks and now that Mona would be a mother with an infant and responsibilities, their relationship would not be the same, Ruth told her daughter. When Ruth suggested Una for the honor, Mona, who had thought Una might be considered too young, readily agreed.

Ruth, however, did not like the fact that Mona wanted Stan's son Karol as godfather. He had played a part in her daughter's escape, and she appreciated what they, father and son, had done, but they were now infringing on her life, and she found it upsetting. Ruth resented how Stan and his family claimed her daughter's affection, and she wanted to distance Mona from them. That the secret Stan and she shared might somehow become exposed was a constant threat, and it frightened her.

Stan was putting her in an awkward position. *Had he told his wife that Mona was his daughter? He has two sons, why does he need to claim my only child? Now his son will be the baby's godfather, attaching another layer of intrusions on her.* That the child, if a boy, would bear Stan's name was another thorn in her side. Now, more than ever, Ruth wanted the child to be a girl.

"Karol lives in Poland! The child will rarely, if ever, see him," Ruth contended. "What kind of a relationship can they have with each other, due to the distance between them?" Mona was adamant.

She would ask Karol to be the child's godfather. Mona believed she owed him that honor.

Ruth, who could not reveal her objections to her daughter, felt suffocated by Stan and his family, and resented their intrusion into her and Mona's life.

When the time had come to bring the child into the world, Mona phoned her mother at work. Ruth left immediately to be with her daughter. The child, however, would not wait, and Mona got a ride from Catherine to the hospital, leaving her mother a note. By the time Ruth got to the hospital, Mona already had the child in her arms. To Mona's surprise, her stoic mother cried with joy that all had gone well, and with relief, as the tension she had experienced, from the time of Mona's phone call to seeing her daughter and grandchild, had left her drained but happy.

The child was not a granddaughter as Ruth had hoped for, but a grandson. Mona, remembering Waheed, wanted a daughter for her mother but was equally happy with her newborn son.

The day before Mona was discharged from the hospital, Mairead Coogan and the knitting group paid her a visit. They brought with them a hand-knitted baby blanket, sweaters, mittens and hats in infant, and toddler sizes, and some knitted animals for her newborn child, whom they declared beautiful. Wanting to know what she would name him, they were told Stanislaw, a name unfamiliar to the group. Mona explained that the child was being named after a wonderful man, who was like a father to her, and who would be arriving the following day with his wife from Poland to visit, to celebrate little Stan's birth. This information puzzled the women, who later among themselves would wonder why a man who was obviously not her father, but acted like a father to her, would come all the way from Poland with his wife to visit her and the child. He must be, they wholeheartedly declared, a wonderful person. Since Stan would be arriving with his wife, he was not Ruth's husband, they decided, and so not Mona's father. The mystery of who fathered little Stan, a person they assumed was living in England, was not made known.

To complicate matters further, this lovely baby boy did not look English or Polish. The child, with a tanned complexion, and with eyes so dark they looked black, did not in any way resemble his mother.

All the women's questions came back to the one question, who was this child's father?

One of the women volunteered to go back to the hospital the following morning, and meet the man whom Mona looked upon as a father, to see if more information could be had through another visit. The women voiced the hope that some details of who fathered the child could be discovered.

The knitter explained her presence as having to be in Kinsale that morning, and while there, she thought she would pay another visit to Mona, and have the opportunity to see the baby again. She met Stan and his wife, and saw a strong resemblance between Stan and Mona. He, however, had a wife and two teenage sons, Karol and Piotr. Therefore, the women did not for a moment consider Stan as a possible father to Mona. Mr. Krakowski and Mona looked alike because they were both Polish with the light complexions, common to many Polish people. The newborn child resembled his grandmother, the women believed.

The knitter deemed Stan and his wife to be very nice people. They, as well as Ruth, thanked her for visiting Mona, and also extended their thanks to all the knitters who had given Mona such lovely gifts for the baby. The Krakowskis had said they hoped Mona would visit them in Poland. The woman felt she had had a very nice visit to report back to the group, but she was disappointed that she had no further information as to who the child's father might be, and so the mystery of who fathered this charming little boy remained unsolved.

Mona had the child baptized before Stan and Ellie Krakowski left for home, with Stan standing in for Karol. Catherine's niece Una, who held the child in her arms throughout the ceremony, was the delighted godmother.

When the child was eight days old, Ruth took Mona and the child to Dublin, where she had him circumcised by a Rabbi.

CHAPTER 17

On Stan's first birthday, a most unusual box arrived for the child. A box so large it had to be moved horizontally into the cottage, for upright it was too tall for the front door. Nobody could guess what it might be. On opening the box, after much struggling with it, Ruth, Mona and little Stan found a large stuffed kangaroo with two of its young in its pouch. When Ruth and Mona stood it upright, its head was just an inch or two from the ceiling. The card attached read, "Happy birthday, son" and was signed with Abdul's full name. This gift cast a shadow over the otherwise joyful event for Ruth. It sent a chill through Mona. While little Stan touched the kangaroo's skin and, stretched his hand into the pouch, the adults spoke in whispers.

"He has found us," Ruth stated with a measure of fear.

"That was bound to happen."

"What will he do, I wonder?"

"We'll just have to wait and see," Mona answered.

"This is embarrassing. What will we tell people when they ask about this very expensive gift?"

"The truth, Mother, that it is a gift from his father."

"Are you sure that is what you want to say?"

"Yes. I will not begin a pattern of lies to my son."

Mona wished Abdul had given a less conspicuous gift—something smaller and more appropriate, like Karol's bear, or practical like Stan and Ellie's warm jacket and pants set. Mona did not volunteer the information, but when asked, true to her word, revealed that the kangaroo was a gift from Stan's father. That stopped all further conversation on the matter except for a few brief comments on the generosity of the child's father.

The neighboring children, having arrived for Stan's birthday, stared wide-eyed at the kangaroo. It frightened some of them, and it caused others to cry. Stan stared at it in amazement for a while, then ignoring it, reached for the furry bear he had received from Karol.

Now that her son was a year old, Mona stopped breast feeding him, and secured work from nine o'clock to five o'clock on Saturdays. Ruth was happy to have a full day to care for her grandson in whom she delighted. Their home was full of love and laughter. Ruth, the practical, no-nonsense woman, who had hoped the child would be a girl, now couldn't imagine life without her grandson, mellowed with joy in this child. Yet she and Mona were disturbed that the giver of the gift had located them. They had hoped he was out of their lives, and it was unsettling to realize that although they had changed their name, and left England to settle in Ireland, he had found them.

"How long do you think Abdul has known we were here in Kinsale?" Mona wondered aloud.

"That's difficult to determine, but he must have someone close by who is reporting back to him," Ruth ventured to say, trying not to unduly stress Mona.

"Should we leave Kinsale?"

"We cannot keep running, especially from a man with so many resources."

"Doesn't it seem strange to you, Mother, that he sent a gift, but did not express a desire to visit Stan?" Mona asked, trying to keep the panic she felt out of her voice.

"I feel he knows our every move, Mona, and with modern technology, he can view all three of us even as we walk down the street."

"That is scary. From here on I'll be suspicious of anyone with a cellphone, assuming they are capturing our images on it," Mona in distress added.

"We're going to have to act as normal as possible. I believe the kangaroo was more than a gift to Stan. It is Abdul's way of letting us know he knows where we are."

How does one act normal with this threat hanging over them? Mona thought, but kept her thoughts to herself so as not to burden her mother with her fears.

The weeks and months passed without any indication that Abdul, or a person hired by him, was present in Kinsale, until Stan's second birthday, when a beautiful lifelike rocking horse arrived for Stan. Again the message read, "Happy birthday, son," but continued with the words, 'When you are older I will give you a real horse.'

At his small birthday party, the children gathered around the horse excitedly waiting their turn to mount it. Stan, who now was very vocal, talked to the horse incessantly. Unlike the kangaroo, he loved the horse, and it became his favorite toy.

Mona, at Stan Krakowski's suggestion, enrolled that autumn at University College, Dublin, and left her Saturday bookkeeping position. She wheeled Stan across the campus in his stroller, and into the classroom where he played quietly until bored, and then fell asleep. He was the only child, and the most popular fellow on campus.

Mona and Colm McGowan met at the University; they liked each other from their first meeting, and became good friends. Colm, a third-year student, took it upon himself to help this beautiful first-year student. He had come to care greatly for her Stan, and could be seen playing with the boy when Mona had a class. When the child grew tired, Colm carried him on his back. It wasn't unusual to see the child asleep in Colm's jacket, or on his sweatshirt on a bench while Colm studied next to him. Others asked Colm why he was getting involved with a married woman, when the campus was awash with very desirable single women. Mona had told him she had left her husband. Colm did not press her further.

On the University campus with all its studying and activities, it was not difficult for Mona to forget the possibility of Abdul's presence in the guise of someone who might be watching her every move. With Colm by her side, she felt secure. She was happier now than she had ever been, even on that magical whirlwind trip to Morocco with Abdul. That was like a dream that she would awaken from, whereas with Colm there was reality. Colm loved Stan, and he was a good man whom she enjoyed being with. *Yes, she was delightfully happy,* she thought, as she walked towards the two men in her life, Stan wrapped in Colm's sweater deep in sleep, and Colm deep in a book.

Colm invited Mona to meet his family over the Christmas holidays, as that was the time he knew with certainty that all the family would be together. Ruth was also invited but declined the invitation, offering instead to babysit Stan. Ruth, Mona, Colm and Stan celebrated Christmas together on Christmas Eve. After dinner Stan opened his gifts of a soccer ball, and shirt and pants with the Cork team's name on it, from Colm and Mona. Stan immediately put on the soccer shirt which delighted him. Forewarned by his grandmother, he knew he could not kick the ball in the house. Warm winter clothes, and books that in quieter moments he asked his beloved grandmother to read to him, were his gifts from Ruth. After Stan had gone to bed for the night, Colm and Mona wished Ruth a Happy Christmas, and then drove up to Monaghan, to spend Christmas Day with the McGowan family.

In passing through O'Connell Street in Dublin, Colm pointed to the General Post Office. "That was where a small band of Irish held out against the British in April of 1916, the Irish Uprising. Yeats wrote of it as 'a terrible beauty was born.'"

After much driving, Colm stated, "We're almost there."

"It's so dark out and there are no lights on some roads. How can you tell where we are?"

"Well, if we go a few miles past the road where my parents live, we'll be in trouble."

"Why?"

"Because we live just a few miles from the border separating the Free State from the gerrymandered six counties in Northern Ireland that the British claimed and insisted on holding onto. Maria looked worried, and Colm glancing at her said, "Have no fear, I'm not going to let that happen. If, however, it were to happen, I'd let you do the talking since you have an English accent. If your mother were with us, she, with her Polish accent, could take charge of the situation."

"Don't toy with mother on her accent. She has had many unsavory comments in England over her accent. Even my school friends outrageously parroted her words."

"Her English is excellent. Does she have anyone to speak to in Polish?"

"Not really. Stan Krakowski, whom I told you about, speaks Polish as does his family, but they all live in Poland. She has, however, since Stan was born, been singing to him in Polish, as she did when

I was very young, and sometimes she forgets, and will say something to Stan in Polish, which baffles him."

They arrived shortly after midnight at the McGowan home. Colm's sister Deirdre had come over from Geneva, where she worked for the U.N., to celebrate Christmas with her parents, Colm, her fifteen-year-old brother Declan, and to meet Mona. This was their immediate family gathering before the grandparents, aunts, uncles, and cousins would arrive on Christmas Day. Mona was glad that they had this time together to get to know his parents, who made her feel very much at home among them, and Declan, a tall, skinny boy who reminded her of Karol. Deirdre and Mona, who shared a room, talked into the early hours of the morning.

Feeling a bit lost among so many relatives of Colm's on Christmas Day, she was nonetheless intrigued by them and the way they included her in every aspect of the celebration. She had gone to Mass with the McGowan's early Christmas morning. Mona had not received Communion, which made Colm's mother think that maybe she and Colm were cohabitating, but then when Colm received the Host, she knew that could not be so.

On the walk back to the house, Colm slowed down and lagged behind his family. Mona followed suit. It was on this crisp cold morning, following the seven o'clock Mass, that Colin asked Mona if she would consent to marry him. She had known for some time that if he asked she would say yes, but was not expecting that question to be asked so soon, nor for the proposal to take place on a small unfamiliar street in County Monaghan.

"Yes," she smiled at him.

"Can I tell the family?" he asked, as happy as a child entering the water on the first warm day of summer.

"Yes," she laughed at his eagerness.

"We'll wait until Mom gets the breakfast on the table, otherwise there will not be any breakfast to be had this morning, and before we would even have a cup of tea, the relatives would have arrived."

Mona smiled at how predictable his mother appeared to Colm. "So it's settled we will tell them after breakfast, and before the hordes arrive, so my mother can enjoy relaying the good news to them, and it will save us from making the announcement a second time."

"That is fine with me. I must, however, tell my mother."

"We'll phone her this very day. How do you think she will receive this announcement?"

"Cautiously. I've told you on the way up here all about my trip to Spain, meeting Abdul, and marrying him, etc., so she has reason to be concerned."

"That is the past. The future lies ahead for us."

"There is always the possibility he may claim Stan."

"You said he has not spoken of doing so. You mentioned he sent the little fellow a gift on his first and second birthday, but otherwise he has not contacted you or the boy."

"That is so. I believe, however, according to their customs, if a man and his wife are divorced, or their marriage has for any reason failed, their child will stay with its mother until the child is of school age. So I know the day will come when my son will be taken from me. I haven't told my mother that, because she has had a hard life, and even without this knowledge, she is fearful that something bad may happen to me or Stan."

"You're the child's mother. Abdul cannot just take the lad from you."

"Abdul has always gotten whatever he has wanted. His family is powerful and very rich."

"There are laws to protect people from such a person as he."

"No law will prevent Abdul from taking what he wants, and he wants our son. I don't know when or how he will do it, but I do know I will be as unable to prevent it, as I was unable to save my first-born from being smothered while the whole household slept. This sword has been hanging over me since Stan was born."

"This is Ireland, not the United Arab Emirates. He cannot take a child from his mother. What if we were to live in some remote area of Donegal?"

"He would find Stan and me even if we lived in Tir-Na-Og, that mythical place in Irish folklore. Ireland is a long way from the Emirates, yet Abdul found us here. He has people watching our every move."

"Have you seen any of these people?"

"No. They perform their job extremely well. Sending gifts to Stan is Abdul's way of letting me know he knows where we are, and that we're being watched."

"Why not go to the police?"

"What evidence could I produce? Abdul has not threatened me, not even communicated with me. He has done nothing wrong. He merely sends gifts to his son. Stan's father is a very charming person, and a diplomat. He will not make a wrong move."

"Maybe the police can set a trap for him!"

"That would be akin to trying to catch one of your leprechauns. "When he determines this should happen, I feel it will all happen swiftly. They will come like a thief in the night. I doubt that Abdul will personally become involved with it. In fact, I believe it will take place without Abdul being in Ireland. In his defense against me, he has these facts. I married him in good faith, and then abandoned him; I was pregnant with his child when I left him, thereby taking his unborn child from him, although I did not know that I was pregnant until the day before I left England, which would not stand up in a court of law. Now I want to prevent him from taking this child from me, when according to his country's customs, the child belongs to him.

We both want the child. We cannot, as Solomon had suggested, 'cut the child in halves.' I suffered a devastating loss when Waheed was murdered, but so did Abdul. My son has asked why his father does not live with us, as his friends' fathers do. How can I tell a child as young as Stan, he is in danger from his own father—a man who, like Santa Claus, brings a wonderful gift to him every year? Colm, I have spent sleepless nights trying to find a way to prevent what I feel will happen, from happening."

"You said he'd try to take the boy as soon as the child is old enough. That gives us about three years to find a solution."

"That is usually the age but he might decide to take my son at any time before that. I have no say in the matter. So I'm left with that terrible unknowable. Do you still want to marry someone who would bring such overwhelming problems into a marriage?"

"Yes. We'll face the good, bad and indifferent together. Speaking of which, we could meet with the local priest while we're here in Monaghan, and ask about getting an annulment of your marriage to Abdul."

Colm hoped they'd be married, and have a child or be expecting a child of their own before Abdul took Stan, so as to lessen, in some small way, Mona's foreseeable sorrow and loss.

"I don't know anything about annulments."

"If one is necessary, it will take about ten months to a year to get both consent and the paperwork involved. But we may not need one as you weren't actually joined as husband and wife in any form of religious ceremony, but rather had a wedding reception. If we need one, we will request it, and give the reason why we seek it, and the Church will handle it all from there. If we do not need an annulment, we can get married whenever we wish."

"When will we be able to meet with a priest?"

"Well, the day after Christmas is a holiday, Saint Stephen's Day in Ireland, and Boxing Day in England. Boxing Day I'm sure you're already familiar with. On the morning after, we can contact the priest and with luck meet with him before we return to Cork."

"I hope he can meet with us on the twenty-seventh as I must get back home to Mother and Stan, and spend some time with them before classes begin."

"We'll tell the priest we must return to Cork early on the morning of the twenty-eighth so we would like to see him as soon as possible. If he cannot meet with us, we can contact the University Chaplain, who may be better able to handle what we're placing in his lap—a girl whose mother is Jewish and ex-husband is Muslim, who now wishes to marry a Catholic!" Colm walked towards his parents' house but stopped as Mona spoke.

"There is something else that might hinder this marriage."

"Good Grief, Mona, you're an enigma. What else could there be?"

"I've never been baptized in any Christian religion."

Colm is speechless for a moment. "So what is your religious affiliation?"

Now Mona was stumped for an explanation.

"Well, actually none. My mother is Jewish but in all the years I was growing up, I didn't know that, for we never attended a synagogue. Stan Krakowski, the man I told you of, who risked his life to rescue me, is Catholic. He came over from Poland to Kinsale for Stan's birth. Stan wanted my son to be baptized into the Catholic Church, with his son, Karol, as godfather. All the Krakowskis are Catholic."

"So the little fellow is Catholic," Colm laughed.

"Well, yes, but he may also be part Jewish. My mother was very annoyed that Stan Sr. wanted to have my son baptized. After Mr. Krakowski and his family left for home, she brought me and Stan to Dublin and had Stan circumcised by a Rabbi. I don't know if it was to somehow erase the baptism or if she believed, which I think she did, that her grandson was Jewish, and so she had him circumcised.

Colm, the tall reddish-haired Irishman, was laughing to such an extent that he couldn't stand up straight, and held onto the wrought-iron railings. "No comedy writer could come up with such as this," he said through the laughter. "Good God, Mona, you are a complicated lady."

Mona was confused. *How serious an impediment is this*, she wondered, *when Colm can laugh at it, or is it the hopelessness of the situation that causes the laughter?*

"Wait a moment, Mona," he asked, as he sat down on the stone wall of the next-door neighbor's garden, so that they could not be seen from his parents' home. "Do you want to take instructions in the Catholic faith, in order to be baptized as Catholic?"

She had never really thought of doing so prior to this moment, but answered, "Yes."

"Are you sure?"

"Both of Stan's godparents are Catholic and wonderful people. Yes, I am sure."

"What if you run into people who are Catholic and not wonderful people?"

"I will still wish to become Catholic."

"Well, you can do all that in Dublin. When classes begin, we will meet with the University Chaplain to seek instructions. After you have taken the instructions, you must then decide if you do indeed want to become Catholic. After you have made that decision we can proceed."

"If after taking instructions, I do not wish to become Catholic, what will the outcome be?"

"That may cause some complications but we will get married regardless, hopefully, within the year."

"Do you still wish to tell your parents of our engagement?"

"Yes, but we won't mention the possible complications, because my poor mother's knees would be sore from constant kneeling in prayer. This is for us to deal with."

Mona, who had not wanted to interrupt the conversation they were having, however, was becoming colder by the minute, and wanted to get indoors from the chilliness of the day, finally mentioned to Colm, "It is cold out here."

"Sorry, love," he said as he put an arm snugly around her as they walked towards the house. "We will not need to wait until Mom has made breakfast to tell them of our plans, for, no doubt, they must be finished breakfast, and are wondering what is delaying us."

"Sit down both of you and have some breakfast," Colm's mother greeted them as she poured out tea, and then filled their plates with eggs, bacon and sausages. Everyone in the house received the news with great joy. The dinner preparations were almost forgotten with the toasting, joking and laughter.

A little over three hours later the extended family arrived, and were given the news of the upcoming wedding. More toasting, congratulations, joking, and laughter followed until Colm's mother, Jane, clapped her hands and said, "The dinner I have worked hard on will be ruined, if you all don't get out of my kitchen, into the dining room and sit down." They did as requested, although throughout dinner, the engagement and the forthcoming wedding, were the chief topics discussed.

Bending towards Mona, to be heard through the noise, Jane said, "Your little boy might like to walk down the aisle as the ring bearer. How old is he?"

"Almost three years old," Mona replied.

"He'll be four years old when you and Colm walk down the aisle," Jane smiled. Colm had obviously told his parents she had a son, and according to Jane's statement, they assumed she was Catholic.

Later in the evening, Colm told his parents he wanted to show Mona where he had gone to school," as he handed Mona her coat, and grabbed his own and headed out the door.

"You want to show me where you went to school? Will it not be closed?"

"That was just a ruse to get away and have a moment alone. There is only so much of my large extended family a person unfamiliar with them can be expected to endure on a first meeting."

"Fine, I'm not familiar with your extended family, and that may take a while, but I'm sure they are all very nice since your immediate family are wonderfully so."

Smiling he said, "I'm so glad I met you."

"And I, in having met you. I had thought about attending Trinity College. I told Una of my plan. She in turn told her aunt Catherine, who suggested I apply to University College in Dublin instead, and so I did. I'm very glad I did. It was Catherine who contacted Mr. Donovan, the man we bought the cottage from, and asked him if his daughter, Ciara, who lives with her husband and two children in Dublin, would give me a room to stay in while I was in Dublin."

"So that is how you came to be living at the Nolan's?"

"Yes, Sunday nights to Wednesday nights. I can go home Thursdays, as you know, after my last class. Since I have only a lecture on Fridays, and I have a classmate who takes notes for me, that lets me have Fridays, Saturdays, and until late Sunday afternoon with Stan."

"There are good colleges down south, why Dublin?"

"My mother brought me to Dublin, and I thought I'd love to live there. Maybe not permanently, but I thought I'd like to attend the University there, and experience the excitement of the City."

"Bored with small town life, is it?"

"Not really. There has always been just my mother and me. I am always amazed by how the lives of the Kinsale people are intertwined. Everybody seems to know everyone else. It's a great place to bring up Stan."

"I'm glad you took Catherine's advice."

"Is there a reason other than it was there that we met?"

"Trinity was established by Queen Elizabeth I of England. Although she was female, only men could attend Trinity in her lifetime, and for centuries after. Only Protestant men were accepted until into the twentieth century, and then about a decade later, women were allowed to attend. So, I would say, it depends on how much of a feminist you are."

"Back in the Elizabethan reign women weren't educated, except for the very few exceptions, unless you want to call doing needlework and taking voice and piano lessons an education." Mona reminded him.

"She could have established the first women's university! What a missed opportunity that was. You should be happy you didn't live in England back then, especially with all the beheadings that were being done. Let's walk back before they send out a search party for us."

Colm's family is very cordial, Colm is wonderful, Stan is a darling, and life is good, Mona felt, as she melted into the happiness of the moment.

After arriving back in Kinsale Mona told her mother all that had happened in County Monaghan. First Muslim, now Catholic! Ruth thought, and then tried to explain to her daughter.

"The Irish religious beliefs and their nationality are entwined. The English tried to 'unhinge' this according to what Catherine told me, but they only succeeded in making the bond tighter. Henry VIII wanted to divorce one of his wives in order to marry another woman. The Pope would not permit it, thereby causing King Henry to decide to make himself the head of the Catholic Church, which then became known as the Anglican Church. In conquering Ireland, they tried to impose this new religion on the Irish, and failed. I believe, however, this will all change in the years to come. All Europe is changing through its influx of foreigners, their beliefs, their foods and their customs."

"I didn't know that you and Catherine spoke of such things."

"Yes. She is a very good friend. The Irish live their past in the present. It is imbedded in them. That too may change in time."

CHAPTER 18

In June, as Ruth and Mona prepared a children's party for Stan, they could not but wonder what Abdul might send the child for this his third birthday. The kangaroo and rocking horse were already taking up too much space in their small cottage, and they hoped that whatever he sent would be smaller in size. Their wish was granted. A card arrived from Abdul stating that Stan should be brought down to Kellagher's stables, where his new pony was being stabled. This caught both women by surprise.

"That man is crazy," Ruth protested. "The boy has just turned three years old. He is too young to ride a pony."

Mona read the card to Stan, who was delighted with the news, and could hardly wait to go to the stables.

At the party, the children and their mothers watched, waiting to see what surprise gift Stan had received this year from his father. On not seeing any unusual gifts, the children became restless. Ruth stood in the kitchen, and was about to put the finishing touches on the cake, but before she could do so, Mona asked the children, "Would you all like to go to Mr. Kellagher's stables and see Stan's new pony?"

Delight shone in the faces of the children as they loudly answered, "Yes." "Can we go now?" they asked. "Can we ride Stan's pony?" "Can I have my picture taken on the pony?"

"Yes, to all your questions," Mona laughed, and turning to the mothers, asked if they would like to escort her and the children to the stables.

"What about the birthday cake and lemonade?" Ruth asked.

"We will have them on our return," Mona answered her, and suggested to the five volunteers, that three lead the way by walking ahead of the children, and the other two mothers walk with her behind the eleven children.

The townspeople smiled at the sight as they passed by, and wondered where the children might be going. One of the children called out to a family member, "We're going to Kellagher's stables to ride Stan's pony." By the time they reached the stables, word of this event had spread through a large portion of the town.

While the children petted and talked to the horse, Mona spoke to Mr. Kellagher, but all he could tell her was what a well-dressed man had told him, that he would be receiving a pony to board. The man, who already knew the cost of boarding a horse at Kellagher's stables, made out a check for that amount for a three-month period. Mona questioned what the man looked like. From Mr. Kellagher's description and also by the way this transaction was handled, Mona had cause to believe the person was obviously from the Emirates, but he was not Abdul. The mysterious man also paid for daily riding lessons for the recipient of the pony.

Mr. Kellagher saw to it that Stan had the first ride, followed by each of the children. He also showed them around the stables, and spoke to them of how to groom and feed a pony. A few of the children enjoyed rubbing down the pony, but declined to ride it.

Approximately two hours later the children were back at the cottage eating birthday cake, ice cream, and drinking lemonade.

One little boy, on leaving the cottage, said "This was the best birthday party ever."

A little girl with fewer words, and more action, kissed Stan on the cheek, and hugged him saying, "Thank you for inviting me." Reminded by the mothers, all the children called out 'Happy Birthday' as they left. Stan was overwhelmed by it all.

"Well, that was a good idea you had Mona, to bring them all to the stables before serving the birthday cake."

"If we had fed them before going there, Mr. Kellagher would have had more than horse manure to clean up," Mona laughed.

"Well Stan, love, you've had a great day, have you not?" Stan laughed and hugged his mother.

"Mona, dear," Ruth said on hearing the wording of that last sentence, "I declare you're beginning to speak like the locals." To which

Mona replied, "Would that be so bad?" Ruth shook her head but didn't answer.

That summer Colm invited Mona and Stan on a trip to the West coast of Ireland. Mona had become very interested in Yeats' poetry, and Colm thought she would like to see where Yeats spent his summers as a child, where he got the inspiration for many of his poems, and where he was buried.

"Have you ever gone camping?"

"No."

"Would you like to give it a try? I have a tent, and two extra sleeping bags you and Stan could use."

"For how long?"

"A fortnight would be nice."

Mona hesitated.

"Aw, you haven't lived lassie until you've slept under the stars."

"What if it rains?"

"We'll be under the tent. If the rain becomes a real downpour, it might wash in under the tent. If that should happen, we'll sleep in the car that night."

"Where will we wash?"

"We always camp near a stream or lake so as to wash ourselves and the utensils we use."

"Utensils?"

"Yes, we'll build a fire, and cook our meals over it."

"I've never cooked over an outdoor fire. You've obviously done this before."

"Yes, my father took us all camping when we were growing up. Once he hired a gypsy caravan."

"So then you slept in the caravan, I presume, not under a tent."

"Yes, but instead of a car, we had a horse. This particular horse had a mind of its own. Sometimes we had to stop in an area where we did not wish to stop, because the horse decided that was as far as it wanted to travel that day."

"Did your mother go with you?"

"Yes and no. She came if we planned to stay in one spot for a week, her preference being along the coast line, which we enjoyed, because we could all go swimming in the sea. She did not like the idea of traveling with a horse leading the way, especially since we had to feed the horse and go and fetch buckets of water for it to drink."

"A wise woman is your mother."

"She is also allergic to bee stings. That causes her to avoid trips into the countryside."

"What did Deirdre think of camping?"

"Oh, she loved it. She also loves horses. The horse might have collapsed from hunger or thirst if Deirdre hadn't taken on the task of feeding and watering it."

"What was your task?"

"I was usually sent to the nearest farmhouse to obtain milk for the tea, and sometimes butter, or cheese or eggs." Declan and dad gathered firewood. Dad worked at getting the fire lit and keeping it lit, which could be a big undertaking if it rained the night before, and all the twigs and wood were wet. Mom, of course, cooked the food, but since this was her holiday as well as ours, other than porridge in the mornings, many a time it was sandwiches for dinner, when we ran out of the homemade soup that Mom prepared before leaving, and we had scrambled eggs or hard-boiled eggs at tea in the evenings." After a pause, Colm continued, "Don't worry, I'll cook porridge in the mornings, or eggs, if you'd rather have them for breakfast, and then to ward off the hunger, we'll eat whatever we can buy along the way."

"So, there won't be a horse to care for?"

"No horse, but we will still need to gather firewood to cook, and keep warm should the evening become chilly. Stan will love it."

"Is he not too young for this kind of holiday?"

"Not at all. One's never too young or too old to have a marvelous adventure."

"Adventure," she laughed.

"Yes, and not only that, but you'll have been to Co. Sligo and seen Yeats' domain, which is why I believe Sligo would be the perfect place to visit. You live in Cork which, of course, is in the South of Ireland, Dublin on the East Coast, Monaghan, where my family lives, is in Northern Ireland, but not within the six counties, and Sligo is in the West of Ireland."

"Do I need a swimsuit?"

"Yes, if you'd rather not swim in your birthday suit."

She ignored the latter part of his sentence. *What will mother think of such a trip?* She wondered.

"All we need to do now is set a date."

"For the first two weeks in August, I'll be filling in for a woman where my mother works."

"Then let's plan on the last two weeks of August. My father has some jobs lined up for me this summer. Some house painting, and other work. I've got some leeway though. I have to tell him what fortnight I will not be available. I'll do that immediately so he can inform the recipients when to expect the work to begin."

"Don't you have to apply in person for these jobs?"

"Normally yes, but not if the jobs are local, as the locals know my dad and me. Also my dad would have my head on a platter if I did not do a good job."

Mona laughed. "You apparently have a good rapport with your father."

He can be tough. He won't do shoddy work, and will not accept shoddy work from those who work for him. He expects me to do a good job, and I try to live up to his expectations."

Stan was very excited when he heard of the trip. Ruth was not.

"What about your riding lessons?"

"Polly won't fit into Colm's car," was his earnest reply.

"Don't you think she'll miss you?"

"Maybe you could go to the stables and talk to her," Stan urged.

"Sorry Stan, she's your horse, not mine."

"Mr. Kellagher will take good care of Polly until I come back," he reassured his grandmother.

Ruth did not share Mona's enthusiasm for going on a camping trip with a young man to whom she was not married.

"You're putting yourself in a precarious position. Are you comfortable with sleeping with a man under a tent out in the wilds?"

"The wilds! It's not Africa, Mother, it's Ireland we're in, and we'll have Stan with us."

"Some chaperone! That child will be asleep by eight o'clock at night."

"I'll place his sleeping bag between Colm's and mine," she answered, barely suppressing her laughter.

Ruth, knowing she was getting nowhere with this conversation, discussed it no further.

* * *

"Sligo, here we come," Colm said as he started the engine. Then he began to recite 'The Lake Isle of Innisfree.' "I've brought a book of his poems to read at night under the stars," Colm said after reciting the poem.

"I can see this is going to be an accelerated course on Yeats," Mona laughed.

That night, after Stan was in bed, they lay under the star-studded sky, and Colm, true to his word, read from his book of Yeats' poetry.

"This is the fourth verse of his Easter 1916 Uprising:

> *Too long a sacrifice*
> *Can make a stone of the heart.*
> *O when may it suffice?*
> *That is Heaven's part, our part*
> *To murmur name upon name,*
> *As a mother names her child*
> *When sleep at last has come*
> *On limbs that had run wild.*
> *What is it but nightfall?*
> *No, no, not night but death;*
> *Was it needless death after all?*
> *For England may keep faith*
> *For all that is done and said.*
> *We know their dream, enough*
> *To know they dreamed and are dead;*
> *And what if excess of love*
> *Bewildered them till they died?*
> *I write it out in a verse —*
> *MacDonagh and MacBride*
> *And Connelly and Pearse*
> *Now and in time to be,*
> *Wherever green is worn,*
> *Are changed, changed utterly:*
> *A terrible beauty is born.*

"That's beautiful," Mona remarked in the silence that followed.

"Yes, too long a struggle and sacrifice makes stones of hearts. Yeats found it personally difficult to reconcile his ambiguity about the 1916 Uprising. He said 'whatever one can say of its wisdom, it will long be remembered for its heroism.' It wasn't well planned. The men who conceived it were not well-trained soldiers."

"On the day it began," Colm continued, "ordinary citizens of Dublin were going about their business as usual. Most Dubliners thought, while watching this interruption in their daily activities, it was madness that a small contingent of men could take on the entrenched well-trained British Army. The people, who stood on the footpaths and watched, did not know at that time, that the Irish citizen soldiers had insufficient weapons and a shortage of bullets. One old lady, it was said, shook her head and prayed, 'I hope none of our boys get shot.' 'They all end up in prison,' another was heard to say."

"The British had been in Ireland since Henry VIII's reign, and had become a permanent, though unwanted, fixture on Irish soil."

"Who were the men Yeats mentioned?"

"They were the leaders of the Uprising, for it was composed of poets and dreamers like Thomas MacDonagh and Padraic Pearse, who yearned to set their country free. They were not the bloodthirsty madmen their detractors would later claim. Pearse found St. Enda's, a uniquely progressive school for Irish boys. The Irish were denied an education in the British-run schools. In St. Enda's school they studied the classics, English and Irish literature, math, science, art, architecture and music. Prof. MacDonagh, a lecturer in English at University College was, like Pearse, a poet. James Connelly was a labor organizer who had spent many years in the United States and savored America's freedom. They, among others, were captured and lined up before a firing squad. Connolly, who was badly wounded, was placed on a chair and tied to it, so he would not fall off. In front of a firing squad all were shot."

"MacBride was not among the group shot that day but he was a patriot. Maud Gonne, the great love of Yeats' life, rejected Yeats and married John MacBride. Yeats afterwards wrote some rather nasty lines about MacBride in one of his poems."

"How long did the fighting last?"

"Just a little over a week. When the people discovered all of the leaders were shot, unrest stirred up among them, and those executed young men, in dying for Ireland's freedom, became their heroes. They had called themselves the Irish Brotherhood. After the execution of these men, recruitments rose. Later on, the Irish Brotherhood would emerge as the Irish Republican Army, better known as the IRA."

"Why didn't they buy more guns and bullets before taking on the British?"

"The British controlled the ports and confiscated any weaponry, which came mostly from France, Spain and the United States, to keep it from getting into Ireland."

"What a beautiful description of war those last lines are, 'Changed, changed utterly: A terrible beauty is born'"

"Yes, many believe so, for those lines are often quoted by others."

"'It is murder, and death, that makes possible the terrible beautiful thing we call physical life. Life springs from death, life lives on death'. That is a line from Padraic Pearse in his <u>By</u> <u>Way</u> of <u>Comment</u>.' 'A terrible beauty is the voice that comes out of the heart of battle.'"

"Would you have fought if you were living at that time?"

"Probably not. Wars don't solve problems, they create them. The Irish, however, were fighting to rid their country of an outside oppressor. Freedom is such a passionate cause. So it's difficult to say yes or no."

"England belongs to the English; Ireland belongs to the Irish," Mona adamantly stated.

"Yes, and once a country takes over another country, or holds onto part of another country, the citizens of that conquered country will continue to want full possession of their native land, and that will be carried down from generation to generation."

"That's sad."

"War is always a great sadness. Yeats also wrote a poignant poem on World War I. Shall I read it for you, or have you had enough of poems of war?"

"World War I! Yes, read it."

"It has only one verse, and is a eulogy to the only son of Lady Gregory, Major Robert Gregory, who was accidentally shot down by the Italian allies. It is called 'An Irish Airman Foresees His Death.'

> *I know that I shall meet my fate*
> *Somewhere among the clouds above,*
> *Those that I fight I do not hate,*
> *Those that I guard I do not love;*
> *My country is Kiltartan Cross,*
> *My countrymen Kiltartan's poor,*
> *No likely end could bring them loss*
> *Or leave them happier than before.*
> *Nor law, nor duty bade me fight,*
> *Nor public men, nor cheering crowds,*
> *A lonely impulse of delight*
> *Drove to this tumult in the clouds;*
> *I balanced all, brought all to mind,*
> *The years to come seemed waste of breath,*
> *A waste of breath the years behind*
> *In balance with this life, this death.*

"Well, what do you think of it?"

"What does he mean, "those I fight I do not hate, those I guard I do not love?"

"Although not mentioned by name, it is well understood from the reference to Kiltartan, that the airman is, Major Robert Gregory, who was a member of the Royal Flying Corps and whose plane is accidentally shot down by the Italian Allies in 1918.. He neither hates the Germans, nor loves the English. Gregory is an Anglo-Irish aristocrat, who has no allegiance either to Ireland or England. To him, his 'country' is very specific and local: 'Kiltartan Cross' where his home, Coole Park Estates, is and his "countrymen" are the poor of Kiltartan, and no matter what the outcome of the war will be, it will not affect them or himself, one way or another. The lonely impulse of delight is any aviator's exhilaration and love of flying. He knows his chances of survival in air combat (the tumult in the sky) are almost nil, but he does not concentrate on the past or the future, only that present delightful moment in the sky into which all else fades."

"Was Yeats well liked and honored in Ireland during his lifetime?"

"Honored yes. He was, however, an aristocrat, which set him apart from the average person in Ireland."

"My mother's life still is greatly affected by World War II. She speaks of her mother, my grandmother and the terrible atrocities that occurred. After Germany's wretched brutalities to her people, Hitler and Stalin made a pact to occupy Poland splitting the country between them. Twin devils, my mother calls them. No nightmare, however terrible, could compare to what went on during that occupation."

"Later, of course, when Germany was defeated and the war was over, the Americans let the Russian army be the first to enter Berlin. Hitler took the easy way out by committing suicide, but the women of the city suffered terribly. The Russian soldiers raped every woman and girl they could find in the city, and the surrounding area. I have no love for the Germans of that period, but I wouldn't want that to happen to any woman."

"You are a forgiving soul."

"But would I be if I had been alive at that time and lived through such horrors?"

"We can never know how we would react if we lived through a particular war."

"World War II still hovers over my mother although it was long over when she was born. It affected her whole family. When she lived in Poland, on Sundays, the only days she had off work, she went back to where my grandmother lived before the war. My mother searched for people of my grandmother's age, seeking their memories of that period, but very few Jewish people remained or returned to Poland. Strangers lived in the house my grandmother once lived in. Mother searched through documents and archives trying to put her family history together. What she found only added to her grief. There was 'no terrible beauty' that came out of WWII for the people living through that war, only death and desolation. Those who survived, or were born to survivors, like my mother, live with unforgiving pain."

"We have to let go of the past. It is as Joyce had said, 'the nightmare of history we try to escape from'" Colm said.

"True. It has, however, affected Mother's and my relationship with each other. We love each other, yet with the best of intentions, we have kept secrets from each other. My mother never revealed that she was Jewish until we came to Ireland. There may be other things she has kept from me in order to protect me. I too have kept things from her to protect her. I never told her that I believe Abdul will someday come for her grandson. I want to protect her from that, and I also secretly hope he will leave Stan with us until my son is in his teen years, so that he will have formed an attachment to us and will, as a young man, visit us whenever he is free and wishes to do so. If Abdul takes little Stan from me while he is very young my son will forget me. And so my mother and I, out of love for each other, and to shield each other from the truth, have built a wall between us."

"I haven't noticed a wall between you and your mother!"

"It's a very low wall. No more than two or three feet from the ground. It has been erected with the very best of intentions. We could step over it, but neither of us have the courage to do so, and so the barrier remains."

"You are just protecting each other, and that is a normal thing to do."

"In our love for each other, we should be more open with each other, rather than protective of one another."

"Life certainly has it complications."

"Yes, and most of which, unfortunately, are of our own making."

"Be that as it may, I hope the little fellow stays with you. He's a great kid."

Mona was silent for several moments until Colm looked up admiringly at the sky.

"What a magnificent array of stars."

"Yes. Out here without street lights or other lights, they really are spectacular. Then lifting up on her elbow, she added, "I think we should say goodnight and get some sleep."

"An excellent idea. Tomorrow we'll be visiting where Yeats, as a young boy, spent his summers with his mother's family, and the houses of his Sligo friends whom he wrote about. Then onto his burial site."

Going into the tent, Mona lay down in the small space on the right of her sleeping son, leaving the larger space on the other side of Stan for Colm. Soon they were asleep

CHAPTER 19

The following morning, Colm built a fire and made tea. He showed Stan how to place the slice of bread on the end of a stick and toast it by the fire. Stan was reveling in this camping experience, and gathering sticks to keep the fire burning was to him an enjoyable game.

Coming back from the lake after washing, Mona was served breakfast by her two admirers. Sitting there finishing his cereal, Stan said, "Let's not go home."

"Grandmamma would be all alone and very sad if we didn't go home."

"Bring Grandmamma here," was the simple solution of this three-year-old."

"We should consult and consider the advice not only from our elders, but also from the youngest among us," Colm laughed.

"Can we play soccer now?"

"We must clean up after ourselves first."

"Go ahead, I'll clean up the breakfast things," Mona offered.

Within an hour, they were in the car.

"Where are we going?"

"Sightseeing."

"What is that?"

"It is when one goes visiting historic sites one may or may not have seen before, and would enjoy seeing."

"What kind of places?"

"Places where famous people lived a long, long time ago."

Stan was bored with this thing called sightseeing. To Stan's way of seeing it, they had spent the whole day looking at old houses that people had let them into and told them all about the houses, and the people who used to live in these houses, and none of the people in these houses offered them lemonade and cookies. Stan was disappointed and hungry.

Tomorrow we take a boat and row on "The Lake Isle of Innisfree.' Today we have just one more place to visit." Colm told the tired boy, as he lifted him on his shoulders.

"One more house?" the child asked dismayed.

"Not a house, a grave site."

Stan did not know what Colm meant and asked, "Can we eat there?"

Laughingly, Colm replied, "No, Stan, but right after we take a look at it, we'll go to a restaurant to eat."

"Good," the boy raised his voice. "Are we going to McDonalds?"

"No, there are no McDonald's in these parts, but I'm sure the restaurant we're going to will have delicious desserts." Having reached the car, Colm lowered his small passenger into the back seat of the car.

They drove until they came to a grassy area. They walked around, and then stood before a Celtic cross. Colm, standing before it with his arm around Mona, recited the last verse of Yeats' poem, Under Ben Bulben.

> . . . *Under bare Ben Bulben's head*
> *In Drumcliff churchyard Yeats is laid.*
> *An ancestor was rector there*
> *Long years ago, a church stands near,*
> *By the road an ancient cross.*
> *No marble, no conventional phrase;*
> *On limestone quarried near the spot*
> *By his command these words are cut:*

Colm then read the last lines of the poem from the gravestone

> *Cast a cold eye*
> *On life, on death*
> *Horseman, pass by!*

Who is this Ben Bulben?"

"See over there," Colm points to the mountain nearby. "That is Ben Bulben."

"Who is the horseman?"

"The horseman denotes an aristocrat. The ancestor was his grandfather."

"Those last three lines on the gravestone sound morbid."

"That is the detachment of the artist looking with a cold eye on life and death."

"Can we climb up the mountain?"

"Not tonight, Stan, it's getting too late," Colm laughingly answered the child.

"Walking back to the car, Mona asked.

"Didn't Yeats write any uplifting poems?"

"Well, he wrote a lot on romance and his relationship with Maud Gonne, but I must admit, they are more woeful than any of the poems we've discussed.

"Are we going to eat now?" the child asked.

"Yes, Stan. That is where we are now heading."

In the restaurant they were seated family style. Three other couples were sitting at the table with them. Colm had been there many years ago. The restaurant was owned and run by a middle-aged couple. Introductions were made, and people asked and told where they were from and why they had come to Sligo. All proclaimed it a most beautiful part of the country. The owner introduced his wife and himself, and then proceeded to take their orders from a limited but nicely selected menu. Stan told all at the table that they were camping, and how he could kick his soccer ball in the large grassy area but not near the camp fire.

The owner brought their food, and as he walked around the table serving them, he recited Yeats' "The Stolen Child" and asked them all to join in the chorus.

. . .

Come away, O human child!
To the waters and the wild
With a faery, hand in hand,
For the world's more full of weeping,
Than you can understand.

Colm was afraid that this poem might be unsettling to Mona, and when he stretched out his hand to her, she smiled and whispered, "It's beautiful."

"Who among you knows the title of that poem, the man who recited the poem asked?" A young man seated next to his girlfriend and across from Mona and Colm, answered and in doing so smiled, for he had impressed his girlfriend.

Stan had just begun kindergarten a few weeks earlier when on a Friday, in late September, Mona set out on the short walk to her son's school at 11:45 a.m., as his class came to an end at noon. Una usually brought Stan to and from school while Mona attended classes in Dublin. Mona picked him up on Fridays, for she loved to see the expression on her son's face when he spotted her, and to know that she was as special to him as he was to her. He was a good-natured boy, and very popular with the townsfolk, the students and teachers. Stan enjoyed school very much and was an eager participant in all its activities.

"A born diplomat," her mother had said of him when at his third birthday party he had settled a dispute between two of his friends. His father's son, was he. Abdul excelled in the Diplomatic Corps, Mona recalled.

Arriving at the school gate, she did not see him, and so waited for him to emerge. Soon all the children had left and there was no sign of Stan. "He must have gotten engrossed in a project and lost track of time," Mona assumed. Entering the school she saw his teacher.

"Has Stan been delayed? I did not see him in the schoolyard."

"No. He has been picked up by his father."

These devastating words had a terrifying impact on Mona. She stood motionless as though all the blood were draining from her body. Suddenly she went limp, and was helped to a bench by two teachers. She was offered water. Everything looked alien to her, even the familiar classrooms had an eerie effect.

"Abdul."

"What did you say?" Mona did not repeat the name.

"Are you all right? Can we call someone for you?" Stan's teacher asked. Mona shook her head.

"I did not question the man who claimed Stan as his son, for he and Stan looked so very much alike, it seemed clear to me that they were father and son," Stan's teacher offered in explanation.

"Other than saying he was Stan's father, did he give you his name?" Mona asked.

"No," the teacher answered after a moment's hesitation.

"Was this man alone? Did he arrive by car? Were there other people in the car?"

"Alone except for the driver. Yes, I believe there was a driver. I only saw the car when he was leaving."

"Please give me a description of this man."

"He looked like your son."

"In what way?"

"He had the same skin tones and black hair. I did not see his eyes as he was wearing sunglasses."

Mona felt Abdul, or anyone he sent to pose as Stan's father would be dressed in western-style clothing, not wishing to stand out among the people here, but she asked so as to be better able to answer questions the police might ask. "How was he dressed?"

"He was beautifully dressed," the teacher answered. "He wore what looked like a very expensive dark-colored pinstriped suit, and a white shirt. I'm not sure what color tie he wore."

"You said he came by car. Did you see the license number of the car?"

"No."

"Why not?"

"I knew of no reason to check that."

"What make car was it?"

"I don't know. It was a black car, rather long in length, I thought."

"You saw Stan get into the car?"

"Yes. The man lifted him into the back seat of the car."

"What was Stan's reaction to all this?"

"He did not seem disturbed. Stan waved to some friends from the car."

What did that man tell Stan? Mona wondered.

"You should get in touch with Stan's father," the teacher advised. "He probably wanted to take him to a football match or an outing."

Get in touch with his father? These people do not understand the gravity of the situation. I've got to reach mother. I must get home. I must call mother, Mona thought through the noise in her head. She handed back the paper cup that had held the water and stood up. Shaken at first, but determined to get home and contact her mother, Mona steadied herself.

"Let me walk you home," the teacher asked but Mona shook her head saying, "I'll be all right. Mother will know what to do." Mona, in gathering her thoughts, assured herself. As soon as she entered the cottage she sat on the chair in the hall where she had left her cellphone, and dialed her mother's place of work. She wished Colm lived closer. She would phone the police immediately after phoning her mother, by which time Colm's class would be over and she would get in touch with him.

On reaching her mother, Mona became very upset in relating what had happened. Ruth became frightened on hearing her usually calm, low-keyed daughter become hysterical. In trying to make sense out of Mona's flood of words and sobbing, she told Mona, "Slow down, darling. Take a deep breath and speak slowly." Out of the jumble of words from Mona, Ruth took what she could and repeated them. "Something has happened to Stan. Did he hurt himself in the schoolyard?"

"Abdul," Mona conveyed the singular word that made her mother gasp.

"I'm coming right home. When I hang up, I want you to phone the police. Can you do that, darling?"

On receiving a yes from Mona, Ruth hung up the telephone.

Mona was about to do as her mother requested but before she could do so, her thoughts were interrupted by the ringing telephone.

Mr. Kellagher called from the stables. He was upset. He told Mona the pony had been picked up early that morning without any advance notice, or explanation. He mentioned that the pony had been groomed, exercised and well cared for. "For what reason?" Mr. Kellagher asked, "did this happen?" Not waiting for an answer he continued, he had been engaged to care for the pony, and paid three months in advance for doing so, including riding lessons. Then abruptly they had come and taken the pony. For what reason were his services terminated?

Mona was at a loss to answer Mr. Kellagher. Mona apologized for what happened, and no, she did not know why that decision was made. The discussion mercifully came to an end.

Abdul, she realized, had meticulously planned all this. He gave little Stan the pony. With such joy Stan and his friends had walked to the stable on the day that the pony had arrived, she remembered. It was akin to a last meal before the executioner strikes. My son's connection to me has been severed.

The telephone rang again. Mona, worried and exhausted by the kidnapping of her son, did not wish to answer it. It kept ringing.

In picking it up, she heard Abdul's voice.

"Hello Maria. As you now know, I have had my son taken from his school. He is being brought back to his family and homeland. Since you cannot enter the United Arab Emirates, you will never again see him in person. I have, however, a proposition to make. I will send yearly photographs of him plus a video whereby you can see him participate in his favorite activities. These I will send yearly, if you give me the names and locations of the people who helped you escape," Abdul stated in calm, gracious, measured tones.

"Where is Stan" He is not yet four years old. He is too young to leave me. Can I see him before you take him?" Mona rapidly blurted out.

"He is already on his way out of Ireland, so it is impossible for you to see him."

"He cannot leave the country; he has no passport. Are you in Ireland?"

"Yes, he does have a passport in his new name. I have seen to that small detail. No, I am not in Ireland."

"What new name? Where are you? Where exactly is Stan? Tell me that I may see him one last time." Mona's words tumbled out in contrast to Abdul's slow, well-paced words.

Ignoring her pleading, he announced, "You may have a week to comply with my request. We will, of course, eventually find those who helped you leave the Emirates, even without your assistance. If that should happen, you will receive no more communication from me, and you will have lost the right to see your son's progress over the years until he reaches his eighteenth birthday. So choose carefully, my dear, between your rescuers and your son." The phone call was disconnected.

Betray Stan Krakowski and his son, or never see my son grow to manhood through photographs and videos? All communication with my son totally cut off. How can I possibly live without ever seeing him again? Mona thought. *How can I betray Mr. Krakowski and his son who risked their lives for me, and who see me as family as I do them? How can Abdul be so cruel?* Mona, struggling with these 'Sophia's Choice" questions, sank into despair.

Ruth would not take the bus but instead hailed a cab as the more expedient way to get to her daughter. Impatient with every red light, Ruth told the driver that this was an emergency, her grandson's life was in jeopardy, and she had to get home. She wished she herself had called the police, instead of leaving that task to her frightened daughter. The driver, seeing a police car stop at the traffic light, got out of his cab, and walked over to the police car, and told the two officers inside that the woman in his cab needed their help. The cabdriver returned to the cab with one of the policemen who briefly questioned Ruth, and then took her to the police car. She tried to pay the cabdriver but he shook his head and said that he was sorry for her troubles, and hoped things weren't as bad as they seemed to be. The police car sped onwards to Kinsale. She tried unsuccessfully to give the police directions to her cottage until in desperation she said, "Donovan's Cottage." In recognition they replied, "We'll be there in no time at all."

The fact that I own the cottage means nothing to these people, it will always be known as Donovan's cottage, Ruth acknowledged.

One of the police officers and Ruth entered the cottage, where they found Mona in a daze. With soothing words, Ruth and the police sergeant tried to get information as to what had happened at the schoolyard from the incoherent young woman, and then Mona became very calm as she stared into space, not seeing.

"She may fall off that chair," the sergeant said. They assisted Mona up from the chair, and guided her into her bedroom, where her mother laid her on the bed. "I will send my partner to the school and check out what happened there," the sergeant stated. "There may be something someone saw or remembered, of what happened this morning." The sergeant walked out towards his partner waiting in the police car, and spoke briefly to him. As the car drove away, the sergeant returned to the cottage.

"A kidnapping," the sergeant said, as they walked out to the kitchen and sat at the table, after Ruth told him Abdul had taken the child. In all his many years in the police force, the sergeant told Ruth, they had never had a kidnapping. On hearing Mona's husband was a Muslim, and of how Mona had escaped from her husband not knowing she carried his child, related to him by Ruth, he knew this was an international affair, not a local incident. To further the investigation, she asked him if he were familiar with the circumstances of the English girl who married a prominent Muslim approximately five years ago. He was. He had, indeed, heard of the marriage of this English girl, and her Muslim husband. She then told him of all that had happened since then, up to their arrival in Kinsale. He was, however, quite surprised to learn that this woman who had made the headlines a few years earlier, had been living unknown to all, in the quiet town of Kinsale.

This was way beyond his jurisdiction, the sergeant knew, and he needed to get all the information to the proper channels. He wished the girl were more responsive. The mother, however, was a great help to him.

"Your daughter needs medical care. Maybe when she breaks out of this, she will be able to give us some useful information. As things now stand, she is incapable of helping with this investigation. She has had a terrible shock, and it will, no doubt, take some time before she'll be able to handle all the pain and horror of what has occurred."

"I will see to it that she receives the best possible care. She is my only child. I live for her."

"I'm sorry for your troubles. Now I must walk up to the school, see what my partner has found, and then file my report." Standing up, he said, "I'll see myself out," and picking up his hat, he left.

Troubles, Ruth thought, *Why do the Irish refer to all harshness and upheaval in life as troubles? When anything goes badly, or when attending a funeral, they extend their sympathy to the family by saying, 'sorry for your troubles.' That uprising they had against the British, they call 'The Troubles.' These people are well advanced in technology, yet they hold on tenaciously to the past. That revolt was very painful to these Islanders, and now all great pain bears that name,* Ruth's mind wandered on. She sat down feeling exhausted. Moments later, she arose and went to her daughter's room. From the doorway Mona appeared to be sleeping. Ruth didn't enter the room for fear that she might awaken her. She stood silently for several minutes before returning to the kitchen, where she made tea.

As much as I loved my grandson, Ruth thought, *if only Mona had gotten an abortion or given the child up for adoption as I had suggested, Mona and I would never have grown to know or love him, and all this pain would have been avoided. Abdul would have left Mona alone, for it was the boy he wanted. Stan Sr. was happy that Mona had decided to keep the child. How I wish he had not interfered in our lives.*

CHAPTER 20

Mona, alone in the house, was returning from the bathroom to her bedroom when the phone rang. Walking towards it, she picked up the receiver but remained mute.

"Maria," the voice said. Is that you, Maria?"

"Maria," she repeated back to him.

"A week has gone by and I have called to ask you for the names of those who aided you in leaving The Emirates. I must have those names in order to keep my promise to you. If you do not comply, it will take a little longer but we will find them. The names, please?"

"Names."

"Yes, the names of those who made it possible for you to leave The Emirates?"

"Emirates."

"Maria, are you sedated?"

Mona removed the phone from her face, looked at it for several moments, then placed it on the table, and walked back to the bedroom. Mona, who had entered into a deep depression, cannot communicate to anyone that Abdul had contacted her, or his proposition. She does not speak and has no appetite.

Ruth, who had been leaving a thermos of hot soup and another of tea on the kitchen table for Mona's lunch, would return home after work to find them untouched. She then began to set the soup and tea and cookies, and some fruit on the table beside Mona's bed, but that too remained untouched.

Mona had not attended classes, nor had Colm heard from her. He phoned Mona, but Ruth answered. She told him all the details of Stan's kidnapping by his father, and of Mona's condition due to what had happened to her son. Colm said he'd drive down after the last class that day to see her. Ruth discouraged such action on his part, by telling him that Mona had not responded in any way since the shock of hearing that Abdul had taken the child out of the country. She assured him that as soon as there was any improvement in Mona's condition, she would phone him immediately. Ruth felt there was nothing, at this point, he could do for his fiancée. Colm, ignoring what he had been told, said he would drive down and should arrive at the cottage between five and six o'clock that evening.

On arriving at their cottage, Colm went immediately to Mona's bedroom, kissed her and taking her hand, sat down on the bed beside her. Sometimes he would lie down beside her. It amazed Ruth when this quiet, soft-spoken young man began a monologue that went on and on about classes, the professors, coming events at the University, anecdotes, and jokes as though he were exchanging information with another responsive being. Mona, however, remained mute. He also spoke of their wedding, and told her they would postpone the wedding, and when she was feeling well enough to do so, they would decide on a new wedding date.

Ruth brought him supper and a light meal for Mona. Before he touched his own meal, Colm patiently assisted Mona, bringing the food upwards to her mouth. To Ruth's surprise Mona ate from the spoon in his hand. Holding a paper napkin under the spoon to prevent spills, he spoke as he served her about everything but the food itself. When she had had enough, he ate his own meal.

When Ruth came into the room to gather the dishes, she found Mona holding his hand with her hand on top of his. Ruth was happy that in her silence Mona had reached out to this unassuming, caring soul, but she also felt a tinge of sadness. *I have always been present in every situation for Mona, but it was not my hand she held but his.* This combination of sadness and joy had become a frequent visitor since Mona's return from Spain.

As the weeks came and went, Ruth admitted, *Colm is a good man. I should be happy Mona has him in her life. It is I who must let go.* Then whimsically she thought, *Mona has had a blond-haired son, and a black-haired son; will her next child, after Colm and Mona marry, be a redhead.*

The young man's positive outlook in adversity has changed my thinking, whereas before he arrived here, I saw only a gloomy forecast for Mona, Ruth realized, *and now I feel hope.* Ruth also admitted that she, who had discouraged his coming to the cottage and seeing Mona in such sad condition, now looked forward to his visits, for the silence in the cottage had been almost unbearable before his arrival. He brought a sleeping bag with him so as to not encroach on their accommodations.

The newspapers and television had extensive coverage of foreign affairs, mostly European, but nothing of the kidnapping. From the police she could get no information of progress, if any, on the matter. She was told they would be in contact with her as soon as they had anything to report. Since Mona was a British citizen, Scotland Yard had been called in and was handling the case. In Kinsale word quickly spread of what had happened in the schoolyard, of the child's father coming to Ireland, from England they presumed, and claiming his son.

People took turns dropping in on Mona during the hours Ruth worked, bringing the girl food and books. They would sit and speak to the mute young woman and encourage her to eat. They brought chocolates, and ice-cream, and joined her in eating the ice-cream. Some read to her. They did all this in an orderly fashion—time to eat, time to break into her silence with talk or readings, and time for her to be alone to rest. They knew Colm's schedule and never visited when he was with Mona. This neighborly care was a great help to the conscientious Ruth who could not afford to take time off from her job.

A Christmas card and letter arrived from Stan Krakowski. Mona made no attempt to open the letter, and so her mother opened it and read it to her daughter. Looking at her daughter, Ruth thought, *I might be reading the phone book for all the reaction I'm getting from Mona*. Then to her astonishment, she saw tears roll down her daughter's cheeks. This was the first sign of emotion shown by Mona since she phoned her mother on the day little Stan was taken from the schoolyard. *A breakthrough,* Ruth thought, and more earnestly than ever, she tried to communicate with the girl, but no words came forth from Mona. *Patience, she told herself. I must be patient. Next week we'll again be keeping our appointment in Dublin with the psychiatrist.* She had contacted the Synagogue in Dublin and asked the Rabbi if he could recommend a psychiatrist for her daughter. This man whom they had an appointment with was, according to the information she received, the best in his field. Mona's condition was evaluated and treatment had begun.

The psychiatrist believes I have kept Mona too sheltered, to the point where she cannot take the initiative, cannot exert herself on her own behalf, Ruth recalled. *I tried to tell him of the bad neighborhood where we lived when she was growing up, and how I wished we could have afforded to move to a better community. Mona's friends were making bad decisions, getting pregnant, marrying jobless young men, and living on the dole in rundown flats in order to get away from their unhappy family life. They did not seem to realize, they were recreating similar lifestyles for themselves, and their offspring.*

I protected Mona from all that with my constant vigilance, strict rules had been for her safety and well-being. Mona never got into trouble. She knew she had to come home immediately after school each day. The psychiatrist faulted me on making all Mona's decisions for her. Yes, perhaps I did, but it was to guide her into making good choices. Learn by example, is what I tried to teach her.

Perhaps the psychiatrist is partly correct. I did encourage her to make good choices. If anything, it was that Mona, unlike me, had never suffered any hardships that would have forged her metal. She was too innocent, completely without guile. She viewed the world's pain from the stage: Othello, Hamlet, and other performances, not from experience. Yes, the psychiatrist was correct in saying I had sheltered her too much. I did it to protect her from the harshness of life. I wanted her to mature at a slower pace, than the young girls in that neighborhood. Was that so wrong? A mother's guilt has no bounds, she thought. *We are born into it at the birth of our first child, and it grows as the child grows, and never ends. It is only when we relive these moments of our past can we, with knowledge gained later in life, try to erase our past mistakes.*

It is our helplessness in this situation that is taking its toll on Mona and me. The police said they are working on it but reveal no progress. Scotland Yard has taken on the case, but as yet they too have come up with nothing. How can we as individuals accomplish anything! Stan is in The Emirates. Possession is nine tenths of the law. My grandson is unreachable while there. Their laws give custody to the father. They deem themselves right.

Four months after little Stan was taken to the United Arab Emirates, Mona was beginning to make progress under the psychiatrist's care. She held onto the psychiatrist's words, that the child was being well-cared for, and although it might be a long wait, she should never give into the idea of not seeing her son again. Until that time, Mona must try to live her life as productively as possible. Although her daughter's condition was still fragile, Ruth was very optimistic at the progress being made. She also knew that Colm, perhaps even more so than the psychiatrist, had helped in her daughter's progress. Mona was now speaking Although using the minimum of words to convey what she wanted to say, to Ruth it was a blessing to hear her daughter's voice. Mona, who had lost much weight, was now eating better and growing stronger.

"Yes," Mona told Colm, she would be returning to the University in the autumn. Colm and Ruth rejoiced at this news.

A fortnight later, picking up the letter that was dropped through the mail slot, Mona saw that it had been mailed from the Emirates. She hastily tore it open and saw a sheet of paper on which the words, "Task completed," were written. For a moment these words did not make sense to her. Then the full impact of their meaning almost paralyzed her. She dialed the phone. Waiting for the call to go through seemed an eternity. Finally she heard a voice on the other end. It was not Stan's but Ellie's voice she heard.

"Mona darling," Ellie said before her voice became suppressed sobs. "I am sorry to tell you over the phone rather than in person, of Stan's death."

Mona did not cry as the shock of Ellie's word penetrated through her whole being and left her numb and immobilized.

"It happened four days ago. Stan and Karol were returning that evening from the hardware store when they were both shot to death." Ellie had to take a few minutes to calm herself before continuing. "The police are baffled. They wanted to know if Stan or Karol belonged to a gang! Of course they did not. Did they owe money to a money lender that they had not paid back? No, we owed no money. Neither Stan nor Karol had an enemy. They were both well liked and were home every evening."

Mona stood in shock as she listened. Ellie blew her nose and sniffled before speaking again. "The police believe the people who did this were professional killers. Just one bullet was fired into each of them, fatally killing them. 'Execution-Style Murders' the newspapers called it. The police are as puzzled as we are. Why my husband and son?" Ellie sobbed. "Perhaps it was mistaken identity one of the police said."

The cryptic message's full impact hit Mona. "I am sorry for your great loss," she managed to say to this new widow who lost both her husband and a son. Mona could not impart to Ellie her well-founded suspicions, knowing that Ellie would expect some kind of justice where none could be had. *Stan, who was like a father to me, was murdered for helping me leave the Emirates. I have ruined so many lives. I am the reason Ellie's husband and eldest son were murdered, and Piotr has lost his father and brother. To my mother who has had a difficult life, I have brought untold sorrow. Colm, whom I dearly love, has witnessed so much pain. My son is lost to me forever. I am the cause of so much grief. It would have been better if I had not been born.*

When Ruth returned home that day, she found her daughter lying on the bed. She was unable to communicate with her. *What could have caused this setback*, Ruth wondered, as she phoned the psychiatrist. Yes, they had an appointment in a fortnight's time, but Mona needed help sooner as she had had a setback. In five days, yes, they would be there.

Ruth found the cryptic words on the table beside the phone, and was as puzzled as Mona had been. Turning over the envelope that lay next to it, she saw the foreign stamp and knew it was from Abdul. "What did these words mean? He completed the task several months ago by taking little Stan from them. What greater pain than that could he inflict on them?" Mona, who just stared ahead, did not answer any of Ruth's questions.

Colm phoned to tell Mona and Ruth that he would not be visiting the coming weekend, as he planned on going home for his mother's fiftieth birthday celebration. Colm's mind was at peace for he did not know of Mona's most recent setback. Ruth did not inform him of Mona's condition. *He should have a week with his family, without worry*, Ruth thought, *He will know soon enough.*

CHAPTER 21

Colm arrived home late on Friday night to find the house in darkness. Would they have begun the celebration tonight, rather than wait for tomorrow, he wondered. No they would have told him, if there had been a change of plans. Why are there no lights on? After searching in his knapsack, he found the house keys and opened the door. Turning on the lights he was greeted by soundless emptiness. He had never before come home to an empty house, and it made him realize how important his family was to him. Where were they? They knew he was arriving tonight. He was beginning to get annoyed by their lack of consideration. Were they playing a trick on him? Then the door opened and Declan stood before him.

"Well, it's about time someone showed up. Where is everyone?" Then seeing how troubled his brother was, his annoyance vanished.

"What's the matter, Dec?"

"I found him," the boy answered.

"Found whom?"

"Dad," the boy choked out the words. Grabbing his brother, Colm led him towards the couch.

"Sit down, Dec, and tell me what happened."

"I found him," repeated his brother as though that explained all.

"You found dad. Where was he?"

"Sitting in his chair."

Colm was confused. He was about to speak when Declan added, "slumped over."

Colm jolted by his brother's words asked, "Where is he now?"

"In the hospital. He's dead," and the younger brother began to cry.

Sitting next to him and holding him in his arms, Colm tried to comfort him. He had lots of questions he wanted to ask, but they would have to wait. Between sobs, Declan repeated, "I found him. Mom was down the street at Mrs. Ryan's house when it happened."

"You and dad were the only ones home," Colm stated to confirm his brother's situation.

"Yes, I thought he was dead but he wasn't. I called the ambulance and did CPR. He had a heart attack, the doctor told us, and he died on the way to the hospital."

"You've had a tough time, Dec. Is Mom still at the hospital?"

"Yes, she told me to go home and wait for you. I found him."

"Yes. I'm sorry I was not here when it happened."

"He died," the boy said in disbelief.

"It was a terrible shock for you to have found him like that. We will all woefully miss him," Colm said as he loosened his grip on his brother. "It was a quick and painless death, Dec, just as dad would have wanted it." The brothers sat in silence.

After a quiet moment, Colm spoke.

"Remember when we were very young how dad brought Deirdre, you and me around to the houses trick and treating on All Hallow's. We were mortified that he came with us, and so he would fade into the background as we knocked on the doors. He was more excited at our accumulation of loot than we were."

"Yes," Declan added, "and he always warned us against eating too much and getting sick."

"When we told him we were old enough to do the rounds by ourselves, he stopped going with us, and I missed him. That was my first indication that being grown up had a touch of sadness to it," Colm, in remembering, added.

"I wish he didn't have to leave," Declan said.

"Remember what he told us when grandma died. He said everyone had to die, some died young, and others got a long time to live, but all had to eventually leave this life, so that others could be born and have a shot at life. Otherwise there wouldn't be room on earth for everyone. We had to be considerate to all those waiting to be born."

Declan smiled through his sadness, which caused Colm to smile.

"I hope the kid that's going to replace dad grows up to be as great a human being as dad," Declan told his brother.

Colm felt badly that Declan was the one to have found their father having a heart attack. It had left a deep, painful impression on his brother. *If only I had arrived earlier and been with Dec and dad when it happened.*

The front door opened. Deirdre and their mother, crippled with grief, entered, followed by her sister, her sister's husband, and others from both sides of the family. There would not be a birthday celebration the following day as planned. His mother, Colm was acutely aware of, would remember her fiftieth birthday with great sadness, and indeed, all her birthdays would be a remembrance of her husband's death.

Colm phoned Mona, and getting no answer, left a message that his father had died, and he planned to spend the week at home to see his family through the funeral and burial before returning to the University or Kinsale.

CHAPTER 22

A few days later, some mail had been dropped into the mail slot. Ruth bent down to retrieve it, and was absent-mindedly sorting it when she came to a letter from Poland addressed to Mona. She ripped open the letter to find a newspaper clipping, and a short note in what she discovered was Ellie's handwriting. In the note, Ellie apologized to Mona for having had to give her the heart-breaking news of Stan's and Karol's death over the phone.

"Oh God," Ruth moaned realizing this was what had caused Mona's relapse. Stan, in risking his life for his daughter, had signed his own death warrant, and that of his and Ellie's son. Ruth wept. In her grief, Ruth wept for Stan Krakowski and the realization that she was completely alone. There was not another soul on this vast planet, not even her daughter, in whom she could share her pain or receive comfort from, for none knew her secret former life nor her tremendous loss.

When I saw Stan in England after so many years, he had changed. He was no longer the young ambitious rigid 'five-year planner' I had known. He had mellowed. This mature Stan I loved even more. Alas, it was too late for he was happily remarried and had two fine sons. I had to distance myself from him. I resented his attachment to Mona for, while he had a wife and two sons, she was all I had. Looking at the photo in the newspaper of Stan and Karol she thought, *if only things could have been different. I made a terrible mistake in taking our daughter from you. Now I have lost you, and my grandson I will never again see.*

If I had not told Mona her father had died when she was an infant, they would have gotten to know each other a long time ago.

Oh what have I done! It all seemed right at the time. How could it have gone so terribly wrong! Thank you Stan, it was very kind of you not to have revealed to Mona that I had left you, and had her believe her father had died. I gave birth to her but you, in ransoming your daughter, paid the ultimate price.

* * *

In late March during a heavy rain storm, when the streets were empty of people, Mona put on her coat and walked out of the cottage. People had been telling her to take a walk, that it would be good for her, and so she decided to do so. Catherine had suggested that, while out walking, Mona should drop in on her, and should she have no clients at that time, they could have a nice chat over a cup of tea and biscuits. Her mother had suggested that while out walking, Mona might like to drop into the library, choose a book or magazine to read, or just sit and rest before continuing her walk.

As she became aware of the wind and pounding rain, she pulled her collar up for protection, walking hatless and in her bedroom slippers through the blinding rain. The heaviest of the rain was causing some streets to flood. The unrelenting rain was disorienting. She had no destination in mind. Soon her bedroom slippers were soaking wet and were beginning to come apart, as she walked in a daze towards the harbor. On reaching the harbor, she stood for several minutes looking down into the sea before crossing over the sea wall, and down into the water.

She felt the water on her feet and then upwards to her knees. She remembered her mother bringing her to the park near where they lived when she was a child. On hot summer days her mother would allow her to wade in the duck pond. The water would come to just below her knees. Other children, some with toy sailboats, also entered the duck pond. The ducks did not seem to mind, and the water felt so good. When the pond got too crowded, the ducks waddled up onto the small grassy island in the center of the pond, taking refuge among the tall grasses and shrubs, where the children were forbidden to go.

Soon the water was at her waist and the waves were trying to topple her over. *Momma, the water is above my knees.* The rain continued to fall heavily downwards and meshed with the sea water, becoming one with it and blocking everything beyond from view. *I am trying to walk to the edge of the pond but I cannot see the edge. The ducks, Momma, are flying overhead, and sound like angry seagulls. Where are you Momma?* Her footing gave way, and she floated along with a feeling of lightness, no constrictions, no sadness, just the sensation of drifting in time and space.

Donovan drove Ruth to view the body. Ruth had the devastating task of identifying the ghostly white face of her dead daughter. *I have lost everything, my beloved daughter, and my grandson. I will wander in the desert until I die, and when I die, my entire family will be extinct. The line will have ceased. I have nothing else to lose.* Nothing left to lose brought a strange kind of freedom, freedom at a terrible price.

* * *

After knocking on the shutters of his son's apartment, the old man waited.

"Father," Abdul uttered in surprise, for his father rarely came to his apartment. "Come in Father."

"You are alone, I see. How is the boy?"

"He will not answer to Zayed, the name of the honorable Sheik Zayed that I have chosen for him. He wants to continue to be called Stan."

"Perhaps you can supply him with a list of names and let him select a new name from among them."

"What an excellent idea. I will do that."

"The boy needs time. Too much has changed in his short life. He must adjust to having a father he had never previously met. Our country and ways are very different from what he has known. And he misses his mother and grandmother."

"He never ceases to bring to mind his mother or his grandmother. He asked to go home. I told him this was his home, to which he replied he wanted to go to his other home where his Momma and Grandmamma lived. Apparently he was not getting the answers he wished from me and sought another source."

"Another source?"

"He asked Jasmine if she could bring him on a plane to see his mother."

"The child is too young, Abdul, to understand the family dynamics. You have just recently entered his life, whereas these two women have always been part of his existence."

"He speaks of Ireland as though it were paradise. What kind of people are these islanders that makes them cling to their tiny country so tenaciously?"

"Home, it is simply home. It is the only home the boy has ever known. I heard the people of that island are a very likeable people. Patience, Abdul, he will adjust in time."

"They are Christians! My son belongs to the Islamic Teachings."

"Yes, and he will remain so."

A moment of silence was shared after which his father spoke.

"I have come to fill you in on the investigation."

"Good, for I also have something to relate to you. Do proceed, father."

"The people who helped Maria escape were two Polish men who worked on the construction site, Maria's father and half-brother. They bear the name Krakowski."

"Her father!" Abdul gasped. I have given orders for Maria's father and his son to be shot! Polish workers—Maria had said her mother who was of Polish origin, told her that her father had died when she was a baby."

"You are ahead of me on this Abdul. I had thought you would wait until I had gotten the full details on these men and why they would risk their lives for a woman whom we both thought was a stranger to them. This is apparently a shock to you. Perhaps you should sit down."

After seating himself, he spoke. "I, who planned every detail of my son's rescue from his mother in Ireland, without any physical harm to me or my family, have shown no mercy to a man whose only offense was to rescue *his* daughter and take her out of the UAE."

"Has the order been carried out?"

"Yes, both father and son have been executed."

"Your only fault was your haste. Impatience is the burden of the young."

"Father, I have always gathered all the facts, and have shown great patience in my negotiations to achieve what was best for the

Emirates. Yet, when the Krakowskis were located, I did not ask what their motives were, but immediately had them murdered."

"Hitherto you never got emotionally involved in your work. You painstakingly worked out all the details from every angle and point of view. Your emotional involvement, in this situation, clouded your thinking."

A silence prevailed for several moments.

The older man broke the silence as he continued to speak of the journey this father and son had made. "Mr. Krakowski, his son and Maria left here and went to Poland."

"Poland," Abdul said, as he remembered Maria and his time in Casablanca. "Maria had said her mother was Polish. Why didn't I make the connection?"

"Why would you have done so? Her mother told Maria that her father had died when she was a baby. After leaving the Emirates, the three of them went to Poland. The father left the son in Poland, believing no doubt that his son was safe, before he and Maria continued on their dangerous journey to France, and then to England. We have seen the record of their flight to France but no airline flight to England. That threw us off, and for a while we searched for them in other European countries, and then realized they had taken the Chunnel to England and from there a boat most likely, for they did not go by plane to nearby Ireland where we found Maria and her mother. Sometime later we located the father and son in Poland as you also did."

"We both, this man and I, were willing to go to great lengths for our children. I did so without danger to me; he did so with great danger to himself. After I had successfully taken back my child, I had Krakowski murdered for doing the same for his.

"Yes, this man showed great love," Abdul's father said. "But Abdul, you did not know of their family connection. You believed you were reprimanding this construction worker and his son, who were guests in our country, for assisting your wife in leaving you."

Abdul did not speak, and after several moments his father continued.

"Perhaps in time you can contact Maria and explain the situation, and offer to make some kind of retribution. You said her living conditions are less than desirable. Maybe you can offer to improve them."

"In my ignorance, Father, I continued this destruction by revealing to Maria that I had eliminated both of the Krakowskis. I did not know, of course, that these two men were her father and half-brother."

"You contacted Maria concerning these two deaths?" his father said in dismay, for he admired Maria and her kindness to the grandson he had neglected.

"I am at a loss in knowing how to make atonement to Maria. She would not accept anything from me. She did not value the Parisian clothes I bought for her nor the jewels I gave her. From what I hear from those who have been watching her, she does not see her poverty as constrictive. She went camping with a fellow University student and my son in a very beat-up old car. They cooked their meals outdoors on an open fire and slept under a tent. She was happy as was our son with that lifestyle." After a moment, Abdul asked, "You once said Maria was a very forgiving person. She took care of Laila's son although Laila had murdered our firstborn. Do you think she will forgive me for what I have done to her father?"

His father was at a loss for words and was very concerned about the effect all this was having on his son. Then Abdul, who had his head downcast, looked up at his father, "There is one thing, Father, that she would appreciate: photographs of our son and a video of his progress throughout the years."

"This offense is so grave, I believe more is required of you. There is one thing Maria desperately wants."

Abdul waited for his father to continue but the older man was silent.

"Surely you do not ask me to give up your grandson?"

His father shook his head.

Abdul, wishing he had his father's patience, mulled over his father's words, and while doing so remembered a riddle his father had placed before him when he was a child. 'Two men claimed the same goat. The goat cut into two would profit neither man, whereas sharing the produce of the goat would provide milk for both families.'

"I could suggest to Maria the following plan: I would send a plane or a plane ticket for her and her mother, and I would provide two-week accommodations for them and our son, twice a year in France, Spain, The Netherlands, Austria or another suitable location of her choice. I doubt very much, that Maria would want to meet with me. Jasmine, however, whom Maria was very fond of, would be willing to accompany Zayed to the chosen location."

"Excellent, and Abdul, let go of your mistakes. Nothing can be gained from your brooding over them."

"I will try, Father. Maria gave me a son. My new wife has given me a daughter. Maria could marry that young man whom she went camping with, and eventually have another son. I will wait a while before contacting Maria, so that the raw edge of her grief may have subsided somewhat. That will give me time to have photographs and a video to send to her along with my regrets, and this plan of reuniting her with our son for a fortnight or more."

"As you say, Abdul, there is nothing else we can do for her. I doubt even Maria will be able to forgive these deaths." The older man thought, *Maria will never contact Abdul after this incident. She will have no desire to have any association with our family and, therefore, Abdul will never know her reaction to this loss and he will get on with his life.*

CHAPTER 23

Colm phoned and heard the heartbreaking news of Mona's death. He came down to visit Ruth.

"I am so very sorry to hear of the death of your father," Ruth told the very likeable young red-haired man standing before her. "Mona had said you are a very close family and you had had a great relationship with your father. It is especially kind of you to come down here so soon after your father's death, while still sorrowing over this tremendous loss in your life."

"I wish I had been here for her after she had that relapse. I loved Mona, I always will."

Ruth revealed to Colm the contents of Ellie's letter, and showed him the newspaper clippings, and the two-word message Abdul had sent to Mona when she was recuperating, which caused her relapse.

"Mona's death was caused by Abdul who in a most insidious manner accomplished that callous deed," Colm stated from the depths of his grief. "She was devastated when he took their son. He got what he wanted, why then did he want to inflict more pain on her?"

"If he had loved her," Ruth questioned, "how could he have caused her so much suffering?"

"Only he knows the reasons for his actions," Colm sadly replied.

Followed by the townspeople and the knitters' group, Colm, with a bouquet of wildflowers in his arms, walked with Ruth, Donovan, Catherine, and Una towards the harbor to the place where the tide had washed the body ashore. Colm stood in silent prayer for several minutes, and then removing the string that bound the flowers, threw the flowers one by one into the sea as he recited the chorus of William Butler Yeats' poem, The Stolen Child.

Come away, O human child!
To the waters and the wild
With a faery, hand in hand,
For the world's more full of weeping
Than you can understand.

They stood in silence for several minutes, until Donovan turned to Ruth and said, "Let me take the four of you to lunch. I told the owner of the restaurant I wasn't sure when we would arrive in order to give you time to be consoled by the town."

"It is our custom to invite all to a reception where people can offer their condolences over a buffet lunch with drinks. Mr. Donovan," Colm told Ruth, "suggested since you're unfamiliar with our ways, you may prefer that the four of us, Catherine, Una, Mr. Donovan and myself take you instead for a quiet lunch."

Ruth, with gratitude, thanked them and accepted Mr. Donovan's invitation. After some time, they eventually broke away from the crowd, and were driven by Donovan, whose car was parked nearby, to a restaurant on the outskirts of town, where they could be alone to relax and eat. They were greeted by the owner of the establishment and seated in a secluded area where they recalled fond incidents in the life of the young woman who was exceedingly dear to each of them.

When his father had been dead a month, following tradition, Colm's family commemorated his father's death by attending a month's mind Mass in his honor. All his extended family, friends and neighbors attended this event. Throughout the Mass, Colm, found himself remembering Mona as much as he remembered his father. He wondered if Ruth's faith had such an event as this. Ruth, too, he believed, should have a special day of love to help her through this still-fresh wound in her life.

A month after Mona's death, a beautiful bouquet of lavender with yellow tulips mixed in arrived at Ruth's cottage. She was puzzled and assumed the deliveryman had made a mistake. Then looking at the attached envelope she saw her name. The note that accompanied the flowers read: 'In memory and gratitude for having known and loved Mona, and for the joy she brought into our lives. Even death cannot destroy our blessed time together.' It was signed Colm.

*   *   *

Should she open it or destroy it unopened, Ruth asked herself *as she gazed at the letter addressed to Maria that she held in her hand. Hasn't that man caused enough damage? Why is he writing her now?* Then Ruth realized that Abdul would have stopped spying on them after he took Stan and most likely did not know that Mona had drowned.

Ruth wanted to destroy the letter but reasoned if she did so, she would never know why Abdul was trying to contact her daughter. *Perhaps something had happened to Stan!* With that thought in mind, Ruth quickly tore open the envelope and read the note.

To be able to see Stan again and to spend some time with him brought tears of joy to her eyes. But, she told herself, *this invitation is extended to Mona and me. Without Mona will Abdul withdraw this kind offer? Most likely he will.* Ruth sat down to ponder this strange turn of events. She could consult with Catherine or Ned Donovan and then decide what course of action to take. She also felt she had no solid grounds for the expectation that Abdul would not withdraw the invitation after he discovered that Mona was dead. Yet she held firmly onto this very weak thread that would bring her face-to-face with her beloved grandson. *Yes, the invitation could be withdrawn, and all my new found hope dashed to pieces. Be that as it may,* she told herself, *the pain of rejection could not compare with the pain of letting go of any spark of hope that presents itself that might make it possible to be reunited with Stan. Yes, she would call the telephone number that was sent to Mona. First she would make herself a hot cup of tea.* She smiled at this action. *I'm becoming like the Irish, I cannot make a tough decision without first having a cup of tea.*

So much weighed in the balance with this telephone call, it made her feel numb. This telephone call would convey whether she would be permitted to see her grandson or that access to him would be forever lost to her. She braced herself for the worst possible outcome while hoping against hope that it would not happen. As she thought on the fact that Abdul had never met her, and that he had not permitted Mona access to her while they were married, Ruth became tense, her courage waning. *Is this telephone call a fool's errand?* She made herself another cup of tea.

Moments after dialing the number that came with the letter to Mona, a voice spoke to her, "Jasmine here." Ruth remembered Mona speaking of Jasmine and it gave her courage to continue. She was relieved that it was Jasmine, not Abdul, who answered the telephone. She remembered to use the name she had when Mona was married to Abdul, and she would also speak of Mona as Maria to alleviate any confusion.

"This is Anna Krakowski," Ruth stated.

"Good evening, Mrs. Krakowski. Is Maria well?" Jasmine asked with concern on not hearing Maria's voice.

"I am sorry to convey the sad news that after her father and half-brother were. . . " She was about to say 'murdered,' but refrained from doing so, "died, and all this happened so soon after her son was taken from her, that Maria fell into a deep depression, and not knowing what she was doing walked into the ocean. Her body was washed ashore on the incoming tide the following morning."

Jasmine was audibly distressed by this news. After a moment, she spoke, "How dreadful, I am sorry, truly sorry. I was very fond of Maria. She was a dear friend, and a beautiful person in every way. I will speak to Abdul and call you back. I am sorry for your great loss. I, who only knew her for a few years, loved her. Your loss is extremely great and on behalf of Abdul, myself and the family, I offer you our sincere condolences. I will call you again later this evening after I have conveyed this extremely sad news to Abdul. Goodbye, Mrs. Krakowski."

Ruth felt the possibility of her being reunited with her grandson had gravely diminished.

Within two hours the telephone rang. The verdict would be handed down, Ruth, feeling her body tighten with tension, picked up the receiver and heard Jasmine's voice. The invitation was still in effect. Plane tickets for two would be sent to her so that she could have a traveling companion of her choosing accompany her. They would be picked up at the landing strip where Stan, who is now being informed of his mother's death, will meet them, and all will be driven to the resort in which they would stay for the duration of their fortnight, and where all their expenses would be paid for by Abdul.

Her grandson would hand her a card on her arrival. In whatever restaurant of the many restaurants in the Resort Complex they chose to dine, they should show this card. It should also be used for their shopping—clothing, jewelry, perfume, cosmetics, etc. The concierge would be instructed to help them if needed, and he would have a limousine within fifteen minutes of their request to take them anywhere they wished to travel. All expenses and purchases would be paid for, and all arrangements set in place for her to travel to France.

"Should you forget your bathing attire, there is a huge selection available at the resort," Jasmine light-heartily said as she ended the telephone call.

CHAPTER 24

When, after a thorough investigation into Mona's life, it was found that the distraught woman had died, Abdul wept. Her love had been pure, he felt. "She sought neither status, nor jewels, nor wealth, and yet I took from her what she cherished most, our son, and then had her father and brother killed."

Over lunch, his father asked, "Do you think it prudent to take the steps you propose, for Zayed to visit with his grandmother? Any obligation you might have felt towards Maria has been nullified by her tragic death."

Abdul remained silent.

"Do you think that this woman, whom you've never met, might convey her belief to Zayed, that you were responsible for his mother's death?"

"No, father, she will not speak of such to Zayed."

"What guarantee do you have from this woman who has been gravely hurt?"

"She knows that should she speak of such things to Zayed, she would lose all access to my son. Never being able to see him again will seal her lips. This woman has no husband, no child. Zayed is her only link to her deceased daughter. I am confident that she will do all in her power to maintain this connection to her grandson, which I am allowing her.

Slowly his father nodded his head in agreement.

Before Ruth had shared the wonderful news of being united with her grandson, she, back to her everyday routine, saw Donovan holding out two tickets. He approached her at the bus stop as she waited for the bus to take her to work.

"I thought you might like to attend Mozart's <u>Requiem for the Dead</u> at the Opera House next Sunday."

"That's very kind of you Mr. Donovan, I accept. Thank you."

"Ned."

After a moment she realized he wished her to call him by his first name. She smiled at him.

"May I make a reservation for the two of us for supper following the performance?" he continued as the bus arrived.

He said the two of us, just the two of us, she thought. Stepping up into the bus, Ruth turned and answered with a smile. "Yes, Ned, that would be very nice," and in the manner of the Irish added, "very nice indeed."

He tipped his cap in acknowledgment.

Ned and Ruth met in Catherine's office where Ruth revealed the contents of the telephone calls. From the selection that had been offered to her, Ruth had chosen the French Riviera as the place to spend with her grandson. Ned would, at Ruth's request, accompany her on this trip.

"We're going to see Stan! Imagine that! Ned said."

"Yes, but we will not go to the country, where Mona lived and gave birth to my grandson." Turning to Catherine she continued, "I doubt if Ned and I will meet Abdul. All my communications have been with this woman called Jasmine who was a friend to Mona and related to Abdul. Mona had spoken highly of Jasmine."

"Now Ruth, would you want to meet this Abdul fellow?" Ned asked.

"In truth, no. Although I've never met Jasmine, as all our conversations were by telephone, yet I believe her to be a very nice person."

"That rascal Abdul."

"Wait a moment, Catherine," Ned injected. "Ruth here wouldn't be visiting her grandson if Abdul objected to such a visit."

"Yes, we have him to thank for this trip to see my beloved grandson."

"Yes, indeed, Ruth," Catherine chipped in. "Besides which, you probably wouldn't know what to say to this man whom you've never met, but who is Stan's father."

"Sometimes I can't believe what is happening. It's like a dream that could pop at any moment into wakefulness and disappointment."

"How in God's name can you waddle in pessimistic thoughts in the midst of one of the greatest moments of your life?"

"Perhaps, Ned, Ruth has had too many disappointments in life to expect the situation to change."

In the silence that followed, Ned put his arm protectively around Ruth.

"I need your advice, Catherine, on what clothes I should pack." Catherine, familiar with Ruth's clothing, and knowing Ruth had nothing suitable to wear, wondered how she could offer assistance without offending Ruth. Ruth was an attractive woman even while wearing that old brown cardigan she constantly wore. All her skirts and blouses had had the life washed out of them. *That grey coat she wears,* Catherine thought, *looks like it came from a charity shop. Her black handbag, a good leather bag, must be older than her daughter and nobody in summer would be carrying a black leather handbag. Ruth has good facial structure and her lovely thick soft brown hair with threads of gray running through it is beautiful.* Catherine offered to accompany Ruth to some good clothing stores.

"There are excellent women's clothing shops here in Cork, or we could take the train to Dublin and visit Switzers or Brown Thomas's, Catherine suggested.

"Oh, my, they're very expensive shops, way beyond my means. Can you suggest other shops that are more reasonable in price?"

Ned chimed in saying, "Catherine, since you manage my rental affairs, I ordain that Ruth will not be paying rent this month or for as many months as needed, but rather using that money for her shopping spree on Grafton Street. I'll drive both of you ladies to the train station, whenever you choose to go."

Before Ruth could thank him, Catherine addressed him. "That's very kind of you, Mr. Donovan. May I also state that you yourself need a decent summer jacket? I know you have a good tweed jacket but it will be totally useless in France at this time of year where a nice linen jacket is called for."

Before Catherine could say anymore, Donovan said, "I have my lightweight corduroy jacket. You can't expect me to go prancing around in one of those light-colored jackets—white or a peculiar shade of green and such!"

"You can get a navy blue linen jacket or a dark tan one, and while you are at it, a couple of lightweight trousers should be added to your wardrobe."

"Aw, Catherine, you want me looking like one of those foreigners."

"No, Mr. Donovan, I want you to be suitably dressed to accompany Ruth on this trip."

Donovan acquiesced.

It looked like the whole town turned out to see the couple off on their trip. Many of the ladies complimented Ruth on how lovely she looked, while the men teased Ned Donovan, asking him whether he had a straw hat and a walking cane.

Ruth and Ned entered the car with words of good wishes for a safe and wonderful holiday, and everyone urged them to enjoy this trip of a lifetime. One of the men in the group called out, "tell us how it feels to live for a fortnight like a millionaire," followed by many calls to tell Stan "we send our love."

At the airport, Ruth turned to Ned and spoke, "This is all so unreal. Here we are with plane tickets to the French Riviera, and, according to Jasmine, we're booked into a hotel suite. We just show the card we will be given, and all our purchases will be taken care of."

"I believe we've gone way beyond the three wishes the Genie usually grants," Ned laughed.

"Oh Ned, I'm not as optimistic as you are. I'm waiting for things to go dreadfully wrong, and having all this whisked away."

"No, Ruth, we're on our way," he answered cheerfully as he took her hand, and they walked forward hand in hand. "Instead of fretting, why not dwell on how great seeing Stan again will be."

"I'm afraid of letting myself get too happy."

"You're afraid things might go wrong, and also afraid of being happy?" Ned asked with a quizzical look on his face.

"I'm so glad you've come with me. I promise to rely on your good judgment and optimism, and enjoy the prospect of seeing my delightful grandson again."

Ruth, true to her word, did so.

"We're not flying Aer Lingus, and I'm not at all familiar with this airline on our tickets." Just then, they heard their names being called out over the loudspeaker, requesting that they make themselves known at the nearest ticket counter. When they arrived there, they were asked to show their passports, and then the woman who had made the request, smiled and said, "Just a moment please," as she made a phone call.

Three men in uniform, one of which looked like a pilot's uniform, arrived within moments. The one they assumed to be the pilot requested to see their passports. He then spoke to the two other men in a language Ruth and Ned did not understand, and these men took their luggage. On seeing his new clothing and toiletries and Ruth's beautiful clothes disappear, Ted thought, *one needs a lot of trust, when traveling into the unknown.*

"What airline will we be taking?" The answer he got was it would be a private plane belonging to the Emirates. Ned was too stunned to put forth any more questions.

"Will they speak English on the plane, do you think?" Ruth asked Ned.

The man with whom they were walking answered. "Yes."

The lettering on the plane looked more like elaborate scroll work than words, Ned thought, as he tried to decipher it.

Soon they were being welcomed aboard. There were several people seated in the small plane when they entered. No women were among them, Ruth noted. Ned smiled as he sat in one of the wide comfortable seats they had been assigned.

"Two of us could be seated comfortably in just one of these seats," Ned whispered to Ruth, aware that the crew, and possibly the other passengers, spoke English.

"Look at all these magazines, and newspapers in English," Ruth pointed out to Ned.

"Well, on my side they're all in what I believe is Arabic, except for the Irish Times. I guess it got here by mistake, and was meant to be on your side." Ted laughed.

Before the meals were served they were not only offered a menu in Arabic and English, but one of the crew explained what each item on the menu consisted of, both food and drink. None of the latter contained any alcohol.

"A nice hot cup of tea would be delightful right now," Ruth said to Ned as she relaxed into her spacious seat. Almost immediately a hot cup of tea, cream, sugar and lemon were placed on the tray before her. Soon the meal followed. As they ate, Ned remarked, "I don't really know what I'm eating, but whatever it is, it's delicious."

As he finished his meal, Ned whispered, "I've heard of first-class passengers traveling with all the comforts of home, and for people like us way beyond, but this I surmise surpasses first-class on a regular plane by all upward notches."

Although the plane's personnel anticipated all their needs and graciously attended to them, they did not have any interaction with the other passengers on the plane. If Stan was not at the end of this flight waiting for them, they would have been happy to have this wonderful experience continue past its expected flight time.

Sitting in the plane, Ruth closed her eyes and reflected on the turmoil that had invaded their lives since Mona, who had lived a very sheltered life, went on holiday to Spain. *I always wanted grandchildren, but had wished Mona had had an abortion to save her from Abdul who would claim the child, and bring calamity into their lives. I could not have foreseen the terrible toll that keeping the child would have on Mona. I believed I was the last surviving member of my family. Now after passing over a trip to Spain due to that country's association with Mona, I am traveling to another country that I have never been to, to see my grandson who will grow to manhood, marry and have children who will also have children, and the line will continue,* Ruth thought, as she drifted off into sleep.

"Maybe it would be best if we let all the other passengers leave the plane ahead of us. In that way, whatever transportation remains, must be for us," Ned suggested.

After all the other passengers had left, Ruth and Ned rose from their seats, and made their way to the exit.

"Your transportation has arrived, and is waiting for you on the tarmac," the pilot told them as he bade them farewell.

On exiting the plane, Ruth and Ned walked down the steps towards the tarmac, wondering what their next step would be.

"There's not a soul in sight," Ruth uttered as she looked at the vast expanse of tarmac.

"Don't fret, dear, they know when we're arriving, and the pilot said our transportation was waiting for us," Ned assured his nervous companion.

"I never thought, Ruth, that one day, I'd be spending a fortnight on the French Riviera!"

Ruth laughed. "I feel like I've mistakenly entered someone else's life."

"No dear, you haven't. All this is happening to us."

"Reality has never been so pleasant."

"Could that be our transportation?" Ned questioned on seeing a lone limousine on the tarmac, and then realizing it had to be waiting for them.

As they set foot on the tarmac, the door of the limousine opened and a beautiful woman whom Ruth believed must be Jasmine, waved to them, and then a young boy emerged and ran towards them, shouting as he ran, "Grandmamma." As he came near, Ruth dropped to her knees, and the boy ran into her waiting arms. For several moments, Ruth and her grandson held each other in a tight embrace. *If only Mona could have been here*, Ruth pondered, in this extraordinary moment. Her sadness and joy mingled and played havoc with her emotions, which she had difficulty keeping under control, but felt she must for the child's sake. *If only this reunion with Stan could have taken place in more normal surroundings for Ned and me; a more familiar place. That would be perfect, but perfection is not meant for us mortals. I am sure the accommodations are excellent, but Ned and I are out of our element here. This is not home. Where is Stan's new home? What is it like?*

Enclosed in his grandmother's embrace, the boy remembered another occasion, when he had asked Jasmine to take him on a plane to the house where Momma and Grandmamma lived. Jasmine said she was sorry that she could not do so. When he was told that he would be visiting his grandmother, he thought he was going back to the home where his Momma and Grandmamma lived.

I know Momma is dead, and that means gone forever. Yet I'd rather go back to where I used to live with them, than to this resort or even skiing in the Alps. Jasmine said I can never go back to Grand-mamma's home again, and that it would not be the same since Momma died. But I will go back when I'm all grown up. I'll go camp-ing again with Colm, and we'll build a fire, cook our food, and sleep under a tent. Will the children at the school remember me?

As she knelt holding the child Ruth silently prayed. *Thank you, God of the Universe, for giving me this moment in time—this two-week visit with my grandson. I promise I will never reveal to this boy that his father, although not intending to, caused his mother's death, not only because it would be a terrible burden for Stan to carry throughout life, and it would cause friction between him and his father, but also because Abdul, whether out of atonement or through great generosity to a now childless widow, has permitted this reunion. There is also the possibility that Abdul truly loved Mona, and he has put all this in place because of that love. I will, however, make known to Stan his heritage. What a heritage that is—a Jewish grandmother, a Catholic grandfather, a father who believes in the Islamic faith. Three great religions—all descended from Abraham. What will this child's destiny be?*

Stan and his grandmother were unaware that the limousine that had brought him to her was now less than a dozen feet from them, and Jasmine was sitting in it with the door open.

Ned, who became a bit flustered when the limousine stopped close by, urgently said to Ruth, "I believe the plane is waiting for us to leave."

With Ned's voice breaking into her thoughts, Ruth released her hold on the boy. *If only Mona could have witnessed this moment,* Ruth thought, but would not give voice to these thoughts, so as not to draw a dark shadow over her grandson, or her wonderful companion, on their precious fortnight together.

Ruth's legs had become stiff from kneeling too long, and would not cooperate as she tried to stand. Ned was immediately there beside her, with his arm around her, as she rose.

Grandmamma needs help in standing. She is getting old. Will she too die? Will other people live in her home? Will the people who will be living in Grandmamma's house return my soccer ball which I left behind?

Will Una, who used to pick me up after school, and tell me she was my Godmother, be there? When I had asked Una what a Godmother was, she said it was a person who would take care of me, if my Momma could no longer do so. Does that mean I could stay with Una and her aunt Catherine?

Jasmine alit from the limousine and as she walked toward them she greeted Ruth. Extending both hands she said, "I am Jasmine. It is so very nice to meet Maria's mother," and turning to Ned, added "and your friend, Mr. Donovan."

"Maria spoke highly of you," Ruth stated.

Jasmine added, "Maria was a beautiful person whom I loved like a cherished sister."

The boy listened to the woman he had once asked to fly him home to see his mother, greet his grandmother with much affection.

"We had better be on our way and find a taxi," Ned said, "for we may be blocking this plane from leaving the runway."

"No," Jasmine smiled, a smile that lit up her lovely intelligent eyes, "that plane will not leave until I'm aboard."

Ned and Ruth, on hearing this, felt more lost than ever, in this world of wealth beyond their imagination.

"The limousine is at your disposal. It will take you to your hotel, and wherever else you wish to go during your stay here." On saying this Jasmine hugged Stan, and then Ruth, and graciously nodded farewell to Ned before walking towards the plane they had only a short time ago exited. Jasmine stopped on the topmost step before entering, and waved to the three of them. They responded in kind. Ruth, realizing that Jasmine had remained in the limousine in order for Stan and her to have those first moments of their reunion alone, called out to the young woman, "Thank you." Jasmine seemed to have heard, or perhaps read her lips, Ruth believed, but she would never know for certain.

CHAPTER 25

The driver of the limousine opened the doors for his passengers. After they entered the limousine, he closed the doors and, having seated himself in the driver's seat, he drove out of the airport.

"Can we assume he knows where to take us," Ned asked Stan.

"Yes, Aunt Jasmine gave him lots of instructions and I too know where we'll be staying."

"You've been to the Riviera before, I gather," Ned states.

"Yes, but I'm not allowed to drive off our grounds and there aren't any pillows in this car to raise me up behind the steering wheel."

"You can drive?" Ned asked, in disbelief.

"Yes, my father taught me how to drive, but I'm forbidden to do so on public roads. It is against the law because I'm under age to do so."

There is an Asian gentleman driving us, in a country we've never been to before, we have no idea where we are going and we have a seven-year-old going on eight with us who knows how to drive.

Turning to Ruth he exclaimed, "What a limousine this is." She laughs.

"Yes, and a spare driver should we need one." They both laugh.

Stan did not know what caused their merriment but their happiness he found contagious. "We have arrived," the boy tells his grandmother and her friend. Getting out of the car, Ned looked upwards.

"So this is what they call a 'skyscraper!'"

Looking upwards, Ned is nonplussed.

"Do they supply the people way up there with oxygen?" Ned asks. Then on a more somber note, "Have you any idea Ruth how much I should tip the driver?"

"Everything has been taken care of, including tips," Stan tells him. My father said since you would not be familiar with the currency of France, everything, including tips, will be taken care of, and the cards you have been given are for all purchases you wish to make here in this country. Of course, at the hotel, we just sign for everything."

As soon as Stan walked into the hotel lobby, he was greeted by a gentleman who told him, "All is in readiness for you and your companions' stay here. Please follow me, Sir." He walked past the main cluster of elevators and around the corner to a single elevator and pushed the button. The door opened and they entered, as the man who had guided them wished them a most pleasant stay.

"Thank you," the boy answered, as the door closed. Immediately they were being transferred to the penthouse suite. Their luggage was there when they arrived, and a porter brought it into their suite.

Our whole cottage could fit in this suite with room to spare, Ruth surmises, while looking around the suite.

"You're not afraid of heights, Ned utters in relief."

Stan was on the telephone. "Tea for three, please, and some strawberries and cream, also a plate of individual cakes. Yes, thank you."

When Stan put down the receiver, Ned remarked, "I have noticed, young man, that you have very good manners. You never fail to say 'please or thank you' to those who attend to our needs."

"Yes, my father insists on it. He does likewise. He believes it's important to be polite to people, especially those who serve us."

"He has taught you well, Lad."

The boy smiled. Room service arrived.

"All this for us," Ruth exclaimed after the food was delivered.

"There is a refrigerator in the largest bedroom," Ned laughed, "but I don't think we'll need to place any of this delicious repast there."

"After we all have our tea, we could do some sightseeing, if you wish, or if you're too tired from your trip here, we could go to the beach. Aunt Jasmine suggested you might like to 'watch the parade go by.'"

"What is the parade in honor of?"

"It's not a real parade, it's just people walking around slowly. Aunt Jasmine said some people just want to have their picture taken. I don't particularly like to have my picture taken," Stan said, as he shook his head, "and my father usually makes sure it is not taken."

Aunt Jasmine will be here to take grandmamma shopping on Wednesday and Thursday."

"Why do they need two days of shopping for clothes?"

"I think, one day might be for choosing clothes they'd like and the second day is for when they change their minds and want to return some of them and get different clothes."

"That sounds about right," Ned laughed.

"I hope they don't want me to go with them," Ned said.

"I don't think so, it's just something women like to do. Waiting for women while they are shopping is very boring."

"Who takes you clothes shopping?"

"Aunt Jasmine used to take me when I was small but now my father takes me."

"What do you think, lad, would be good entertainment for us men while the women folk are shopping?"

"I can't go swimming without my father being present, but we can look at any movie even the most recent ones here in the room, or sports, or anything you'd like."

"Great, why don't you choose us a movie for us to watch?"

* * *

Jasmine arrived on the assigned day to take Ruth clothes shopping. Ruth worried that Jasmine, a beautiful young woman who wears clothes that are both elegant and expensive, might bring her shopping in stores that did not cater to the sturdy clothes her lifestyle required.

Apparently, the salespeople were expecting them and took them into a private room that looked like a large formal living room. Wine and a variety of nuts and slices of fresh fruit were placed in front of them.

"We'll start with coats," Jasmine told Ruth.

The clothes that were brought for Ruth to choose from were of elegant design, fashionably cut, stylish, yet practical. Many of them were trimmed in fur at the collar, cuffs and hems. *These good people apparently are not aware of the amount of rain we receive in winter, in the Emerald Isle,* Ruth thought, as she visualized herself waiting at the bus stop in a downpour as she had done on many occasions. Pay attention, she reminded herself, as more clothes, magnificent in color and design, were placed before her from which to choose.

"They are all so lovely, it is difficult to choose one."

"Take as long as you need." The patient Jasmine told her. "Just select several coats that you think you might like, try them on here and later in the comfort of your suite. Ask Ned's opinion and if you find that you are not absolutely delighted with anything in this selection, we'll have the hotel return them for us, and we will go to other stores tomorrow."

"I don't wish to encroach on your time and busy schedule."

"I'm at your disposal today and tomorrow. Now pick at least three, four or more of the coats that appeal to you." Ruth is flabbergasted.

"One coat is sufficient."

"No, Ruth, you must choose at least three or I will feel I have failed you in this endeavor."

Encouraged, Ruth said, "I'll take the purple one with the high black fur collar, as it is absolutely magnificent, and the emerald green with the brown fur along the hem and cuffs, which is equally beautiful in color, material and design."

"Excellent choices, each of them looked beautiful on you. If, however, you decide you'd rather have some others than you have tried on, we'll have the hotel return them, and we'll shop in another store, until we find what you'd like."

"I would like you to consider the black coat with the grey fur trim and its matching grey fur hat," Jasmine said, "as a gift from me."

Ruth was about to protest when Jasmine made eye contact with the saleswoman, who had kept a discreet distance from the two women, and pointed to the three coats.

"Rather than go directly to another store for dresses, skirts and blouses, let's have some afternoon tea."

"That would be delightful," Ruth agreed, for as wonderful as such an activity was, she found herself too tired in having to choose from such a variety of clothing.

Over lunch, the conversation turned to Maria.

"Abdul truly loved Maria," Jasmine told Ruth. "It was all a terrible misunderstanding. When Abdul discovered that the people who made it possible for Maria to leave him, were guest workers in our country he was naturally enraged, and had them killed, not knowing this man and his son who enabled her leave the Emirates were her father and half-brother. It was a dreadful shock to Abdul, even more devastating that his actions caused Maria's death. He was unable to function for a long time after hearing of Maria's death. So huge were the misunderstandings that caused that terrible tragedy," Jasmine revealed to Ruth. Before continuing, Jasmine drank some wine.

"Abdul blames himself solely for Maria's death and, of course, the death of her father, your ex-husband, and his son. We cannot undo the past but it is Abdul's hope that these yearly fortnights spent with your grandson until he is thirteen years old and ready to enter boarding school, will sustain you through the immense sorrow you bear."

"I deeply appreciate his generosity to me." *The possibility of my meeting Abdul while I am here, I doubt will happen.* "Please convey to . . ." she finds it difficult to say his name, "Stan's father, my gratitude for being able to see my grandson, which is greater than words can express. You too, Jasmine, are a major part of making these visits possible and I thank you most deeply. Maria spoke highly of you. I'm so glad she had your friendship in those troubling days after her firstborn son's death. I cried for her when she revealed that terrible incident to me. Now, as Ned said, 'Maria is beyond pain.'"

The women finished their lunch and left the restaurant in silence, grateful and feeling less burdened for having had this discussion.

How much has Stan been told of his mother's death, Ruth wonders. *What version of this terrible tragedy and of his father's involvement has been revealed to Stan? If Stan in the coming years, asks questions of me, I will not involve his father, partly because his father has permitted me yearly access to my grandson, but most of all because those dreadful facts would hurt Stan deeply and damage the good relationship he has with his only remaining parent—a father whom he loves and respects.*

Jasmine broke into Ruth's thoughts saying, "There is a store just a short walk from here, where, I believe, you will like their clothing—elegant but simple dresses, skirts, blouses, and sweaters, etc."

"It will be good to walk after all that sitting but what about your driver?"

"He will follow us," Jasmine laughed. He is used to my rambling whether shopping or walking on the beach."

"You do not wear the very strict clothing of your womenfolk!"

"Did you not notice that the entrance we used was used by women only? We were in the part of the store and the restaurant that caters to women only. All salespeople were likewise, women. Should my husband be with me, we would go to stores that cater to both. I have on many occasions gone into men's stores to purchase blazers, bathing trunks, etc. for my two sons and I always have been treated with the utmost courtesy. I'd rather go there if possible."

"You wear a scarf only covering your head!"

"Nobody, it seems, would dare to accost me," Jasmine laughed.

"I hope you won't be offended if I ask you a personal question." Getting no negative feedback from Jasmine, Ruth dashes ahead, "Did you choose your own husband, your relationship with him is apparently excellent?"

"No, my father chose him. I could not have chosen a better spouse. I think my father saved me from myself. I'm a bit, what my father calls 'head strong.' I am very fortunate in having a wonderful father, and a most endearing husband and three remarkable children," Jasmine smiled, then continued, "Maria and Abdul chose each other. Our ways were foreign to Maria and she was homesick—losing that beautiful child in such a despicable manner became too much for her to endure."

"Why wasn't I allowed to be with her at that most heart-breaking time of her life?"

"Abdul's education in England gave him a mistrust for 'mothers-in-law'"

"In what way?"

"He saw them as being overbearing."

"How many of his friends' mothers-in-law did he meet that bore that title."

"Probably no more than one or two, but those encounters apparently were enough for him to perceive all European mothers-in-law as interfering with their adult children's lives and he was told that it became worse if there were children involved."

"One or two people, in his eyes, condemned all women on the continent with married children, and through his erroneous belief, Maria was deprived of her mother at the lowest point in her life."

"Not just Abdul, his friends living there thought likewise," Jasmine spoke in his defense.

I may have jeopardized my visiting rights with my grandson, Ruth worried. *I must not speak on this matter further for I'm getting too emotional and should I continue, my visits with Stan might come to an end.*

Jasmine had questions of her own.

"How did Maria and her father connect in the Emirates? If it is too painful for you to speak of, let it go. I will not trouble you with it again."

After a pause, Ruth spoke. "It goes all the way back to Poland." Jasmine is surprised but keeps her silence as Ruth continues with her and her deceased husband's life together and her journey to England and the birth of Maria, right up to Maria's disappearance on a trip with fellow workers to Spain, of Maria's and her father's trip to England and then hers and Maria's boat trip to Ireland, where they thought they would be free, by fishing boat so as not to be detected. "After his work was done, my ex-husband returned to his wife and sons in Poland."

Jasmine listened attentively while the older woman spoke and through the moments of intense silence that followed. The two women with tear-stained faces never made it to the stores that Jasmine had planned to take Ruth. That would be put off for another day.

CHAPTER 26

Ruth, now in her late fifties, and Ned in his sixties, both sat by the fire on a cold rainy evening. Although it was late spring, the weather was wintry. They were not expecting anyone to be out on a night like this, when they heard a knock on the door.

"It must be important for a body to come out on a night like this," Ned observed as he stood up and walked towards the door.

On opening it, Ned saw a young man standing there covered in rainwear. Ruth rose and walked towards the door.

"Come in. Is it directions you are in need of," Ned asked.

"No, I believe, I have come to the right place and knocking his rain hood off his head, asked, "Surely you remember me."

On hearing his voice, Ruth gasped, "Stan" and catching her breath, added "Come here child, come here."

As Ned stood aside to allow their guest to pass, he told Ruth, "No child is this, he's a young man."

Helping him remove his raingear, Ned asked, "To what do we owe this marvelous surprise?"

Wordlessly, Ruth flung her arms around the sixteen-year-old youth. Then regaining her voice uttered, "Stan, Stan," the words came to her partly in a sob and partly in wonder.

"Since our terrific holidays with you came to an end when you were thirteen years old, and were sent to a boarding school, I wondered how you were doing and were you happy as you approached the brink of manhood. Thank you for all the cards you sent over the years, they brought great joy into our lives," Ruth told him while silently recalling the cards his mother had written to her but which were never mailed.

"Sorry, I didn't get in touch with you, save for those cards. My father has kept me very busy learning the family business, which means traveling a lot with him; plus preparing for college entrance exams, etc. I'll be attending college in the U.S. this coming autumn. I wanted to attend Trinity College, Dublin, but father said, "No." I was also accepted at Cambridge but that too he rejected—too close to Ireland and, he assumed, too many distractions."

I'll put the kettle on for tea," Ned announced, which Ruth, caught up in the joy of the occasion, neglected to do.

"Thank you, Ned."

They spoke into the early hours of the morning when Ned finally drew their attention to the time saying, "Let us let this young man get some sleep."

"Before I do so, I'd like you to have this business card with my telephone number on it, should you need to contact me at any time. No matter where I am, I can be reached at this number."

Ned takes the card, and thanks him.

Now warmed by the fire and fed with a light supper, Stan entered the room he slept in as a boy, with his rocking horse and stuffed kangaroo standing by, and he fell into a restful sleep.

Breakfast was no sooner over when they heard a knock on the door. Then the door opened and Una popped her head in.

"I gave you all as much time as my curiosity would allow," she told the group. "When I saw that beautiful motorcycle, I knew Stan must have come home."

"Come in dear, come in," Ruth called to her.

"How could you have kept his homecoming a secret?" she laughed as she threw her arms around Stan's neck.

"Grandmamma and Ned didn't know I would be arriving, "Stan laughed. Even I did not know if I could arrange it. After my last meeting in London, my host wanted me to join the group at the end of the session at their Club. I thanked them and told them I had to make a trip to Ireland."

'The Emirates have business in Ireland?' they questioned.

'No. I plan to visit my grandmamma who lives there,' I replied, which completely confounded them and brought an end to their questions."

"You've grown to manhood, yet you are the same Stan as always," Una declared.

"You are more beautiful than ever. How is your Aunt Catherine?"

"She is married and living in Dublin, Ned added. We were saddened to lose her but happy that she married a fine young man and they now have a son. Una, here, has taken over her aunt's Real Estate Agency."

By noon, more knocking is heard and the door is opened to neighbors streaming in, each bringing a food item or something to drink. Stan is hugged by all who entered the cottage. They arrived singly or in groups until it seemed that the whole village had squeezed into the cottage. The last to arrive was the local bar owner carrying Irish whiskey. "Since all my customers are here, I thought I'd join you all," he laughed as he opened the bottle of whiskey.

Some soul began to sing and soon everyone joined in.

"I was just dropping in for a short visit," Stan told Ned but I have decided instead of leaving this evening for the airport, I'll wait until tomorrow morning."

News of Stan's return spread rapidly. His young friends from his kindergarten days came and on seeing how crowded the cottage had become, waited outside by Stan's motorcycle for a moment with Stan. When Una informed Stan of the small group outside, he managed to disentangle himself from the crowd and meet with the group of his one-time fellow students. The conversation quickly turned to the motorcycle and Stan offered each of them a ride before they said goodbye.

As the party seemed like it might linger throughout the night, Ned, calling the neighbors to attention, spoke, "Stan has a long trip ahead of him and needs a good night's sleep before his drive to Dublin and his long flight home."

After much handshaking, hugs, and best wishes, with the hope that he would visit Ireland in the not-too-distant future, they returned to their homes.

"Thank you," a tired Stan told his equally tired hosts. I again feel like that young boy who used to live here."

* * *

As the years passed, Ruth's health began to fail. She survived "a bout with pneumonia" as Ned called it, but she did not return to her former good health. It was ten years since she last saw Stan, although he telephoned frequently on the telephone he had installed in their cottage. Now, homebound, Ruth lives partially in the past. The painful past has now become a more friendly place to visit—her early years with her husband, her beautiful daughter which brings great happiness and also much sadness into her life. She grieves silently over Maria's death and the death of Maria's father and half-brother. Ruth thinks of Stan's wife and the devastating pain she had to endure—two innocent men, husband and son, murdered. So much pain—at times it seems like a lifetime of pain. Then her mind turns to her grandson and his wonderful surprise visit. Sometimes the losses seem to outweigh the joys and so, she tells herself, she must hold on tightly to her great fortune in having met and married such a marvelously kind husband as Ned. Secretly she hopes her grandson will again come and visit. Then, losing hope that that will happen, she rebukes herself saying, her beloved grandson has a full and busy life. She must not despair of seeing him again.

After she suffers a stroke, and her ability to speak becomes difficult, she shuns visitors. What saddens her most is that Ned's activities are greatly reduced by her illness. He is a people person stuck in a tiny cottage with her, who remains mostly silent, knowing how difficult it is for her to be understood. Yet, he is the soul of patience.

His daughter-in-law comes in once a week to clean the house, and drop off hot meals for her and Ned four times a week. Ned tells his daughter-in-law that he is capable of cooking for his darling Ruth and himself, to which she laughingly replies, "Sure it is just as easy to make dinner for four as it is for two, and when I'm here feeding Ruth, cleaning the cottage and doing the bit of wash, you can use that time to have your walk and drop in on your friends."

"Now I don't want to add to your work," he protests.

"Don't go looking a gift horse in the mouth."

"Women!"

"I insist you keep in touch with your friends, they miss you."

"Now, I've got both of you, Ruth and yourself, telling me how to live my life."

In a caressing voice, Kara tells him, "Pop, caregivers need to be taken care of too. You won't be much help to Ruth if you wear yourself out. So for Ruth and yourself let others help you. Beginning tomorrow, Teddy will come over and join you in your daily walk which you have been neglecting. Before Ned can protest, she continues, "You must get back to your daily walk. It will give you and your son time together, which will do you both good, and it will make Ruth happy too."

"Women, you can wear a fellow down," yet it was obvious that Ned was enjoying the conversation and the prospect of getting out of the cottage more while knowing that Ruth was being cared for. Knowing that he is not going to win any argument with his daughter-in-law, Ned acquiesces. Grabbing his hat, Ned looks in on Ruth before leaving the house.

Looking in at Ruth, Kara tells her, "Well, I got him out of the house."

"Thank you, love. I closed my eyes when I heard him approach the bedroom to make it easier for him to leave. God knows that man needs a break. You may have to urge him back to a somewhat more normal life a couple more times. He needs his friends, a chat, and some laughter, and to know what is going on in the neighborhood—these vital ingredients."

"Your speech has much improved over the past few weeks."

"Yes. Ned has been patiently helping me with words. I'm afraid I got lazy and used my hands instead of my voice. I know I speak very slowly but I have to find the words. Ned is blessed with an abundance of patience and I'm fortunate to be the recipient of his boundless patience. He and you both wait for my words rather than speak them for me and that's a great help."

"I'll make us a cup of tea before I leave," Kara says as she pours water in the tea kettle.

"Thank you, love. I'm going to have Ned pick up some sandwiches at the pub in the evenings and we'll have them for supper. That will free him from preparing the final meal of the day. You are tired working all day and need to relax in the evenings."

"It's no trouble at all," Kara protests.

"Now that my speech has improved, I want to get back to some kind of normalcy.

"You will. You've worked very hard on your speech. You have always been an independent soul. I have no doubt that you'll make a good recovery."

"Thanks, Kara."

Kara, who has been making the tea while conversing with Ruth, pours out a cup of tea for each of them.

After the young woman leaves, Ruth picks up the previous evening's newspaper and speaks the words out loud so that she can hear and adjust her pronouncement of each word.

* * *

Ned and Ruth, some years later, were sitting at the kitchen table finishing their supper when a knock was heard. Looking towards the door, Ned and Ruth wondered who can be calling on them so late in the evening. Rising, Ned walked towards the door. On opening it, the last bright rays of the summer sun clothed the couple standing before him. The woman's appearance brought Ned back to many years ago. The woman reminded him of Jasmine. *The sun is playing tricks,* he thought. He was stumped for a moment until the young man, whom he had not paid attention to, spoke. On hearing his voice, he threw his arms around Stan. Regaining his composure, he opened the door wide and was about to call to his wife, but Ruth on hearing the word 'Stan' was suddenly standing behind him.

"Stan," she gasped!

"Yes, grandmamma, it is I and this is my wife and daughter." The girl who was Stan's wife, was dressed in a pink silk suit and she had a pink gauze-like scarf covering her head, but not her face.

Ruth threw her arms around Stan and he returned her hug. Not knowing the protocol for greeting an Arab woman, Ruth threw caution to the wind and hugged the woman and child. Gaining her composure, Ruth bade them enter. The young man, in his early thirties, stood before her with his hand on his wife's back, and gently guided her and their child into the cottage.

"God be praised," Ned uttered as he closed the door behind them.

"Stan all grown up and with a beautiful wife and daughter," Ruth spoke as she marveled at the young couple.

"Well, aren't you going to offer us a cup of tea," Stan jokingly asked, which caused Ruth and Ned to relax with their most unexpected guests. Turning to his wife, he introduced her to his grandmamma, Ruth, and her husband, Ned, and, in turn, them to her.

Ned pulled out a seat for Stan's wife and Ruth, and the three of them sat down at the table while Ned filled the teakettle and put it on the stove; then he took down the biscuit tin of cookies that were kept for special occasions.

"Could I hold the baby," Ruth asked as she sat down in her comfortable armchair. The young woman handed the baby to Ruth who lovingly took the child in her arms.

"What name does she have?"

Before his wife could answer Ruth, Stan says, "Guess!"

"Oh I could not guess any name from your country."

"You don't need to," Stan replies, "her name is Maria."

Tears flowed into Ruth's eyes and for a few seconds she was unable to speak.

"She is, of course, named for my mother."

"You were so young when you were taken..."—then Ruth stopped fearing she might have offended Stan or his father, corrected herself, saying, "you were young when you left here.."

"I remember it clearly, and how I rebelled against my father. He is, however, a very good father and I revere him, but I'm still a bit of a rebel—it must be my Irish early life experience.   Since my dad is a born diplomat and I have followed him into the Diplomatic Corps, he listens to my side of an argument and I to his, and we weigh both sides and come to a mutual agreement—well, most of the time." Stan laughed and they all joined in.

Since his wife had not spoken, Ruth asked Stan, "Does your wife speak English?"

"Yes, she does, plus three other languages. I met her at University."

He smiled at his wife, who smiled in return.

"She has never been outside the Emirates except to attend University. This country, its people and your little cottage are all a new experience for her. She could not believe that with my father's wealth, I could have lived here in this cottage, my first home, and a place dear to me."

Ned, who had left the room for a few seconds, returned with a soccer ball.

"My ball," Stan uttered in disbelief. He took the ball and dribbled it on the worn wooden floors of the cottage. Then holding it in his arms laughingly said, "unbelievable! Absolutely unbelievable!"

"Well, are you ready to take it back with you?" Ruth asked.

"If my wife and I have a son, I will fly back here and claim it."

"Then I pray you have a son," Ruth told them.

"Who would like another cup of tea?" Ruth asks.

"I would, thank you," Ned replies.

"And I too," Stan added.

"Would you like some more tea?" He asked his wife.

"No, thank you. The tea and biscuits were very good," she answered with a smile.

"Little Maria is a very good, non-fussy child," Ruth told the young mother.

"Yes, and a good traveler," the younger woman added.

"I'd say, she would need to be, as you both travel a lot."

"This is our first trip with our daughter because she is so young, but Zayed," then corrected herself, "Stan, and I would not have taken her on such a long trip except that he hoped to fly into Ireland to visit you, his grandmother and your husband and show you our daughter who bears his mother's and your daughter's name."

How much does she know, Ned wonders.

"We are delighted that she is named for my daughter who died when Zayed was quite young." Trying to uplift this downward flowing conversation, Ruth spoke, "If I had known that Zayed was married and had a daughter, I would have knitted an outfit for this beautiful great-grandchild of mine."

Seeing how overwhelmed with joy Ruth was by this visit, Ned, looking at Stan's wife, spoke. "Our joy overflows, nothing could surpass this visit of the three of you being here, or the fact that this beautiful child is named for Stan's mother." *Maria, whose beautiful eyes are neither those of Abdul, Maria, nor the child's parents, but rather an unusual shade of dove grey.* Then on a lighter note, he turned to Stan and stated, "You must have gotten a lot of objections on your choice of a name for your beautiful daughter!"

"True. Actually it was my father's backing my decision to name our daughter a non-Arabic name that silenced all objection to it. My father is held in high esteem by our extended family."

Due to this visit being a close family visit, and also due to Ruth's poor health, friends and neighbors did not come to the cottage.

Within a fortnight of this family visit, Ruth suffered a massive stroke and died.

The whole village attended the funeral service in the local church. The Rabbi, whom Ned had invited, from the synagogue in Dublin, where Ruth had gone on High Holy Days, also attended. The Parish Priest and the Rabbi would speak at the funeral. Ruth would be buried in the family plot where Ned's first wife had been buried.

Ned had telephoned Stan of his grandmother's death.

Ned shook hands with everyone present but did not see Stan among those who had gathered for the funeral. It was Una who drew Ned's attention to two lone figures standing beside a black limousine on a hillside. After receiving condolences from his friends and neighbors, Ned looked towards the hill where two well-dressed men stood. The younger of the two men walked towards Ned and embraced him. They held each other closely for several minutes until Ned broke the silence. "Is the man with you your father?"

"Yes, we were in France when I received your message that Grandmamma had died and we immediately flew here. You must, of course, have met my father when I was a child and you and grandmamma came to the Riviera."

"Neither Ruth nor I, whom your father kindly brought to that wonderful resort, ever met him," Ned told Stan. "It was the beautiful lady, Jasmine, who met us and showed us around."

"Come, let us remedy that right now, for I would very much like you and him to meet each other."

The two men walked towards Abdul. Now that Ned had been given the opportunity to meet this man who brought such sorrow into Ruth's life, yet is the beloved father of her grandson, Ned wondered what to say to him.

As they came close, Abdul addressed Ned.

"Your wife was an extraordinary and well-liked woman."

"Yes, that she was," Ned nodded in agreement.

"My son feels so much a part of this beautiful country," and as he spoke, he reached out and shook hands with Ned.

While the two men were speaking, Una walking towards Stan asked, "What is your most memorable event of your early childhood in Ireland?"

Stan laughed, then answered, "There were so many happy times," then after a pause he added, "perhaps the most memorable one was my camping trip with my Mom and Colm, a truly remarkable man who made Mom very happy."

After bidding farewell to Abdul, Ned walked towards Stan and Una.

"Death is a universal sorrow. None of us escape it," Ned told the younger man as they hugged each other. This was an exceptionally sad goodbye as both Ned and Stan knew, with Ruth, Stan's only relative in Ireland, now gone to her grave, Stan would not be returning to Ireland.

As Stan walked towards the black sleek limousine, Abdul looked ahead, and seemed transfixed at the beautiful landscape that rolled down to the sea. Suddenly the sky darkened and a heavy downpour of rain occurred. Looking down into the village, Abdul saw a bare-headed blond young woman walking in the rain towards the sea. It was as though Maria was walking towards the rippling waves. Then suddenly the woman entered one of the cottages and the street was empty.

"The book, *Finley's Tale: The Bond of Love*, is a creative, humorous type of ecclesiastical allegory . . . This book indicates that Lutheran theology's intent goal of declaring the Gospel of Jesus Christ to a sinful world is not opposed to Christians enjoying wholesome humor."

—Alvin J. Schmidt, Ph. D.
Author of *How Christianity Changed the World* (2004);
Hallmarks of Lutheran Identity (2017), plus ten other books

"I love Finley and Ruby! The Osterhagens are true Christians and put up with so much. They make a good team. You have captured much truth in a magical way. Keep up the great writing! I'm a big fan!"

—Sonia (Sunny) Carlsen Fedak
daughter of Kurt Carlsen, the captain of the Flying Enterprise

After hearing countless quips about "church mice," this may be your first chance to read one's diary in detail! Though "Finley" is make-believe, author Sandra Voelker has obviously seen church life up close, both the petty and the heart-warming side. She also paints a very touching and human picture of the pastor and family at "Historic St. Pete's." This could be amusing reading for church people, especially if they're the types who don't mind poking a little fun at themselves!

—Pastor Robert Bugbee
Past President, Lutheran Church-Canada

This is a unique perspective of church life: an array of many-coloured characters, observed in penetrating detail by some extremely inquisitive and unusually brilliant church mice. The storytellers go through the church, the parsonage, and the church year in their curiosity to know just what makes this place tick. One wonders while reading, what would Finley see in my congregation?

—Kelly Klages
Artist, author, and pastor's wife
Morden, Manitoba

Sweet. _ _ and heart-warming!

—Dr. Bruce Kotowich
Director of Choirs, University of Windsor

"Through the eyes of church mice, observations are made. Using their voices, author Sandra Voelker has told in diary form delightful and divine stories about life in a church, in a parsonage, and life as a pastor, the pastor's wife, and their children. The reader meets a variety of personalities (aka church members) and becomes involved in both church and town incidents, problems, and occasions. Open the pages now and enjoy a journey that is perceptive, evokes compassion, causes smiles and laughter, reveals wisdom, and touches the soul. In other words, enjoy a bit of real 'heaven on earth.'"

—Rev. Dr. David H. Ritt
President and Bishop Emeritus
English District, Lutheran Church – Missouri Synod

"Under the observant eye of Finley Newcastle (aka F.N.), the church mouse living at Historic St. Pete's Church, the comments and activities of Pastor Osterhagen, his wife Aia, their family and congregation are carefully recorded. Thank you, F.N. You put a smile on a reader's face as you record life in the parsonage and bring to mind the ups and downs, trials and triumphs of the church as a family of families… warts and blemishes, sweetness and grace. I love it!"

—Rev. Steve Wagner
Associate Pastor, Concordia Lutheran Church, San Antonio, Texas
Past Director, *Pastoral Leadership Institute*

"A charming 'tail' revealing a church's congregational life through the sharp eyes of its own church mice. A delightful read!"

—Mount Olive Lutheran Church's Monday Night Book Group
Rochester, Minnesota